Richard wore only his nightshirt, rumpled and loose, and yet somehow revealing far more than his usual dress did—because beneath all that snowy linen he was...*naked*.

The darker shadows beneath the fabric, the way the linen draped over his body, left no doubt, and Jane's cheeks flamed at the realisation.

Hastily she looked back up to the safer territory of his face. Or perhaps it wasn't. In all the time she'd been in His Grace's employment she'd never seen him this dishevelled, his hair loose around his face and his jaw roughened with a growth of darker beard, his whole expression without its usual reserve and control. It was unsettling, seeing him without his guard like this, and it made him less like His Grace and more simply like any other man.

A large, scarcely dressed, and surprisingly handsome man that she'd just summoned from his bed.

Heavens preserve her—what had she *done*?

THE DUKE'S GOVERNESS BRIDE

Miranda Jarrett

First published in Great Britain 2010
Large Print edition 2011
Harlequin Mills & Boon Limited,
Eton House, 18-24 Paradise Road, Richmond, Surrey TW9 1SR

© Miranda Jarrett 2010

ISBN: 978 0 263 21849 7

Harlequin Mills & Boon policy is to use papers that are natural, renewable and recyclable products and made from wood grown in sustainable forests. The logging and manufacturing process conform to the legal environmental regulations of the country of origin.

Printed and bound in Great Britain
by CPI Antony Rowe, Chippenham, Wiltshire

Miranda Jarrett considers herself sublimely fortunate to have a career that combines history and happy endings—even if it's one that's also made her family far-too-regular patrons of the local pizzeria. Miranda is the author of over thirty historical romances, and her books are enjoyed by readers the world over. She has won numerous awards for her writing, including two Golden Leaf Awards and two *RT Book Reviews* Reviewers' Choice Awards, and has three times been a Romance Writers of America RITA® Award finalist for best short historical romance.

Miranda is a graduate of Brown University, with a degree in art history. She loves to hear from readers at PO Box 1102, Paoli, PA 19301-0792, USA, or at susan@susanhollowayscott.com

Novels by Miranda Jarrett:

RAKE'S WAGER
THE LADY'S HAZARD
THE DUKE'S GAMBLE
THE ADVENTUROUS BRIDE*
SEDUCTION OF AN ENGLISH BEAUTY*
THE SAILOR'S BRIDE
  (in *Regency Christmas Weddings*)

*linked by character to
  The Duke's Governess Bride

Chapter One

If a Woman has any Mind to be wicked, Venice seems to be the last Place in the World to give her better Sentiments.

—'Miss N', to the actor Thomas Hull, 1756

Venice—January 1785

Most English gentlemen came to Venice to be amused, whether to view the antique paintings, or to wear a long-nosed mask and dance at the carnival, or to dally with a courtesan in a closed gondola. But Richard Farren, the fifth Duke of Aston, wasn't here for idle amusement. He had come to Venice for one reason, and one reason only. He'd come for the sake of love.

Turning the collar of his heavy Melton travelling cloak higher against the wind, Richard smiled as he imagined again what his friends in London must be saying of him now. That he was a sentimental fool, surely. That he'd lost his wits, most likely. That the love he was travelling so far to offer would never be returned in equal measure—ah, there were doubtless a good many wagers being made about that, too. So be it. He'd only been able to tolerate a couple of months of loneliness at Aston Hall before he'd given in, and taken off on this journey. But then, caution and care had never been his style, and he wasn't about to change now. Nothing ventured, nothing gained—that seemed to him not so much a time-worn adage as a good, sound philosophy.

He leaned his arms on the rail of the little sloop, staring out at the wavering dark outline of the shore. This passage from Trieste to Venice was the last step of his long journey, and he'd stood there much of the day, preferring the damp and chill on the deck to the close, fishy stench of the cabin below. Besides, he'd doubted he'd have been able to sleep even if he'd tried. After so many weeks travelling by land and sea, and hard travelling at that, his destination was now only hours away. By nightfall, all his doubts, all his worries, would at last be put to rest—or, if Fate went against him, they'd only have begun.

'His Grace is eager to reach Venice.' The sloop's

captain joined him unbidden at the rail. 'His Grace is happy we make such good speed, yes?'

'Yes,' Richard said, hoping that brevity would make the man leave him in peace.

But the captain only squinted up at Richard, pushing his greasy cocked hat more firmly on his head against the wind. 'His Grace is brave to sail in winter, yes? Ice, snow, wind, *brr.*'

The captain hugged his arms over his chest to mimic a man warming himself. In return Richard only nodded. He knew perfectly well the perils of travelling at this time of year. He had embarked from England so late in the season, almost in winter itself, that crossing the Continent to Italy through France and the Alps was out of the question. He'd had no choice but to travel by sea, around Spain and Portugal and into the Mediterranean, until he'd become heartily sick of the company of sailing men like this one.

'Once you're at Venice, your Grace, you stay,' the captain continued. 'No more journey until spring. No Roma, no Napoli, no Firenze, no—'

'Quite,' Richard said, his impatience with the man's company growing by the second. He didn't need a list of every landmark city in Italy to know that he'd be winterbound in Venice. He was rather counting on it, in fact, given the pleasing female company that was waiting for him there.

'But his Grace will find willing friends in Venice to warm him, eh?' The captain winked slyly, studying Richard from his thick dark gold hair to the toes of his well-polished boots with obvious approval. 'A great English lion like his Grace will have many ladies, eh?'

Richard said nothing, choosing instead to stare out at the water and let the rascal draw whatever unsavoury conclusions he pleased. His dear wife Anne had been not only his duchess, but his best friend and his dearest love, and when she had died, he'd sworn no other woman could possibly replace her in his life. That had been fifteen long years ago, and the pain lingered still.

'I can tell you the house of the best courtesans in the city, your Grace,' the captain was saying. 'I know what you English lords like, eh? A woman who will bring you to such joy, such passion, such—'

'Enough,' Richard said curtly, the voice he always used with recalcitrant servants, dogs and children. Why did everyone on the Continent believe English peers were in constant rut, panting after low women in every port? 'Leave me.'

The captain hesitated only a moment before

bowing and backing away, and, with a grumbling sigh, Richard turned back towards the horizon. The sloop was drawing closer to the harbour now, the outlines of the city's skyline sharpening in the fading light of day. Richard could make out the famous pointed bell tower of San Marco's, looking precisely the way it did in the engravings in the books in his library at Aston Hall. There was much else beginning to appear from the misty dusk, of course, places Richard supposed he should have recognised as well, but his mind was too occupied with the coming reunion to concentrate on anything else.

He remained on the deck against the urging of his manservant to come below to ready himself for shore, and he ignored the same suggestion from the captain as the crew finally dropped their anchor. Soon he'd be hearing the merry laughter that meant the world to him, and feel the soft girlish arms flung around his shoulders in the embrace he'd missed so sorely these last months.

As the sloop entered the harbour proper, a flurry of small boats came through the mist towards them, odd long skiffs that reminded Richard more of the punts at Oxford than the usual longboats, with the oarsman standing high in the stern-sheets—or what would be the stern-sheets in an English boat. Foreigners had a different name for everything.

'What are those skiffs, Potter?' he asked his secretary as the man joined him at the rail.

'Gondolas, your Grace,' said Potter, supplying the proper word in his usual helpful manner. Like some small, bustling, black-clad badger, the secretary had ducked from the path of the sailors to join Richard, while the rest of the English party, Richard's manservant and two footmen, saw to his belongings below. 'Gondolas are the common means of travel throughout Venice, rather like hackneys in London.'

'Then pray hail one for us directly,' Richard said. 'The sooner we're off this infernal sloop and on dry land again, the better.'

At once Potter nodded, bowing over his clasped hands. 'I am sorry, your Grace, but before we can venture into the city, we must clear customs.'

'Customs?' Blast, he'd forgotten that every last city and village in Italy considered itself its own little country, complete with a flock of fawning satraps who expected to have their palms greased. *'Customs.'*

'I fear so, your Grace,' Potter said. 'That building on the promontory is the Dognana di Mare, the

Customs House of Venice, your Grace, where we must go—'

'Where *you* must go, Potter,' Richard said. 'You see to whatever needs seeing to, and pay whatever fees the thieving devils demand. I'll proceed directly to the ladies.'

Potter's expression grew pinched. 'Forgive me, your Grace, but surely you must realise that the customs officers will expect you—'

'They can expect whatever they please,' Richard said, 'I've more important business this night than to bow and scrape to their wishes. They may call on me tomorrow, at a civil hour, at the—the, ah, what the devil is the place called?'

'The Ca' Battista, your Grace,' Potter said. 'But if you please, your Grace, we—'

'Ca' Battista,' Richard repeated the house's name to make sure he'd recall it, and nodded with satisfaction. Though he'd no notion what the words meant, they had a fine, righteous sound to them. 'Tell the drones in the Customs House to come to me there.'

'I beg your pardon, your Grace,' Potter persisted, 'but Venice has a very poor reputation in its treatment of English visitors. Venice is a republic, and their officials have little respect for foreign persons of rank, such as yourself. It can be a place full of danger, your Grace. This city is not London, and—'

'But I am not a foreigner,' Richard said. 'I am an English peer. Now a boat, Potter, one of your gondolas, at once. At once!'

Soon after Richard was, in fact, in a gondola, seated on a low bench against leather cushions, his long legs bent at an ungainly angle before him. Yet he couldn't deny the swift efficiency of this peculiar vessel as it glided into one of the channels, or canals, that divided the city and served as a type of watery streets. On this evening, the canal seemed muffled in mist and fog and the endless lapping of the wavelets against the buildings, with the striped poles used for mooring like so many drunken demons lurching through the waters.

Without a city's usual bustle and clatter from horses, carriages and wagons, the canals seemed oddly quiet, so quiet that to Richard the loudest sound must surely be the racing of his own heart. His long journey, and his waiting, was nearly done.

'Ca' Battista, *signori*,' the oarsman announced as the gondola slowed before one of the grandest of the houses: a tall square front of white stone, punctuated with balconies and pointed windows frosted with elaborate carvings, which sat so low on the dark water that it seemed to float upon it. The gondolier guided the boat in place before the house's landing, bumping lightly against the dock. Roused by the noise, a sleepy-eyed porter opened the house's door and held up a lantern to peer down from the stone steps.

'Stop gaping, man,' Potter shouted as Richard clambered from the gondola. 'Go to your mistress and tell her that the Duke of Aston is here.'

Still the servant hesitated, his face full of bewilderment. With an oath of impatience, Richard swept past him and through the open door, his long cloak swinging from his shoulders. The entry hall was a hexagon, supported by more of the tall columns and pointed arches. A pair of gilded cherubs crowned the newels at the base of the staircase, the steep steps rising up into the murky gloom. The floor was tiled, the walls painted with faded pictures, with everything dismally half-lit by a single hanging lantern. There were no other servants to be seen besides the single hapless porter; in fact, Richard had no company at all except his own echoing footsteps.

He swore to himself with furious disappointment. He was angry and tired and cold, but most of all, if he were truthful, he was wounded to the quick. This was hardly the welcome he'd expected. Where were the kisses and tears of joy? Hadn't the land-lady received his letters? Why the devil weren't they prepared for him? Blast the infernal Italian post! He knew he'd gambled by coming all this way on impulse, but damnation, he'd paid for the lease of this wretched, echoing house. Wasn't that enough to earn him at least a show of affection in return?

'The English lady, most excellent one?' the porter asked breathlessly as he finally trotted up behind Richard. 'You wish to see her?'

'Who the devil else would it be?' At least the man had worked out that much. In fact, Richard was here to see two English ladies, not just one, but he'd credit the mistake to the porter's general con-fusion. 'Go, tell her I'm—'

'A thousand pardons, but she waits for you.' He pointed behind Richard. 'There.'

Richard whipped around, gazing to where the man was pointing. At the top of the stairs stood a woman, indeed, an Englishwoman, but neither of the ones he'd so longed to see. She was small and pale, her eyes enormous with shock in her round little face. Her hair was drawn back severely from her face and hidden beneath a linen cap, relieved only by a narrow brown ribbon that matched the colour of her equally plain brown gown. She clutched at the rail, clearly needing its support as she struggled to regain her composure after the shock of seeing Richard.

'Your—your Grace,' she said, and belatedly curtsied. 'Good evening, your Grace. You—you took me by surprise.'

'Evidently,' he said, his voice rough with urgency. 'I'm tired, Miss Wood, and eager to see my girls. Please take me to them directly.'

'Lady Mary, Your Grace?' she asked with a hesitation that did not please him, not from the woman he'd trusted as his daughters' governess. 'And Lady Diana?'

'My daughters,' he said, taking another step towards her. His daughters, his girls, his cherubs, the darlings of his heart—who else could have made him come so far? Solemn, dark-haired Mary, the older at nineteen, and Diana, laughing and golden, a year younger. Could any father have missed his children more than he?

A second woman came to join the governess, dark and elegant, a lady dressed in widow's black. Most likely this was the house's owner, he guessed, their landlady Signora della Battista.

'My journey has been a long one, Miss Wood,' he said, 'and you are making it longer still.'

'Your daughters,' the governess repeated with undeniable sadness, even regret. The older woman spoke gently to her in Italian, resting her hand on her arm, but Miss Wood only shook her head, her gaze still turned towards Richard. 'You did not receive my letters, your Grace, or theirs? You do not know what has happened?'

'What is there to know?' he demanded. 'I've been at sea, coming here. The last letters I had from you were from Paris, weeks ago, and nothing since. Damnation, if you don't bring my girls to me—'

'If it were in my power, your Grace, I would, with all my heart.' With her hand once again on the rail, she slowly sank until she was sitting on the top step, so overwhelmed that she seemed unable to stand any longer. 'But they—the young ladies—they are not here. Oh, if only you'd been able to read the letters!'

A score of possibilities filled Richard's heart with sickening dread: an accident in a coach, a shipboard mishap, an attack by footpads or highwaymen, a fever, a quinsy, a poison in the blood. Long ago he'd lost his wife, and grief had nearly killed him. He could not bear to lose his daughters as well.

'Tell me, Miss Wood,' he asked hoarsely. 'Dear God, if anything has happened to them—'

'They are married, your Grace,' the governess said, and bowed her head. 'Both of them. They are married.'

Chapter Two

'*Married?*' roared the Duke of Aston. 'My daughters? Married?'

'Yes, your Grace.' Jane Wood took a deep breath, and told herself that the worst must now be over. Surely it must be, for as long and as well as she'd known the duke, she could not imagine him becoming any more incensed than he was at this moment. Nor, truly, could she fault him for it. 'Both have wed, and to most excellent gentleman.'

'Most excellent rascals is more likely!' His handsome face was as dark as an August thunderstorm, and she realised to her surprise that his expression was filled with as much disappointment as anger. 'Why did you not put a stop to these crimes, Miss Wood? Why did you permit it?'

'Why, your Grace?' She forced herself to stand, to compose herself to give her answer. In his present state, the duke would see any kind of confusion as weakness and incompetence. Rather, *further* incompetence. His Grace never expected to be crossed, and his temper was legendary. After nearly ten years in his service, Jane knew that much of him, just as she knew that the surest way to calm him was to present the facts in a quiet and rational manner. That had always proved successful with him before, and there was no reason to believe it wouldn't again.

She took another breath and lightly clasped her hands at her waist, the way she always did. She shouldn't have let herself be so shocked. She wasn't some callow girl, but a capable woman of nearly thirty. A calm demeanour was what was required now, she told herself firmly, a rational argument. Yes, yes—rationality and reason. Not a defence, for she believed she'd done nothing wrong, but the even, well-reasoned explanation of the events of the last few weeks that she'd been rehearsing ever since she'd come to Venice from Rome.

But she'd always expected to be delivering that explanation in the duke's sunny library at Aston Hall, in Kent, once she herself was safely returned to England, and long after he would have read his daughters' letters. She never imagined he would have come charging clear across the Mediterranean like a mad bull to corner her here on the staircase of the Ca'Battista.

'Permit me to summon the watch, Miss Wood,' said Signora Battista in indignant Italian, standing beside her. 'Or at least let me call the footmen from the kitchen to send this man away. There is no need for you to tolerate the ravings of this lunatic!'

'But there is, *signora,*' Jane murmured swiftly, also in Italian, 'because he is my master. I am employed in his household, and rely upon him for my livelihood.'

'Livelihood!' The *signora* made a sharp click of disdain. 'What manner of life can there be with an intemperate male creature such as this one?'

Swiftly Jane shook her head, appalled by such disrespect. She was most fortunate that the duke was proud, as only an English peer could be, of speaking no other language than English, and hadn't understood the other woman's comments. Hurriedly she shifted back to English herself.

'Your Grace,' she began, 'if you please, may I present Signora Isabella della Battista, the owner of this fine house? *Signora,* his Grace the Duke of Aston.'

To Jane's dismay, the *signora*'s nod of acknowledgement was also calcuated at the precise angle to signify exactly where a parvenu English duke of only two or three hundred years' nobility stood in relationship to her, a member of one of the most ancient families of the Republic of Venice who was at present so unfortunately impoverished that she was in need of rich travelling foreigners as lodgers.

'Madam,' the duke said curtly to the *signora*, too caught up in his own anger to perceive her slight. 'Damnation, Miss Wood, come down here where I can see you properly.'

Jane grabbed her skirts to one side so she wouldn't trip, and hurried down to stand before him.

Or, rather, beneath him. In the half-year since she'd last seen him at Aston Hall, she'd forgotten how much taller he was than she, and how much larger, too. The duke had a presence that few men could match, a physical energy that seemed to vibrate from him like the rays from the sun. While most men of his rank and age masked their emotions behind a show of genteel boredom, he let them run galloping free. The results could make him either the very best of men, a paragon of charming good nature and generous spirit, or the very worst of devils, when his temper triumphed. Everyone acquainted with the duke knew this to be so, from his daughters to his servants, his neighbours, even his pack of hunting dogs.

As, of course, did Jane. And there was absolutely no doubt as to which side of the duke now held sway.

'Explain, Miss Wood,' he ordered curtly. 'Now.'

'Yes, your Grace.' She took another deep breath, and forced herself to meet his gaze. 'Your daughters have both wed most excellent gentlemen, your Grace, gentlemen of whom I dare to believe you yourself will approve upon acquaintance.'

'Then why the devil didn't they wait to ask me properly?' the duke demanded. 'Gentlemen, hah. Only the lowest rascal steals away a lady from her family like that.'

'In ordinary circumstances, they would have, your Grace,' Jane agreed, blushing at what she must next say. 'But once your daughters had…ah…become their lovers, it seemed best that they wed at once before—'

'My girls were *ruined?*' the duke asked, sputtering with horror.

'Not ruined, your Grace,' Jane said. 'They were—they are—in love, and love will not be denied.'

'It would have if I'd been here,' he said grimly. 'Their names, Miss Wood, their names.'

'Lady Mary wed Lord John Fitzgerald in Paris—'

'An Irishman? My Mary let herself be seduced and wed to an *Irishman?*'

'A gentleman of Irish birth, your Grace,' Jane said firmly, determined to defend the choices that both her charges had made. 'His lordship is a younger son, true, but his brother is a marquis.'

'An Irish peerage is as worthless as muck in a stable!' the duke cried with disgust. 'At least if the thing was done in Paris with a Romish priest, then I can have it dissolved as—'

'Forgive me, your Grace, but they were wed properly, before an Anglican cleric,' Jane said. 'Lady Mary herself was most conscious of that.'

Pained, the duke closed his eyes. 'If Mary's thrown herself away on an Irishman, then what kind of scoundrel has ruined Diana?'

'Lady Diana's husband is Lord Anthony Randolph, your Grace, brother to the Earl of Markham.'

'Another younger son, when with her beauty and breeding, she could have had a prince!' He shook his head with despair. 'At least he's an Englishmen, yes?'

'His father was, yes. His mother was from an ancient Roman family of great nobility, which is why his lordship has resided in that city all his life.'

'A Roman by birth, and by blood,' he said, bitterness welling over his words. 'An Italian, draped with an English title. An Italian, and an Irishman. My God.'

'I beg you, your Grace,' Jane said softly. She loved his daughters, and because of that love, she owed it to them to try to make their father understand. 'These are good and honourable gentlemen, worthy of—'

'Miss Wood.' He cut her off as surely as if the words had been wrought of the steel. 'I trusted you with my dearest possessions on this earth, and you—you have carelessly let them slip away.'

'But, your Grace, if I might explain—'

'No.' Pointedly he turned away from her. '*Signora,* pray show me to my rooms. I will dine there, alone, as soon as your kitchen can arrange it.'

Signora della Battista knew when to put aside her animosity, especially towards the gentleman who had leased her entire house in the winter, a season of few travellers. The Venetian republic was famous for its mercenaries, and the *signora* was no different.

'This house is honoured beyond measure, most excellent sir,' she said in English. 'My finest chamber shall be at your disposal, and my cook will prepare his very best to tempt you. This way, if you please.'

As Jane watched the duke follow the *signora* up the stairs, she saw how his usually squared shoulders sagged with weariness and discouragement, how the jagged white salt-stains from the sea worn into his once-elegant dark cloak seemed to illustrate just how long and arduous his journey here had been. She deeply regretted disappointing him, and though she knew better, she impulsively hurried up the stairs after him.

'Your Grace, if you please,' she said softly. 'If I might speak to you further, to explain and—'

'You've explained more than enough for tonight, Miss Wood,' he said, brushing her away. 'If you've any sense left at all, you should prefer to wait until tomorrow to hear what else I shall say to you.'

This time, Jane did not follow. Instead she remained behind, alone on the staircase, listening as the voices and footsteps of the duke and the *signora* grew fainter before they finally faded away.

It couldn't have gone any worse with his Grace, short of him tossing her into the Grand Canal. Perhaps, Jane thought with growing despair, his Grace was saving that for tomorrow. In any event, she should prepare herself for the worst. Lady Mary and Lady Diana had assured her that their father would understand, and that he couldn't possibly blame Jane for their choices. Yet already she'd seen that he could, and he would.

She had failed in her duty, failed in a way that in her entire life she'd never failed before. She had put the wishes of her charges ahead of their parent, an unforgivable sin in any governess. Yet still she believed she'd acted in the interests of both sisters. Wasn't that the first order of her responsibilities? To put the welfare of her charges before everything else? But because of it, she was sure she'd now be turned out here in a foreign country, without references, or worse, with damning ones from the duke.

Slowly she climbed the rest of the stairs and headed down the long hallway to her room. She'd already dined earlier with the *signora;* there was nothing left for her to do this evening beyond preparing for her seemingly inevitable departure in the morning.

Like all the lesser rooms in grand Venetian houses, hers lay between the elegant bedchambers that were to have been occupied by the duke's two daughters. One of these faced the front of the house, with tall windows and a balcony that overlooked the Grand Canal, while the other faced the house's rear courtyard and private garden. Although comfortable enough, Jane's chamber was undeniably intended for a servant, with a lesser view of the Rio della Madonnetta. Depending on the hour and the cast of the sun, candles were necessary, and the tiny stove for heat did little to relieve the winter damp either.

Always frugal, Jane lit only the single candlestick beside the small bed. She set her two trunks on the coverlet, and briskly set about emptying the clothes-press and chest of her belongings. Given the humble nature of her wardrobe, packing her clothes into the trunks took no time at all, and only her letters now remained to be sorted. She changed from her gown into her nightshift, brushed out her hair from its customary tightly pinned knot and wrapped an over-sized wool shawl around her shoulders against the chill. Then, with fresh determination, she scooped the bundled papers into her arms and headed for the front bedchamber.

Once Signora della Battista had understood that Jane had arrived alone, without the English ladies who had been expected, she'd given the governess leave to use the other two bedchambers as well. It was of no concern to the *signora* who occupied them; she'd already been handsomely paid in advance long ago by the duke's agents.

But for Jane, the luxurious bedchambers had only added to the dream-like quality of her visit to Venice. Each room had exuberant carved and gilded panelling and swirling paintings of frolicking ancient goddesses and cupids. Huge looking-glasses reflected the view of the canal and the garden, and magnified the dappled light off the water as well.

Jane hadn't gone so far as to sleep in either of the huge bedsteads—each more like a royal barge than a mere bed—but she had permitted herself to spend time in the rooms, and she'd taken to writing letters at the delicate lady's desk overlooking the Grand Canal.

Now she set her papers on the desk's leather top, and settled in the gilded armchair. First she turned to the journal that had accompanied her ever since they'd left Aston Hall late last summer. This tour of the Continent had been planned to put the final finishing on the educations of Lady Mary and Lady Diana before they returned to London society and, most likely, suitable husbands and marriages. The trip was also meant to restore the reputation of Lady Diana, singed as it had been by a minor scandal. Her father had decided that a half-year abroad would serve to make people forget Diana's misstep, and Jane had guided the girls with the mixed purpose of education, edification and whitewashing.

To Jane it had been a glorious challenge. She'd begun by recording her impressions each day in her journal in precise short entries, from their crossing to Calais, the carriage across the French countryside to Paris and then on to Italy, to Florence and Rome and finally here to Venice.

But those initial brief entries had soon blossomed

into longer and longer writings as Jane had suc-
cumbed to the magic of travel, and the journal bristled with loose sheets of unruly scribbled notes and
sketches that she'd hurriedly tucked inside. But that
wasn't all. Pressed into the journal were all kinds of
small mementos, from tickets and playbills to wild-
flowers. Jane smiled as she rediscovered each one,
remembering everything again. Not even his Grace
could take such memories away from her, and with
special care she tied the journal as tightly closed as
she could.

Yet there'd been far more to her journey than me-
dieval cathedrals, and this was to be found in the
letters she'd received from Lady Mary and Lady
Diana since their marriages. These were filled with
rare joy and the happiness that each of them felt
with their new husbands, and so much love that
Jane's eyes filled with tears.

How she missed her ladies, her girls! Jane had
thought she'd been prepared for their inevitable
parting, the lot of all governesses; she just hadn't
expected it to come so soon. As much as she'd enjoyed Venice, she would have much preferred it in
their company, the way it was originally planned.
But love, and those two excellent young gentlemen,
had intervened, and though Jane would never wish
otherwise for Mary and Diana, there were times

when her loneliness without them felt like the greatest burden in the world. The two newlywed couples planned to meet here in Venice for Carnivale later in the month, and at their urging, she'd decided not to risk the hazardous winter voyage back to England, but remained here instead to see them once again. They'd convinced her that, since everything had been long paid for, she might as well make use of the lodgings, and she'd hesitantly agreed. But now, everything had changed.

She'd never expected the duke to surprise her like this, or to make so perilous a journey on what seemed like a whim. Yet as soon as she'd seen his face, she'd understood—he'd missed his daughters just as she missed them now, and he would have travelled ten times as far to see them again. She'd been stunned by the raw emotion in his face, the swift transition from anticipation to bitterest disappointment. At Aston Hall, he never would have revealed so much of himself; he was always simply his Grace, distant and omnipotent, a deity far above mere governesses.

Yet tonight, she'd glimpsed something else. Loneliness like that was unmistakable, as was the love that had inspired it. Didn't she suffer the same herself?

Swiftly she tied the letters together once again.

Better to go to bed than to sit about weeping like a sorrowful, sentimental do-nothing. She climbed into her bed, blew out the candle and closed her eyes, determined to lose her troubles in sleep.

But the harder she tried to sleep, the faster her restless thoughts churned, and the faster, too, that her first sympathy for the duke shifted into indignation on behalf of Mary and Diana.

She could just imagine him, snoring peacefully in the huge bed in the front bedchamber upstairs. Even asleep, he'd be completely resistant to the notion that his daughters might be happy with men of their own choosing instead of his. He didn't want to hear their side. He'd already made his decision, and he was so stubborn he'd never change it now, either.

He wasn't just a duke. He was a bully and a tyrant to his own daughters, and it was time—high time!—that someone stood up to him on their behalf.

She flung back the coverlet and hopped from her bed, grabbing her shawl from the back of the nearby chair. She gathered the ribbon-tied letters from Mary and Diana into her arms and, before she lost her courage, hurried from her room and up the stairs to the duke's chambers. The rest of the house was silent with sleep, and by the pale light of the blue-glass night lantern hanging in the hall, her long shadow scurried up the stairs beside her.

She stood only a moment at the duke's tall, panelled door before she thumped her fist. She waited, her bare feet chilled by the marble floor, heard nothing, then knocked again. In truth, she was only summoning the duke's manservant, Wilson, or perhaps Mr Potter, but she'd still make her point.

The *duke*. Hah, more like the Duke of Intolerance than the mere Duke of Aston, to say such impossibly cruel things of his own new sons-in-law, without so much as the decency of—

'Yes?' The door swung open, not just a servant's suspicious crack, but all the way. 'What in blazes—Miss Wood!'

She gasped, clutching the letters more tightly in her arms. Not Wilson, or Potter, but the duke himself stood in the open door, scarce a foot apart from her. Clearly she'd roused him from his bed, and from a deep sleep, too, for he was scowling at her as if he wasn't quite sure who she might be. She understood his confusion; she'd never seen him like this, either. He wore only his nightshirt, rumpled and loose, yet somehow revealing far more than his usual dress did because beneath all that snowy linen, he was... *naked*. The darker shadows beneath the fabric, the way the linen draped over his body, left no doubt, and Jane's cheeks flamed at the horrible realisation. To make matters worse, the throat of the shirt was unbuttoned and open to reveal his chest and a large thatch of dark curling hair, his sleeves were pushed up over his well-muscled arms, and his stocky legs and large, bare feet showed below.

Hastily she looked back up to the safer territory of his face. Or perhaps it wasn't. In all the time she'd been in his Grace's employment, she'd never seen him this dishevelled, his hair loose around his face and his jaw roughened with a growth of darker beard, his whole expression without its usual reserve and control. It was unsettling, seeing him without his guard like this, and it made him less like his Grace, and more simply like any other man.

A large, scarcely dressed and surprisingly handsome man that she'd just summoned from his bed.

Heavens preserver her, what had she *done?*

Chapter Three

The duke stared down at Jane, clearly not pleased to find her standing at the door to his bedchamber in the middle of the night.

'Miss Wood,' he said again, sleepily rubbing his palm over his jaw, 'why are you here? I thought we'd agreed that in the morning—'

'Forgive me, your Grace, but this could not wait,' Jane said, speaking to him more firmly than she'd ever thought she'd dare. 'It is most important, you see.'

'But it can't be more than two hours past midnight,' he protested. He was looking downwards, not at her face, and his scowl had become less perplexed, more thoughtful. Belatedly she realised that if she'd noticed he wore nothing beyond his nightclothes, then he was likely noticing the same of her. Yet instead of being mortified or shamed, she felt her irritation with him grow. How could he let himself be distracted in this idle fashion when so much—so *very* much!—was in question?

'Forgive me for disturbing you, your Grace.' She raised her chin, and impatiently shook her hair back from her eyes. 'But your daughters and the gentlemen they wed deserve that much from me, your Grace, and I would never forgive myself if I didn't speak on their behalf.'

His frown deepened, his thick, dark brows drawing sternly together. 'No gentlemen would steal another man's daughters. They are rogues and rascals, and I will deal with them accordingly.'

'Your daughters would not agree with your judgement, your Grace.'

'My daughters are too young to realise their folly, mere girls who—'

'Forgive me, your Grace,' Jane interrupted, her voice rising with uncharacteristic passion, 'but they are women grown, who know their own hearts.'

'"Their hearts," hah,' he scoffed. 'That is the sorriest excuse for mischief in this world, Miss Wood. When I consider all the sorrow that has come from—'

'Such as your own marriage, your Grace?' she demanded hotly. 'That is what I have always been told, and by those who would know. Did you not follow your heart when you wed her Grace, and at the same age as your daughters are now?'

His face froze, his anger stopped as cold as if he'd been turned to chilly stone.

And at once Jane realised the magnitude of what she'd done and what she'd said. The late Duchess of Aston was often mentioned at Aston Hall, and always with great affection and respect, and sorrow that she'd died so young. Her beauty, her kindness, her gentleness, all were praised and remembered by those who'd known her, and over time in the telling the duchess had become a paragon of virtue, a veritable saint. By an order so long-standing that its origins had been forgotten, no one spoke of her Grace before the duke. It was terribly tragic and romantic, true, but it was also the one rule of the house that was never broken.

Yet this was Venice, not Aston Hall. Things were different here, or perhaps it was Jane herself who was different after having been away for so many months. Either way she likely wasn't a member of the duke's household any longer, and certainly not after this.

'Forgive me for speaking plainly, your Grace,' she said. The words could not be taken back now, nor, truly, did Jane wish them unsaid, not in her present humour. 'But how can you not wish the same contentment for your daughters that you found with—?'

'You presume, Miss Wood,' he said sharply. 'You have no knowledge of these matters.'

'I know the young ladies, your Grace,' she insisted, 'and what brings them joy and happiness.'

'I know my own daughters!'

'You may know them, your Grace, but you will never know the gentlemen they love, not so long as you remain so—so set against them.'

He drew back as abruptly as if she'd struck him. 'Love,' he said, practically spitting the word. 'What do my daughters know of love? What can you know of it, Miss Wood?'

'I know what I have read for myself in your daughters' own words.' She thrust the bundled letters into his arms, making him take them. 'I know they are happy, and that they love the gentlemen they chose as their husbands. And *that* is what I know about love, your Grace.'

She curtsied briskly in her nightshift, then retreated without waiting to be properly dismissed. He did not try to stop her, nor did she look back.

She ran down the steps to her room, her shawl billowing out behind her shoulders. She closed the door to her bedchamber and took care to latch it. For what might be the last time, she sat at the gilded desk before the window, curling her feet beneath her and pressing her trembling palms to her cheeks.

She stared out at the mist rising from the canal and waited for her breathing to calm and her racing heart to slow. The night was still and quiet, with no sounds coming from his Grace's rooms upstairs. By now he must have returned to his bed to sleep. By now, too, he would have made up his mind regarding her future. Which was just as well, for she'd decided it, too.

With a sigh, she reached for a clean sheet of paper and a pen, and began to write her letter giving notice to the Duke of Aston.

'Your Grace!' Bleary-eyed, Wilson hurried out from the shadows, his striped nightcap askew over one ear and his nightshirt stuffed haphazardly into his breeches. 'Forgive me, your Grace, I did not hear you call.'

'I didn't.' Richard still stood in the doorway to his rooms, scowling down the stairs where Miss Wood had vanished. She'd appeared like a wild-haired wraith, and disappeared like one, too, so fast that he wondered now if he'd dreamed the whole thing. 'I answered the door myself.'

'Oh, your Grace, you shouldn't have done that,

indeed you shouldn't have,' his manservant said, scandalised. 'It's not safe, not in a queer foreign place such as this.'

'I'm safe enough, Wilson,' Richard said. 'Besides, it was hardly some brigand come to the rob me. It was Miss Wood.'

'Miss Wood, your Grace?' asked Wilson, clearly astonished. 'Our Miss Wood? Come here, at this hour? Why, your Grace, I'd scarce believe it, not of Miss Wood.'

'Nor I,' Richard said. 'Yet here she was, and in a righteous fury, too.'

He glanced down at the two bundles of letters she'd left with him, each tied neatly with ribbons. Of course they'd be neatly tied, just as he was certain they'd each be folded back into their seals and sorted in precedence of the date they'd been received. That was the way Miss Wood always did things, with brisk, predictable order. But there'd been nothing orderly or predictable about her outburst just now—not one thing.

'She must've had a powerful strong reason, your Grace,' Wilson said, hovering like the old nursemaid he very nearly was. 'It don't seem like her in the least.'

'It didn't, indeed.' Earlier this day he'd barely noticed Miss Wood at all, except to register that she was in fact the same governess he'd trusted with his girls' welfare. She'd simply been Miss Wood, the woman that had lived beneath his roof for nearly a decade, the same stern, plain Miss Wood that would have cowed him into obedience as a boy and had gone completely unnoticed by him as a man.

Or had until now. He'd never seen her as he just had: looking younger, much younger and more beguiling, her hair not scraped back beneath a linen cap, but loose and tousled like a dark cloud over her shoulders, her usually pinched cheeks flushed with emotion, her eyes anything but serene. Gone, too, was the strict shapeless gown, with her body bundled and barricaded within. Instead she'd been clad in only a worn linen nightdress that had slipped and slithered over her shoulders, and had revealed far more than it hid, likely far more than she'd intended. As a man, there was no conceivable way he could have overlooked the heavy fullness of her breasts, or how the chill had made her nipples tighten enticingly beneath the linen.

He grumbled wordlessly to himself, a kind of mental shake, and pushed the door shut with his elbow. God knows plenty of scullery-maid seductresses would flaunt themselves before their masters to secure extra favours, but he wasn't that kind of master, and Miss Wood wasn't that kind of servant—which had made this evening all the more unsettling. He'd always thought of her as a dry old virgin, scarcely female, and now—now he saw that she wasn't. Not at all. No wonder he couldn't forget how she'd looked, standing there with her little toes bare to lecture him about love.

About *love*. Miss Wood, coming to rouse him from his bed to challenge him in her nightdress. Damnation, what was it about this infernal Italian air that seemed to turn everything upside down?

'Here you are, Your Grace,' Wilson said, holding his dressing gown out before him. 'Put this on, and warm yourself. This is a perilously damp place, your Grace, all this water and musty old plaster, and I won't have you taken ill from standing about. Now here, let me take those papers from you.'

'No, I'll keep them,' Richard said, ignoring the dressing gown and returning to his bed, or rather, the bed that had come with the room. No respectable Englishman would ever consider such a bedstead as 'his', not when it was tricked out with gilded swans and crimson hangings shot with gold thread. All it required was a looking-glass overhead in the canopy and a naked whore or two to make it fit for the priciest brothel in London.

Grumbling, he let Wilson pull the coverlet up and plump his pillows as he picked up the first package of letters, the ones that had come from his older daughter Mary. One look at that familiar, girlish penmanship, and he forgot all about Miss Wood and her bare feet.

How could his girls marry without his consent? How could they abandon him like this, without so much as a by your leave? How could they possibly have changed so fast from his little girls in their white linen dresses and pink silk sashes into women grown and wed to other men?

'Ah, your Grace,' Wilson said, beaming. 'Letters from the young ladies?'

'That will be all, Wilson ,' Richard said curtly. 'Leave me.'

Leave me—that was what his girls had done, hadn't they? He'd come all this way for them, yet they'd already gone.

He waited until Wilson had gone, then slowly opened the first of Mary's letters and tipped the sheet towards the candlestick on the table beside the bed. It felt strange reading letters not addressed to him, like listening at a keyhole or behind a fence, practices no gentleman would do.

Yet as soon as he began to read, he heard the words in Mary's voice, as clearly as if she were in the room speaking to him, and his heart filled with emotion. The letter seemed to date from early autumn, soon after her marriage, after Miss Wood had continued on to Italy with Diana and left Mary behind in Paris with her new husband.

Ah, Mary, his dear Mary. Mary had always been his favourite of his two daughters. It wasn't that he loved her any more than he loved Diana, for he didn't, but Mary was easier to *like* than Diana. With her calm, thoughtful manner and pleasing serenity, Mary was the opposite of her impulsive and passionate sister. For better or worse, Diana took after him, while Mary favoured her mother, and as she'd grown older, Richard had come to rely on Mary to handle things about the house that had once been his wife Anne's domain. Even now he'd put off making certain decisions at Aston Hall—new paint for the drawing room, improvements that Cook wanted in the kitchen—telling himself that they could wait until Mary came home to guide him.

Except that now, as he read, he learned she wasn't coming home. No, worse—that home for her no longer meant Aston Hall, but wherever this Irish-born rascal she'd married took her. He learned that though this man seemed to have some sort of income, he'd no proper home for Mary beyond bachelor lodgings in London. Instead they seemed to be content to live like vagabonds in Paris—in *Paris!*—dining out and wandering about day and night. To be sure, their lodgings were in an excellent area that even he recognised by name, and at least Mary had enough of a staff to be respectable. Richard could learn that much from the letters, and know his Mary wasn't in any need or want.

But as he read on, Richard discovered that Mary had found more than simply respectable lodgings in Paris. In this Lord John Fitzgerald, she also seemed to have discovered a man who shared her interest in musty old pictures and books and long-ago history: a man who could make her happy.

And Mary *was* happy. There wasn't any doubt of that. Every page, every word seemed to bubble with unabashed joy in her new life and her new husband. Richard couldn't recall the last time she'd been as jubilant and light-hearted as this, not since she'd been a small girl before her mother had died.

Diana's letters were shorter, less thoughtful, and full of the dashes and false starts that made her writing so similar to her speech, darting here and there like a dragonfly over the page. Her new bridegroom, Lord Anthony Randolph, was delicious, and sought endlessly to please her. Their life together in his native Rome was full of music and friends, parties and other amusements. She'd ordered a new gown, a new hat, yellow stockings to his lordship's delight. He'd given her a talking bird from Africa. Like her sister, she was happy, more happy, she claimed, than she'd ever been in her life. She was also already four months with child.

His *grandchild.*

Richards groaned, and let his daughter's familiar girlish signature blur and swim before his tired eyes. He wasn't even forty, yet tonight he felt twice that. Oh, he'd learned a great deal from the letters. He'd learned that though he'd always done his best to make his girls happy, these unknown young men had succeeded far beyond his lowly paternal efforts. He'd learned that, no matter that his daughters had been the very centrepiece of his life, he really didn't know them at all, not as they were now. He'd learned that Mary and her husband were likely even now on their way here to Venice to meet Diana and her husband, and together to bid their favourite Miss Wood farewell before she sailed away for England. But the blistering greeting that Richard would have offered them earlier wouldn't happen. Not now, not after he'd read these letters.

Because what he'd learned the most from them this night was exactly what Miss Wood had predicted: that his darling girls had somehow changed into women in love, blissful, heavenly love, with the men they'd chosen as their mates for life.

And he, their father, had been left behind.

Chapter Four

Giovanni Rinaldini di Rossi stood close by his bedchamber window, watching. It was early for the Englishwoman to come calling on him, impossibly early by Venetian standards, yet there was Miss Wood, hurrying across the bridge towards his house. She walked briskly, with the determination and purpose with which she seemed to pursue everything, her plain dark skirts rippling around her legs. He knew ancient, widowed matriarchs who dressed with less solemnity than this little English wren did. Almost like a nun, she was, and the thought made him smile. No wonder he found her so desirable.

Without shifting his gaze, he idly touched one fingertip to the chocolate powder floating on the foamy top of his cappuccino and tapped it lightly on the tip of his tongue to taste the sweetness. Like so many of the windows in Venice, this one was designed for seeing without being seen, for mystery rather than clarity. The glass was not set in flat panes, as was done in other places, but in small round bull's-eyes framed in iron. Miss Wood would have no idea he was standing here, or that he'd been watching her ever since he'd glimpsed her in the gondola. A pretty deception, like everything else that made life interesting.

He shifted to one side so he could watch her as she waited at his door. She'd pushed back the hood of her cloak, and now he could see how the chilly early morning air had pinked her cheeks and the tip of her nose.

There were never any of the usual female artifices of powder or paint with her, none of the little false ways of hiding from a man. She was always as she seemed, fresh as new cream. Despite her age, he'd stake a thousand gold sequins that she was a virgin. He could sense it. She'd be as untouched as any young postulant, really, and he'd always a weakness for debauching convent flesh.

It was this utter lack of guile that had tempted di Rossi from the moment Miss Wood had appeared one morning in his drawing room, her letter of introduction in her gloved hands. Seduction, corruption, ruin or simply a worldly education in pleasure—it would all amount to the same thing for him. She was a governess of no social standing or family, a foreigner, in truth no more significant than any other servant. He could do whatever he pleased with her without consequences.

Now he watched as she entered his house, the door closing after her, then he smiled, and considered the delicious possibilities she presented like a gourmet before a rich feast. Though clearly she'd the body of a woman beneath that grim, shapeless gown, in her heart she still had that innocent's trust in the goodness of men. Teaching her otherwise was proving to be the greatest diversion he'd had in years.

Jane perched on the very edge of the chair. No matter how she tried, she could never quite relax on the delicate gilded chairs here in Signor di Rossi's drawing room. The red-silk damask cushions seemed too elegant to sit upon and the artfully carved legs in the shape of a griffin's clawed feet seemed too delicate to support any grown person. She was certain, too, that the chairs were very old and very valuable, like everything else in the *signor*'s house, and she would hate to repay his hospitality by being the clumsy Englishwoman who broke a chair.

Once again she drew her watch from her pocket

to check the time. She realised that calling here so early in the day could be interpreted as an affront, especially by the *signor,* who had the most refined manners she had ever encountered in a gentleman. But the hour could not be helped, not if she wished to offer both her thanks and farewell. As much as she'd enjoyed his company these last weeks, her time for the idle pleasures of art and conversation were done.

Restlessly she smoothed her skirts over her knees. She'd already accomplished much this morning, making her plans for life beyond the Farren family. She had decided to stay here in Venice rather than return to England, where her likely lack of references from the duke would be an impossible handicap. With the assistance of the English ambassador here, she had already found new lodgings with a Scottish widow that were both respectable and inexpensive. The ambassador had also promised to help her find a new place with a family with children here, either English or Italian. Failing that, she could be a companion to a widow or other elderly lady. She couldn't afford to be particular. She'd little money of her own, certainly not enough for the costly passage back to England. No wonder her situation was a complicated one, and vulnerable, too. Given his Grace's fury last night, she could return to the Ca' Battista and find all her belongings bobbing in the canal outside by his orders.

'Ah, Miss Wood, *buon giorno, buon giorno!*' Signor di Rossi entered the room with the easy self-assurance that generations of aristocratic di Rossis had bred into his blood. 'You cannot know how a visit from you pleases me.'

He was too dark, too exotic by English standards, but here in Venice Jane thought he was the very model of an Italian gentleman. He was perhaps thirty, even thirty-five. Over his shirt and black breeches he wore a long, loose dressing gown of quilted red-and-gold silk. With the pale winter sunlight glinting on the gold threads, the extravagant garment floated around him as he walked, more like a king's ceremonial robes than a gentleman's morning undress while at home. By contrast, his olive-skinned face seemed almost ascetic, his cheekbones and nose sharply defined. His black hair was sleeked back into a simple queue, and his dark eyes were full of welcome as he reached out to take her hand, and lift her up from her curtsy.

'You are most kind, *signor.*' Jane smiled, flushing with embarrassment as he held her fingers a moment longer than was proper in England. 'Most kind. You always have been that way to me.'

'But that is hardly a challenge, Miss Wood,' he

said, motioning for her to sit. 'Not between friends such as we, surely?'

Purposefully she didn't sit, determined to keep the visit short, as she'd intended. 'I am honoured that a gentleman so grand as yourself would consider me as such, *signor*.'

'Please, Miss Wood, no more.' He waved his hand gracefully through the air, the wide sleeve of his banyan slipping back over his arm. 'You speak as an Englishwoman who has had the misfortune to have spent her life in the thrall of your English king. Venice is a republic, her air free for all her citizens to breathe. If I wish to call a gondolier, or a fisherman, or an English governess my friend, then I may.'

As experienced as Jane was at masking her feelings, she couldn't keep back a forlorn small sigh at that. She'd miss her time with Signore di Rossi, discussing the beautiful paintings that his family had collected over the centuries. She'd met him soon after she'd arrived in Venice, through a letter of introduction meant for the duke's daughters. This was the customary way that well-bred English visitors could view private collections on the Continent, a day or two walking the halls of palaces and country houses with a watchful housekeeper as a guide. But to Jane's surprise, the *signor* had shown her his pictures himself, and invited her to return the following day, and every day after that.

And the *signor* was speaking the truth. He *had* treated her as a friend, almost as an equal. He had respected her observations about art so much that he'd sought her opinions as if they had actual merit. No other gentleman had listened to Jane like that before. Was it any wonder, then, that her visits here to him had become the most anticipated part of her day?

And now—now they must be done.

'Let me send for refreshment for you,' the *signor* continued as he stepped to the bell to summon a servant. 'It's early, yes, but not so early that I cannot play the good host to my favourite guest. A plate of biscotti, a cappuccino, a dish of chocolate, or perhaps your English tea?'

'Thank you, no, *signor*,' Jane said, though sorely tempted. She'd come to adore Venetian chocolate in her time here, and it would be one of the things she'd miss most when she returned to England. 'You are most generous, most kind, but I cannot stay.'

He turned on his heel and stopped, one black brow raised with surprise. 'How do you mean this, Miss Wood? How can you come, and yet not intend to stay?'

'Exactly that, *signor.* I've come only to thank you, and to—to say farewell.'

'No,' he said firmly. 'I shall not permit it. I've something special and rare to show you today, a manuscript book, drawn by hand four hundred years ago in a Byzantine monastery. The artistry will steal your breath, Miss Wood, with each parchment page brought to life with ground lapis and gold leaf and—'

'Forgive me, *signor,* but I cannot stay,' she repeated. She had to tell him the truth; putting it off like this was not making her task any easier. 'My master, his Grace the Duke of Aston, unexpectedly arrived in Venice last evening, and he—he is most displeased with me. I have given my notice to resign my place in his service, and must find another directly.'

'No!' He rushed back to her, the scarlet silk billowing after him. 'What manner of man is this duke, to be displeased with you?'

'He is a very great man in England, *signor.*' Jane sighed, thinking of how different the gruff, broad-shouldered duke was from the man before her, like comparing a great shaggy roaring lion to a sleekly self-possessed jaguar. How could she fairly describe the hearty, noble *Englishness* of his Grace to a gentleman as elegantly refined as Signore di Rossi? 'I still believe that I did what was best for his daughters, but because His Grace was expecting to find them here in Venice with me, he was…distraught.'

'For that he has cast you out?' the *signor* asked. 'For doing your duty as best you could?'

'I did not wait for him to dismiss me,' Jane said with care. To fault the duke felt disloyal; besides, when she remembered how shocked he'd been, she could almost excuse him. 'But because I felt it was inevitable, given the degree of his unhappiness, I chose to give notice first.'

Di Rossi stared at her, openly aghast. 'Yet from your telling, the daughters love you as if you shared the same blood.'

'They did love me,' she said sadly, for that, too, was true. Mary and Diana did love her, and she them, but their father loved them, too, and she thought again of the sorrow and pain she'd seen on his face last night. 'They *do*. But it is their father, not they, who decides my fate, and I'd rather not wait to hear his judgement.'

The *signor* frowned and shook his head. 'That is barbarously unfair, Miss Wood. To punish you for the sins of the daughters!'

'Daughters in my safe-keeping. I was their governess. I was to watch over them, and keep them from harm.'

'Love is not harm.'

'Love without a father's consent is,' she countered wistfully. 'At least it is if the father is an English peer of the realm.'

He shook his head. 'This puts me in mind of an ancient tale, of a Roman messenger put to death for bringing ill news of a battle to his emperor.'

'Forgive me, but it was a Spartan messenger.' She smiled sadly. 'You see how it is with me, *signor*. I cannot help myself. I am a governess bred to the marrow of my bones.'

'Ah, *cara mia*,' he said. 'You were a woman before you ever were a governess.'

Cara mia: my dear. Jane's cheeks warmed, even as she drew herself up straighter into her customary propriety. She'd learned early in her trip that gentlemen on the Continent tossed about endearments much more freely than Englishmen, yet this—this felt different.

'These last weeks have been most enjoyable, *signor*, that is true,' she said, as briskly as she could, 'but it is past time I put aside my idleness, and found another place where I can be useful.'

'To fill your eyes and feed your soul with the beauty of great paintings, the works of the finest masters—that is not idleness,' he countered. 'That is useful, Miss Wood, more useful than recalling the lesson of the Spartan messenger.'

'A well-fed eye does nothing for an empty stomach, *signor*,' Jane said, her sadness and regret rising by the second. The end would always have come in time, of course. Even if Mary and Diana had remained with her, they would have been bound to sail for home at the end of February; their passages home had been booked for months along with the rest of their itinerary. But this way, with so little warning, somehow seemed infinitely more wrenching.

'I must work to support myself,' she began again. 'I've no choice in the matter. Being a governess is not so very bad, you know.'

'Yet a governess is not a slave, chained to his oar in the galleys,' he reasoned. 'Even an English governess. No matter who employs you next, you'll have a day to yourself each week, yes? Even the lowest scullery maid has that. A day you can come here to me?'

'But a governess is expected to set a certain tone of propriety and behaviour, *signor*,' she said. 'Calling on gentlemen would not be considered as either.'

'Then don't call,' he said with maddening logic. 'I shall meet you elsewhere in the city by agreement. A hooded cloak, a mask, and the thing is done. No one shall ever know which is the governess, which the great lady. Venice is the best city in the world for assignations, you know.'

Any other time, and she might have laughed at the outrageousness of such a suggestion. 'I am very sorry, *signor,* but I cannot do that, either. My reputation must be impeccable. I have no resources of my own, you see, nor any—'

'Miss Wood.' Gently he took her hand again, though this time from affection, not the polite necessity of assisting her. She understood the difference at once, and tensed in response.

He smiled over their joined hands, his fingers tightening ever so slightly around hers.

'Signor di Rossi,' she protested, startled. 'Please. Please!'

'Know that you have a friend in Venice,' he said, his voice rich and low. 'That is all. Know that you are not without resources, as you fear. Know that you are not…alone.'

Was it a dare, an invitation, an offer? Or simply an expression of fond regard between acquaintances and nothing more?

'Goodbye, Signor di Rossi,' she said, barely a whisper. 'Goodbye.'

She pulled her hand free, turned away and, without looking back once, fled.

Chapter Five

'Blast these infernal foreign clerks,' Richard said, finally giving voice to his exasperation. He'd scarce sat down to his breakfast before the officials from the Customs House had descended upon him, and it had taken the better part of the morning for him and Potter to settle their questions and finally send them on their way. 'They're so puffed with their own importance; they do believe they're as grand as his Majesty himself. Did they truly believe we'd try smuggling rubbish in our trunks?'

Potter made a small bow of agreement. 'The Venetians are most particular about their trade, your Grace. They have such a long tradition of trade by sea, that they are most watchful guarding their port.'

'Their entire city's a port, as far as I can see.' Richard sighed, and reached for his glass again. Despite the canals and rivers everywhere, he'd been

warned for the sake of his health to stay clear of the
water for drinking, and from what he'd seen floating about beneath his window, he instantly agreed.
Instead he'd been advised to drink the local wine,
a rich, fruity red from the nearby Veneto that was
surprisingly agreeable, even when accompanied by
drones from the Customs House. 'At least we satisfied them that we're no rascally rum-smugglers,
eh?'

Potter smiled. 'Quite, your Grace.'

'Quite, indeed.' Richard nodded, then sighed
again. What lay next for this morning—or what was
left of it—wouldn't be nearly as easily resolved. He
didn't enjoy admitting he was wrong any more than
the next man did. 'Ah, well, now for the rest of my
business. Pray send in Miss Wood to me.'

'Forgive me, your Grace,' Potter said with a delicate hesitation, 'but that is not possible. She's not in
the house.'

'Not here? Of course she's here. Where the devil
could she be otherwise?'

'I do not know, your Grace.' Potter stepped forwards, instantly producing a sealed letter in that
mystifying way of all good secretaries. 'But she did
leave this for you to read at your convenience.'

Richard grabbed the letter from Potter's hand.
'I cannot believe Miss Wood would simply dis-

appear,' he said, cracking the seal with his thumb. 'She's never been given to such irresponsibility. It's not like her.'

'I expect she'll return, your Grace,' Potter offered. 'It isn't as if she's run off. All her belongings are still in her room.'

'Well, that's a mercy, isn't it?' With a grumbling sigh Richard turned to the neatly written page. A single sheet, no more, covered with Miss Wood's customary model penmanship. If she'd been upset by their exchange last night, she wasn't going to betray it with her pen, that was certain.

'Damnation,' he muttered unhappily. 'Thunder *and* damnation! Potter, what does she mean by this? You read this, and tell me. What's she about?'

Quickly the secretary scanned the letter, and handed it back to the duke. 'It would seem that Miss Wood has given notice, Your Grace, effective immediately.'

That was what Richard had thought, too, but hadn't wanted to accept. 'But she can't resign, Potter. I won't permit it.'

Potter screwed up his mouth as if he'd eaten something sour. 'You can't forbid it, your Grace, if she no longer wishes to remain in your employment. As Miss Wood herself writes, with the young ladies wed and gone, there's little reason for—'

'I know what she damn well wrote, Potter,' Richard said crossly. He set the letter on the desk and smoothed it flat with his palm. When he'd first heard that his daughters had married, he'd been ready to banish Miss Wood from his sight for the rest of their combined days on this earth. But once he'd read the letters from his daughters, he realised that Miss Wood was the last link he might have with them.

The last link. Lightly he traced her signature with his fingertip. He thought of how hard she'd tried to make the news as palatable as possible to him last night, how she'd tried to ease both his temper and his sorrow. She'd done her best for his girls in this, the way she always had, yet she'd also done her best for him. How many years had she been in his household, anyway? He couldn't remember for certain. It seemed as if she'd always been there, setting things quietly to rights whenever they went awry, looking after his girls as loyally as if they'd been her own. He could hardly expect more, nor would he have asked for more, either. Surely he must have told her so, somewhere in all the time that his daughters were growing up. Somewhere, at some time, he must have, hadn't he?

Hadn't he?

'Miss Wood is still a young woman, your Grace,'

Potter was saying, stating the patently obvious as he too often did. 'No doubt she is already looking towards her future, and a position with another—'

'I know perfectly well how young she is, Potter,' Richard said, and as soon as he spoke he remembered how she'd looked last night, her hair loose and full over her shoulders and her eyes wide and glowing with the fervour of her argument. Oh, aye, she was young, a good deal younger than he'd remembered her to be. Now he couldn't forget it, and his confusion made his words sharp. 'Nor do I need you to tell me of her future.'

Potter sighed, and bowed. 'No, your Grace.'

'Miss Wood's future, indeed,' Richard muttered, pointedly turning away from Potter to gaze out the window. Nothing had prepared him for losing his girls as abruptly as he had, and now he'd no intention of letting Miss Wood go before he was ready. 'As if I'd so little regard for the young woman that I'd turn her out in a foreign place like some low, cast-off strumpet.'

'Your Grace.'

He swung around at once. Miss Wood herself was standing there beside Potter, her gloved hands neatly clasped at her waist and her expression perfectly composed.

'Forgive me for startling you, your Grace,' she

said, 'but Signora della Battista told me you wished to see me directly. I have only now returned, and I came to you as soon as I could.'

He nodded, for once unable to think of what to say. Hell, what had he been saying when she'd entered? Something unfortunate about strumpets and being turned out.

'Potter, leave us,' he ordered, determined not to embarrass her any further. 'I will speak to Miss Wood alone.'

The secretary backed his way from the room, and shut the door after him. Miss Wood continued to stand, her expression so unperturbed that Richard found himself unsettled by it.

'Sit, Miss Wood, sit,' he said, waving his hand towards a nearby chair. 'That is, if you wish to.'

'Thank you, your Grace.' She sat with an unstudied grace, the slight flutter of her plain woollen skirts around her ankles reminding him painfully of her nightshift last night in the hallway.

Unaware of his thoughts, she sighed and glanced down at her letter, still open on the table before him.

Her smile became more forced, its earlier pleasantness gone. 'I suppose you wish to discuss terms, your Grace. I can be gone from this house by nightfall today, if that is your desire.'

'It most certainly is not!' he exclaimed, appalled. 'Look here, Miss Wood, what I was saying when you came in—I didn't mean you, or that you were to leave.'

Her eyes widened with bewilderment, and she flushed. 'Forgive me, your Grace, but I don't understand. When I entered just now, you were looking through the window, saying nothing.'

'Very well, then, very well.' He cleared his throat to cover his discomfort. That was a fine start to things, stammering out an apology when none was needed, like some tongue-tied schoolboy. 'I've no intention of sending you off to fend for yourself without any warning. It's not right, and I won't have it said that I'd do such a thing to any woman in my employment.'

'You're very...kind.' Now her smile was tremulous with an uncertainty he'd never seen from her before, and that touched him at once. Little tendrils of her dark hair had escaped from beneath her linen cap, doubtless coaxed into curls by Venice's perpetual dampness, and reminding him again of last night. Why had he always believed her hair to be straight and uninteresting before this?

'It's not kindness,' he said as firmly as he could. 'It's my duty to you, in return for how well you have served my daughters.'

'It *is* kindness, your Grace,' she said carefully, 'and I thank you for it. But I cannot continue here, a governess with no charges to govern. It would not be right.'

'And I say it is.' To prove it, he took her letter and tore it in two. 'There. We'll forget about this notice, and you can continue with the same wages. I'll have Potter settle the particulars, to make sure I'm not in arrears with you for the quarter.'

'But for what, your Grace?' she asked. 'Before you arrived, I could continue to stay here until I took the passage for home because I was following my orders as we had arranged last summer. I could continue as I was, because I'd no reason not to, even without any responsibilities. But now that you *do* know my situation, everything changes. To accept wages from you for being idle would be perceived as unseemly, your Grace.'

Her cheeks had remained pink, and he wondered if she, too, were remembering last night. Had he surprised her as much as she had him? Had she been aware of him as a man, and not just a master? Is that what she meant by 'unseemly'?

'You've been in my household for years, Miss Wood.' A thousand memories of her with his daughters came racing back to him—more, really, than he had of the girls with his wife. All he asked now was that she share that with him for another fortnight. 'You are in many ways a part of our family, you know. Certainly my two daughters feel that way towards you.'

With triumph he saw the brightness in her eyes that meant unshed tears. She wouldn't go now, not so long as she thought of Diana and Mary.

He lowered his voice, softer but no less commanding. 'Please, Miss Wood. No one would question it if you remained here another few weeks.'

But instead of immediately agreeing, as he'd expected, she shook her head. 'Forgive me, your Grace, but I believe they would. A governess is always vulnerable to talk.'

'No female servant has ever come to grief in my household,' he declared proudly, 'and I defy anyone to say otherwise. That shall not change, Miss Wood. I give you my word of honour.'

'I thank you, your Grace.' She rose, and he stood, too, on the other side of the table with her torn letter lying between them. 'But I must refuse. I have no choice, not if I hope to be at ease with myself. I cannot remain here to take money from you for doing nothing in return.'

'Nothing?' Swiftly he turned away from her again and back towards the window, unwilling to let her see his surprise at her refusal. When was the last time anyone had refused him like this? What more did she wish from him, anyway? What more could he offer her?

'For the sake of my girls, I would ask you to stay,' he said to the window. 'Reconsider, and stay. Please.'

Yet she did not answer, and he sighed impatiently, clasping and unclasping his hands behind his back.

'An answer, Miss Wood,' he said. 'Damnation, you can at least grant me that courtesy, can't you?'

No answer came, not a word, and with a muttered oath he swung around to confront her.

And to his chagrin, learned that she had left him and he was already alone.

With feverish haste, Jane packed the last of her belongings into her travelling trunks. Despite the luxury and comfort of this house and the hospitality shown to her by Signora della Battista, the sooner she left this place, the better. No matter how much the duke insisted she stay, she could not remain here with him. She could *not*. It was as simple, and as complicated, as that.

She muttered with frustration, a rolled-up stocking clutched tightly in her hand. She had anticipated this tour across the Continent so much. Likely it would be the one time in her life she'd be able to see the places and paintings she'd only read about in books. While most tutors to noble families had travelled to France and Italy, very few governesses ever left their schoolrooms, and she'd counted on these new experiences to increase her value to families who'd hire her in the future.

But what she hadn't counted on was how this trip had altered her.

The changes had been imperceptible as they'd happened, or at least they'd been so to her. When she studied her reflection in the looking-glass, she appeared much the same as she always had, with more thoughtfulness than beauty in her face. She wore the same clothes as when she'd left Aston Hall, and pinned her hair back into the same tidy knot as she had since she'd been a girl. She still wore no scent, no ornaments or jewels, no extra little enticements designed to beguile. She dressed for sturdy, respectable practicality and nothing else.

Nor could she say exactly when or how the changes had occurred. Was it because she'd been forced to step so far beyond her usual place in life, and accept more responsibility for herself and her young charges? Was it the art she'd seen in the galleries here, frankly sensual images of pagan love among the ancient Greeks and Romans, of writhing nymphs and satyrs, of Romish saints in the throes of exquisite ecstasies, that had subtly marked her? Or had the proximity to the heated affairs of Mary and Diana affected her, too, softening her, burnishing her, making her less like her familiar spinster self and more receptive to male attention, even admiration?

Because that was what had happened. Not only was she noticing gentlemen with more interest than she ever had before, but they were noticing her. To be sure, Signor di Rossi was Italian, and by his nature much given to emotional displays, but for him to have proposed assignations had stunned her. The very word sounded beyond wicked. She would be thirty on her next birthday, well beyond the impulsive age for making *assignations* with gentlemen. Wasn't she?

Then why had she seen his Grace in an entirely different light last night? For ten years he had been her master and no more, the father of her charges and little else. She had admired him from afar, of course; there was much about him to admire. But once she took the letters to his room last night, everything between them seemed to have shifted. When he'd opened the door himself, she hadn't thought of him as her master the duke, but as a large, tousled man roused from his bed.

She'd been acutely aware of his physical presence, glimpsed outside his nightshirt, of the muscles of his bare forearms and the curling hair on his chest like the naked Roman gods in the paintings by Tintoretto. His unshaven jaw bristled with a night's worth of whiskers, and his uncombed hair had fallen across his forehead. She'd stood so close to him that she'd smelled his scent, the warmth of his skin combined with the faint fragrance of freshly washed bed-linens. He'd looked at her, too, looked at her as if he'd never seen her before, with admiration and interest and with desire for her as a woman, too, if she were being honest. In her confusion, she'd looked down to avoid his scrutiny, and had seen the shocking intimacy of his bare feet, so close to hers that their toes could have touched.

And then he'd spoken of his daughters and love and desire and she'd heard the passion in his voice, the urgency of his emotions, so great that she'd had no choice but to run away, just as she'd run away from him now, both times without his leave or her own common sense.

She groaned, and hurled the stocking into the open trunk. What if he'd guessed her thoughts? She'd come to his bedchamber door last night shamelessly in her nightshift. She'd told him this morning that she couldn't take his wages without earning them, and of course he'd seen no reason to her objection. The duke was a man in his prime, and bound to make conclusions. And what if his Grace had the same wanton notions towards her that she'd felt towards him? Considering it—considering *him*—was enough to make her flush all over again. No, she'd no choice. She had to leave this house now, *now,* before she was thoroughly disgraced by her own wicked self.

She slammed the lid shut on her trunk. She would go to the Scottish widow, and put aside for ever the pleasure of viewing pictures on the arm of Signor di Rossi. She would live as chaste a life as she could until she found a new place. She'd drink no more wine, nor view inflammatory pictures. She would again be the model of English propriety. She would be lonely, too, but she'd been lonely before, it would be nothing new to her. The consequences if she chose otherwise would be far more grievous.

She heard the rap at her door—doubtless the porter come to collect her things.

'Uno momento, per favore,' she called, hurrying to gather up her cloak. She paused in the doorway between her little servant's bedchamber and the more extravagant one meant for a lady, gazing for the last time at the unforgettable view of blue sky, shimmering canal and tiled rooftops framed by the

window's curving arches. It was unforgettable, too; she'd carry it in her memory for ever, and she lingered to savour the sight a moment longer.

'Miss Wood.'

She jerked around. His Grace stood in the open door, his hand resting on the latch, surprising her just as she had done to him earlier.

'You left before we could finish,' he said, coming to join her. 'We weren't done.'

'I believed we were, your Grace.' She wasn't exactly frightened of him, but she was wary: of him, and of herself.

'We weren't,' he said, folding his arms over his chest. 'You say you won't remain with me and be paid for being idle.'

'Yes,' she agreed. 'That is what I said.'

'Then what if you remain as my guest? You'll receive no wages, no money. There's no sin to that, is there?'

She raised her chin, more determined than ever. 'Idle tongues would still see sin, your Grace, whether I were paid a thousand pounds or none at all. It would be so with any woman beneath your roof.'

'Damnation, it's not as if we're alone,' he said. 'The house is full of servants.'

She didn't answer. She didn't have to, not with her resolve so evident in every inch of her posture.

He grumbled, a sound she knew was his way of masking an oath in the company of ladies. He began to walk slowly around her, not exactly pacing, but thinking, considering. She recognised that about him as well.

'You speak Italian, don't you?' he asked at last. 'You can manage the lingo here?'

'A bit, your Grace,' she admitted. 'I am not precisely fluent in the language, but I have learned enough to make my wishes understood.'

'Well, then, there's the solution,' he said as if that explained everything. 'You can remain here as my translator. You can take me about the city and show me the sights.'

'But I—you—already have a bear leader hired for that purpose,' she protested, naming the professional guide who had presented himself with a flourish the morning she'd arrived, 'a native Venetian named—'

'I do not care what the fellow is named,' he said grandly. 'I would rather have you, Miss Wood, to guide me, and teach me what I should know of Venice.'

'Oh, your Grace, I am hardly qualified—'

'You know more than I,' he said, smiling proudly

at his solution. 'That's qualification enough. You are a governess, a teacher by trade.'

'Your Grace, please—'

'I do please,' he said, and stopped his walking. By accident he stood framed by the arch of the window, his dark blond hair turned gold by the sun, as much a halo as any English peer would ever have. Yet he also stood beside the bed, that extravagant, opulent, sinful bed, and there was nothing angelic about that whatsoever.

'In those letters you gave me to read from my girls,' he continued, 'they said they'd be here in a fortnight. They're expecting to see you then, and they'll have my head if you're not here to greet them.'

'Was that all you gleaned from those letters, your Grace?' she asked, appalled. She had given him the letters so that he'd learn of the love his girls had found with their new husbands, and the happiness as well, but now it seemed he'd read them and learned nothing. 'An itinerary?'

'Two weeks, two short weeks,' he said, ignoring her question. 'Surely you can tolerate my company for that time, until they arrive, and then—then you may go as you wish.'

'Why does my presence matter so much to you?'

she demanded. 'Surely you can tell me that, your Grace. Why should you care at all?'

'Why?' He turned slightly, just enough so that he caught the reflections from the water, ripples of light across his face that robbed it of all his certainty, his confidence.

'Why?' He repeated the single word again as if mystified by how exactly to reply. His smile turned crooked, too, or maybe it was only another trick of the shifting light. 'Why? Because my girls, my finest little joys, have grown and left me. Because you, Miss Wood, are my last link here on the other side of the world to them, and to the past that I'd always judged to be happy enough.'

'Oh, your Grace,' she said softly, bewildered by such an unexpected confession. She took a step towards him, her hand outstretched on impulse to offer comfort. 'Oh, I am sorry, I did not intend to—'

'Damnation, because I do not wish to be entirely abandoned here alone,' he said gruffly, the truth clearly so painful to him that he could scarce speak it aloud. 'Is that reason enough for you, Miss Wood? Is it?'

Now when she looked at him, she saw neither the overbearing master she'd always known, nor the lusty male she'd encountered last night. What remained was sorrow, loss and resignation, all the proof she needed that what he'd said was true: that he did not want to be left alone.

And neither, truly, did she.

'I'll stay, your Grace,' she said softly, daring to rest her hand on his arm. 'Until your daughters arrive, I'll stay.'

Chapter Six

The following morning, Richard woke slowly, letting himself drift into wakefulness from the pleasing depth of unconsciousness. He'd slept much more soundly the second night in the Ca' Battista, and he wasn't entirely sure why. The bed was every bit as uncomfortable the second night as the first, the sheets still smelled of the damp, the fireplace still smoked with every stray gust of wind, and the peculiar little plaster cupids that surrounded the painting in the ceiling still seemed to be watching him with their sightless plaster eyes.

He smiled drowsily up at them, rolled over and buried his face once again in the musty pillow-bier. Cupids, hah. Miss Wood surely would have something to tell him about small, fat, naked boys with wings who hovered, laughing, over a gentleman's bedstead when he—

Miss Wood. That, or rather she, must be the reason

he'd slept so much better. Having an Englishwoman like Miss Wood here in Venice with him made all the difference, and knowing she'd stay would put any man's mind at ease. She'd help him learn all the little things he'd somehow missed about his daughters, and explain to him what he didn't know about their lives, just as she'd once kept him abreast of their progress in the schoolroom. It had all made perfect sense, and he'd never been in any real doubt that she'd agree to remain. Now he'd have to thank her for a good night's sleep, too.

Or perhaps not. She was prickly about such things, and she might take such a compliment the wrong way, and say it was too scandalous. He grinned, and rubbed his palm over his unshaven jaw. He could show her real scandal, if she were agreeable—he was a man, after all, still in his prime. Not that he'd test any woman with so little respect, of course. Ever since his wife had died, he'd prided himself on being in control of his passions for the sake of her memory, limiting himself only to the occasional visit to a discreet house in London.

Yet there was something about this new side of Miss Wood that he found peculiarly tempting, a spark behind her prim control that hinted at more. How he'd like to kiss that severity from her mouth, and muss those tidy petticoats of hers a bit!

He chuckled, imagining how she'd react, how indignant she'd be, how shocked. Lord, what possessed him to think such thoughts of a governess? Chuckling still, he pushed himself up against the pillows. High time he rose, anyway. His manservant Wilson would be here soon with his breakfast.

Exactly on cue, Richard heard the chamber door open and shut and saw the flash of sunlight behind the bed curtains that announced Wilson's arrival. The curtains of the bed opened, the rings scraping on the metal rod overhead, and there was Wilson's gloomy face to greet Richard's day, the same as it had been for years.

But on this morning, there seemed to be a change in the never-changing routine. Wilson glared, as usual, but his gnarled hands were empty, without Richard's customary cup of steaming coffee.

'What's this, Wilson?' Richard asked. 'Where's my brew?'

'There's none, your Grace,' Wilson said, his expression sour, 'not that I'll be bringing you, anyways. If it were my deciding, I would, but it's not, so's I won't, and there's no help for the change from where I can see it.'

'No riddles, Wilson. It's far too early for that.' Exasperated, Richard swung his legs over the side of the bed. This made no sense. He was always most particular about beginning his day with the same breakfast. Wilson knew his ways better than anyone, and had personally made certain that Richard had had his customary breakfast even on the long voyage from Portsmouth, when his shirred eggs had required the presence and supervision of three miserable laying-hens. 'Where the devil is my coffee, you lazy sot? And where's the tray with the rest of my breakfast?'

Wilson groaned, and held up Richard's dressing gown. 'I told you, your Grace, it's not for me to decide,' he said almost primly. 'It's that Miss Wood who's doing all the deciding this morning.'

'Miss Wood?' Richard thrust his arms into the waiting sleeves. 'What does Miss Wood have to do with this?'

'Everything, your Grace.' Wilson's wounded pride finally gave way in a torrent of outrage. 'On account of her telling me it was wrongful for you to eat an English breakfast in your chambers while you was in Venice, she told me you had to come down to her and eat what they eat here, foreign-like, no matter that you never do and never would. That was what I told her, your Grace, that you liked what you liked for your breakfast, but she'd hear none of it, and told me you'd already agreed to do as she said. As *she* said, your Grace, and you a duke and a peer and she a governess and daughter of a two-penny preacher from Northumberland!'

'Her antecedents matter little to me, Wilson.' Richard whipped the sash twice around his waist, tying it snugly with the determination of a warrior readying his sword belt for battle. 'But as for interfering in my breakfast—*that* is another thing entirely.'

He threw open the door and marched down the stairs to the floor with the more public rooms. Halfway down he wished he'd stopped long enough to find his slippers—the polished treads of the carved marble staircase were infernally cold beneath his feet—but he wasn't about to retreat until he'd settled this with Miss Wood.

Following his nose and the pleasant scent of cooked food, he found her in a small parlour to the back of the house. The room was taller than it was wide, with narrow arched windows and a domed, gilded ceiling that made Richard feel like he stood at the bottom of some eastern gypsy's jewel box. Two squat chairs covered in red were set before the little round table, likewise covered with a red cloth, only added to the sensation that he'd blundered into someone else's exotic nightmare.

Except that sitting at the red-covered table was

Miss Wood, as unexotically English as any woman could be.

'Good morning, your Grace,' she said cheerfully, rising to curtsy. 'I'm glad you chose to join me for breakfast.'

Glowering, he chose not to sit. 'There was no choice involved. You bullied my manservant, and refused to let him do his duty towards me.'

'What, Wilson?' She raised her delicate dark brows with bemusement. 'Your Grace, you grant me supreme powers if you believe I ever could bully Wilson into doing—or not doing—anything against his will.'

Richard's scowl deepened. She was right, of course. 'Are you saying that he chose to disobey me?'

'Oh, no.' Her smile became beatific. 'Rather I should say that I am most honoured that you have chosen to join me for breakfast in the Venetian manner.'

'This is not as I wished, Miss Wood,' he said, shaking his head. 'Not at all.'

'Oh, but it is, your Grace,' she said. 'Last night you hired me to act as your guide while you were visiting this city, and to teach you what I'd learned myself of Venice. This is our first lesson, you see, to experience how a Venetian gentleman begins his day.'

Richard looked down at the array of dishes laid out on the table before her. There was a plate with paper-thin slices of ham arranged to overlap like the petals of a flower, and an assortment of fancifully shaped breadstuffs. Beside her cup was a chocolate-mill and a smaller pot of hot milk.

'Please, your Grace,' she coaxed, turning the armchair beside her invitingly towards him. 'As you see, everything is in readiness for you.'

Everything, hah. He retied the sash on his dressing gown more tightly with quick, disgruntled jerks, and sniffed while trying still to look unhappy at being crossed. He couldn't deny that the rich assortment of fragrances that had first drawn him were tempting, or that his empty stomach was rumbling with anticipation. But likewise he liked his habits, his routines, and a breakfast that lacked eggs, strawberry preserves and well-roasted black coffee was not part of his habit.

'Miss Wood,' he began, determined to steer things between them more to his liking at once, before they'd escaped too far beyond his control. 'I know you mean well, Miss Wood, but I am afraid that—'

'Oh, your Grace!' She was staring down at his

bare feet with the same horror that most women reserved for rats and toads. 'Oh, your Grace, your poor feet! These stone floors are so chill on a winter morning. Come, sit here beside the *kachelofen* and warm them at once while I prepare your chocolate.'

She bustled forwards, taking him gently by the elbow to guide him to the chair with such concern and efficiency that he could not shake her off without being rude.

'Here now, I'm not some greybeard to be settled in the chimney corner,' he grumbled, even as he let her do very nearly that. 'And what the devil's a *kachelofen?*'

'This,' she said, pointing to an ornate object behind the table. He'd thought it was a tall cabinet or chest, but now that he was closer, he could see that it was made not of painted wood, but of sections of porcelain, fantastically moulded and glazed with curlicues and flowers. He also realised that the thing was giving off heat most pleasantly, far more than the grate in his bedchamber had, and automatically he shifted closer to warm himself.

'A *kachelofen's* a kind of stove, much beloved by Venetians,' she explained, holding her palm over the nearest surface to feel the heat for herself. 'They claim a good *kachelofen* will warm a room better than an open fire, require less wood and be safer as well.'

'Safe, you say?' he asked, not because he really wished to know, but because it seemed rude to her not to make an enquiry or two.

'Oh, yes,' she said eagerly. 'For a city surrounded by water, the Venetians are powerfully afraid of fire. Only the glassmakers are permitted to keep furnaces, because it is necessary for their trade and therefore necessary for the economy of the city.'

'You're full of useless information for so early an hour, Miss Wood,' he said, though the pleasing warmth from the whatever-it-was-called was easing his temper.

Nor was she offended. 'There is no such thing as useless information, your Grace. Only information whose usefulness is yet to be revealed. Consider how useful a *kachelofen* would be in the north corner of your library at Aston Hall. You could set the fashion in the county.'

'What, for foreign kickshaws and foolishness?'

'For efficiency, your Grace, and being clever and forward-thinking,' she suggested. 'The people here do understand how to make their lives more agreeable, and there would be no sin in borrowing the best of their notions. But then I would imagine your Grace has already considered it, yes?'

'Ahh—yes, yes, of course.' He studied her with fresh surprise. His recollection of Miss Wood with his daughters was of her being reticent, speaking only when first addressed. He'd never heard her be quite so…loquacious before. More surprising still, he realised that he rather liked it.

In fact, he liked sitting here, wearing his night-clothes in cosy domesticity with his daughters' governess, in a room too lurid for most London bagnios. He suspected he was called many things about the county at home, but 'clever' wasn't a word he'd heard often, and to his surprise, he rather liked that, too.

'Perhaps one of these would be of use,' he said, regarding the *kachelofen* now as an ally. 'It does keep off the cold better than a grate.'

'Indeed it does, your Grace.' She returned to her own chair, and began to busy herself with the chocolate-mill. 'Now that you're warming your-self from the outside in, we must see to warming you from the inside out as well. This, your Grace, is how every proper Venetian gentleman begins his day, and likely the improper ones as well.'

He watched her briskly twisting the rod back and forth between her palms to mix a froth into the dark mixture, her little hands moving with confident dexterity. He wished she hadn't mentioned those improper gentleman, considering how improper his own thoughts were at the moment.

'Chocolate's well enough for those fellows,' he said finally. 'But I'd as soon have Wilson fetch me my usual coffee.'

She paused, and glanced up at him without raising her chin. 'You could, your Grace. You could. But if you did, it would be disappointing.'

It was the evenness of her voice that stopped him. No fuss, no excess of emotion, only that quietly stated disappointment.

'Would you be disappointed, Miss Wood?' he asked softly. Now with the idle pleasantries of the *kachelofen* done, he found he cared more about her answer than he'd wish to admit. 'If I chose my old ways, would you be disappointed?'

But instead of answering, she lowered her gaze back to the mill. 'I ask only that you try it, your Grace. This chocolate is far different from that served in London. Cocoa, sugar, cinnamon, vanilla. You will taste the difference at once.'

'How did you come by all this knowledge of yours, eh?' he asked, still sceptical. 'You've not been here so long yourself.'

'I listen to whomever will speak to me, your Grace, and I learn wherever I might,' she said, carefully filling a second cup for him. 'Signora della

Battista and her cook. The gondoliers who pilot the gondolas and the old monks who show me the paintings in the churches. Here now, take care, and do not burn your tongue.'

She set the little cup before him, and Richard looked down at it so glumly that she laughed.

'Faith, your Grace, I've no wish to poison you,' she said. 'You look like a small boy faced with a foul-smelling physick.'

He sighed dolefully. 'If I drink it, will you let me have my coffee afterwards?'

'An entire pot of Wilson's best, if you wish it,' she said. 'But you must make an honest effort, else I won't take you anywhere today.'

'I suppose there's no help for it,' he said, manfully taking up the cup with fingers too large for the dainty porcelain handle. 'Must obey the governess.'

Though he tipped the cup to drink, the chocolate was almost too thick to do so, not quite a pudding, nor a drink, either. What it was for certain was wonderful, redolent of spices and flavour, warm and rich, and exactly sweet enough to satisfy. It delighted his tongue and his stomach, the pleasurable sensation of contented well-being spreading through his limbs as well. She was right: he'd never tasted anything like it, and he tipped the cup again, wanting more.

'Should I send for Wilson's coffee now, your Grace?' While her expression was studiously impassive, her eyes shone bright with amusement in the grey winter sunlight. 'Or would you care for another dish of chocolate?'

He held his cup out to be refilled. 'You tell me, ma'am.'

She laughed and poured the chocolate. As he drank again, she took a two-tined fork and plucked up a piece of the ham. The meat was sliced so finely that she could twist it into a rosette on the tines of the fork, offering it to him.

'That looks as thin as the sorry ham they serve at Vauxhall Gardens,' he said, turning suspicious again. 'Flimsy, tasteless rubbish, unfit for any man.'

'It's not the same, I assure you,' she said. 'It's far, far more delectable than that, and not at all like that thick, fatty bacon you devour at home. *Prosciutto,* it's called. Try it now, while the chocolate lingers on your tongue, and let the flavors mingle.'

This time he trusted her, taking the entire twirled rosette of ham from the fork into his mouth. Magically, the saltiness of the meat melded with the fading sweetness of the chocolate to make something entirely different. It seemed that beyond the spices of the chocolate and the spices of the ham's curing, he could also taste the dark mystery of the cocoa along with the sweet summer grasses that the pig had eaten. He'd never tasted anything like it, especially not for breakfast. It was not only beyond his experience, but beyond his powers to describe as well.

She knew it, too, her mouth curving up in a mischievous, knowing grin as she twisted the fork into the ham once again. '*That* is how Venice tastes, your Grace, or rather, how it tastes so early in the day. We can have another lesson at each meal, if you please.'

'Oh, it pleases me,' he said. He took another sip of the chocolate, but instead of reaching for the fork with the ham, he leaned forwards and opened his mouth. She hesitated only a moment before her smile blossomed into a grin, and she fed the ham to him. He made a rumbling sound of happiness as he chewed, and finally winked at her by way of thanks.

Startled, she sat back in her chair, the fork still in her hand, but then she laughed softly, too, as much at her own surprise as with him. Best of all, she blushed, her cheeks turning nearly as rosy as the cloth on the table.

If this was his breakfast lesson, why, he could scarce wait for dinner.

'Who taught you this?' he asked, intrigued by the notion of his prim English governess indulging in something as sensuous as this unexpected combination of ham and chocolate. Or rather, a governess he'd mistakenly judged to be prim. Clearly there was far more to her than he'd ever realised before. 'Where did you learn it?'

'It's scarcely a secret, your Grace,' she said, so deftly dodging his question that at first he didn't realise she'd done it. 'The Venetians do relish their chocolate. Why, two hundred years ago, cocoa beans were of as much value as gold coins.'

'More fool them, I say.' He reached for another fork to finish the ham. He'd had the rare pleasure of her feeding him before, but he didn't wish to test her—or himself—too far by expecting her to do it again. There were limits, limits he'd already come close to crossing, and besides, he was hungry. 'Chocolate for gold!'

'For other things, too, your Grace.' She lowered her voice to a conspirator's whisper. 'They say there was a time when a slave could be bought for the sum of a hundred cocoa beans.'

'A man's life for beans?' he asked as he ate. 'That doesn't seem a fair price.'

'But 'tis true,' she said. 'I had it on the best authority. And more—that a dozen cocoa beans would buy the luscious favours of the most wanton courtesan in all the city for a night.'

Richard choked on the ham.

'Do you need help, your Grace?' she asked frantically as she rushed to stand behind his chair and began thumping him on the back. 'Wilson! Wilson, come at once! His Grace is in distress!'

'Hush, hush, I'm fine,' Richard sputtered, gasping for breath. 'Now sit, and be still.'

She sat, barely, on the edge of the chair with her hands clasped tightly in her lap and her face screwed up with concern. 'You are certain you are recovered, your Grace? You are sure?'

'Of course I am,' he said, taking a deep, heaving breath. 'You took me by surprise, that was all.'

'I, your Grace?'

Damnation, what right did she have to look so astonished? 'Yes, you, Miss Wood. To hear you speak, ah, to speak with such freedom—'

'Of the courtesans?' she helpfully supplied. 'Venice is famous for them. Or should I say infamous? You may not be aware of this, your Grace, but it is a historical fact that at one time there were more courtesans in Venice than in any other city in Italy.'

'In the past, you say?' The historical past meaning yesterday, he supposed, when he'd not even disembarked before the whores had come rowing right up to the boat. Either Miss Wood was a complete innocent, or she must have the blinders of all polite women in place to have missed them.

'Yes, your Grace, the past,' she continued charmingly, falling back into her schoolroom manner. 'The courtesans then were like the great ladies of other places, living as high as queens. They must have been very beautiful and accomplished, for all that they were—were not very nice women.'

'Oh, no, not at all.' Deliberately he helped himself to a bun. A round bun, about the size of his fist, bristling with plump raisins and glazed with white sugar icing. Exactly. If he concentrated on the bun, on each and every infernal raisin, then perhaps he could not be thinking the thoughts he was thinking about his daughters' governess.

'But then history is often like that, your Grace, isn't it?' she continued, blithely unaware. 'Our own British history's not always as honourable as it should be, though I don't believe even wicked old Henry Tudor tried to barter cocoa beans for courtesans.'

'Who told you of the, ah, value of cocoa beans?'

he asked. 'I trust it wasn't the bear-leader hired in my name.'

'Signor Gaspari?' She smiled at the notion, a chink in her schoolroom manner. 'Oh, no, your Grace, he is the very soul of decorum. No, I heard it from another, though I cannot recall exactly where.'

In those few moments, Richard sensed more than she was telling. Could she have met someone here during the few weeks she'd been here alone, someone who'd taught her how to taste chocolate and ham together and to speak so easily of courtesans? Could that be the reason that she seemed so different from how he remembered her?

Could the ever-respectable Miss Wood have had an intrigue?

He studied her with new thoughtfulness. She might not be a young girl any longer, but there was an intelligence and animation to her, an eagerness, that gave beauty to her features in a way that he'd never noticed before. In the silvery winter light of Venice, she looked more delicate than he'd remembered from the bright country sunshine of Kent. Here she returned his gaze levelly, without hesitation or fading deference, and that was different, too. She *was* beautiful, really, with her round little face and luminous blue eyes.

'Do you be needing me, your Grace?' Wilson stood in the doorway, clearly peeved at having been called down for what he perceived as a fool's errand. Behind him hovered Signora della Battista and one of her footman, her expression filled with more curiosity than concern. 'We heard Miss Wood shouting, your Grace, loud enough to raise the very dead, and—'

'No one's dead, Wilson,' Richard said curtly, pushing his chair back from the table without looking at Miss Wood. He felt foolish now, almost guilty, for no reason at all. 'And no one's in any need of help, either.'

Wilson glanced pointedly at the chocolate pot. 'None of your coffee, your Grace?'

'No.' Likely he looked a great fool, too, sipping hot chocolate with a governess in his nightclothes. 'I am finished with breakfast, and I'll be dressing now for a day out of doors.'

'Out of doors, your Grace?' Wilson asked. 'On the water?'

'Out of doors, Wilson, and on the water, and into the very sky if it pleases me to do so.' Richard nodded, striving for nonchalance as he walked past them, or at least as nonchalant as he could be in his bare feet and dressing gown. 'In addition to the proper clothes, I'll ask you to arrange what is necessary for keeping warm while in the open. Miss Wood will be my guide, and I will be going wherever she suggests.'

Chapter Seven

'I've heard enough tales of that infernal bell tower, Miss Wood,' the duke said. 'No more *campanile*, if you please.'

Jane looked at him sideways, using the hood of her cloak as an excuse to keep from turning her face fully towards him. She wasn't sure if she could, anyway, she was that close to being frozen stiff. The coals in the tin foot warmer beneath her petticoats had long ago lost their warmth, and with it she'd lost the feeling in her toes as well as in her fingers. The weather had turned much colder overnight, and the breeze that came down the canals from the open sea felt less like the customary summery caress and more like an icy slap.

Yet the duke had insisted they survey the city by gondola. On other, balmier days, Jane had thought a gondola was a fine, elegant method of travel. She'd come to love gliding through the watery streets, with the gondolier at his oar behind her and Signor Gaspari sitting at her feet while he described everything they saw.

But this morning was different. Without Jane's knowledge, poor Signor Gaspari had been summarily dismissed. As the duke's new guide, Jane had at once volunteered to sit in the guide's place on the plain bench, but the duke wouldn't hear of it. Instead she must sit with him, beside him, as uneasy equals. His Grace insisted. There was no argument.

And sitting on the gondola's cushioned bench with a man as large as the duke was, well, *intimate.* No matter how Jane tried to ease herself apart from him, the sleek narrowness of the gondola's design pushed them together, and she couldn't help touching her arm against his arm, her leg against his, her hip against his. The way that Wilson had tucked them in together beneath fur-lined rugs as if they were in bed only made the arrangement cosier still.

In retrospect, it had been her own fault, feeding the duke the ham with the chocolate at breakfast. She'd intended it to be instructional, not seductive, but his Grace had clearly misinterpreted, and considered the simple gesture as something more than she'd ever meant it to be. It was not as if he'd attempted any new familiarity, or said anything to her that was disrespectful, but she sensed the difference just the same in how he looked at her, even listened to her speak.

Somehow she'd lost that invisibility that servants had in most households. He'd stopped treating her like a governess, but as a person, or worse, as a woman, and however subtle the change might be, it still unsettled her. How was she supposed to respond? What was she to say, to do, to think, sitting like this with his thigh pressed shamelessly against hers beneath the rug? She sighed with agitation, her breath coming in a little pale cloud before her face.

'Forgive me, your Grace,' she said, finally answering his question. 'But isn't that the reason you asked me to attend you in this way? To learn about Venice? Surely there is no single landmark in the city that contains as much history as the *campanile* at San Marco.'

'I'm sure,' he said, shifting his body more squarely towards hers. His face was ruddy from the chilly air, his dark gold hair tossing lightly beneath his cocked hat of dark grey beaver. He didn't seem affected at all by the cold, partly because of the heavy cloak he wore over his coat, but mostly, Jane suspected, because he was simply of warm and hearty temperament, accustomed to riding across the lands around Aston Hall in every kind of weather. Now he yawned, stretching his arms before him. 'I do believe I've learned enough for one day.'

He wasn't smiling, making it impossible for Jane to tell if he was speaking in teasing jest, or perfect seriousness.

'I'm out of practice with learning, Miss Wood,' he continued ruefully. 'These days my head can accept only so much knowledge, and no more.'

She doubted that. 'Then I must be the poorest of teachers, your Grace, if, after one morning, your head is already stuffed beyond capacity.'

'I didn't say that, did I?' he asked with a smile. 'It's more a question of the topic than the teacher. I'm sure if you spoke of something other than history, then I might again be your best pupil.'

'What subject is more pleasing, your Grace? Mathematics, philosophy, geography—'

'Something more personal, perhaps,' he said. 'Something of more interest to us both. Such as why you permitted my daughter Mary to fall in love with this man Fitzgerald.'

Jane caught her breath. So this was the true reason for this junket, to give him the opportunity to interrogate her. She'd not escape from him here. In a gondola in the middle of the Grand Canal, she was as good as trapped, and they both knew it.

'I didn't mean to surprise you,' he said. 'That is, I did mean to surprise you, but not in a malicious way. I wish to know the truth, that is all, and without permitting you the time to contrive a practised answer that would—'

'I have told you nothing but the truth in regard to both your daughters, your Grace,' she said swiftly. 'Lord John has a great deal in common with Lady Mary, and she with him. There was no "permission" to their attachment at all, and I do not believe I could have stopped their friendship even if I'd tried. Mutual interests led to a delight in one another's company, and love soon after followed.'

She hadn't meant to run on so long, but he'd listened, and he hadn't interrupted, either, the way he usually did. He'd simply...*listened,* and now that she'd realised it, she blushed.

'The short of it, your Grace, is that they fell in love,' she said, 'and I am certain that neither has ever been happier.'

'In love, you say?' he repeated, watching her so closely that her flush deepened further. 'You speak as if from your own experience, Miss Wood. You have been in love yourself?'

'I, your Grace?' she asked, stunned. However was she to answer so personal a question?

'Yes, you, Miss Wood,' he said. 'Surely you must have some experience with love yourself if you were so quick to recognise it in my daughters.'

'Love.' She could not bear his regard any longer, and in confusion lowered her gaze to her frozen fingers.

'Aye, love,' he repeated, more softly. 'Is there something wrong with your hands, Miss Wood?'

'They are cold, your Grace,' she said. 'It is my own fault.'

'But easily rectified.' He lifted the edge of the fur-lined rug, inviting her to slip her hands within. 'Here, tuck them in. I'll warm them fast enough.'

She shook her head, determined not to succumb to such a scandalous temptation. To let him warm her hands against his body, beneath luxurious fur!

'Thank you, no, your Grace,' she said, still addressing her fingers and not him. 'Next time I shall put aside my vanity, and wear my heavy woollen mittens.'

'You won't speak to me of your old loves, will you?' he asked. 'I am sorry. Last night I realised that, despite all the years you have been in my employ, Miss Wood, I know very little about you.'

'But you do, your Grace!' she exclaimed. 'You

know that I was born in Hertfordshire, that I was schooled by my father, that I speak French and read Italian, that I can teach mathematics for ladies, composition, painting in watercolours, and—'

'That is nothing,' he said with such an all-encompassing sweep of his arm that the gondola rocked from the force of it. 'Anyone who reads your references will know that much. But it was not until last night that I learned your eyes are the same shade of blue as the lilacs that grow beneath the dovecote, back at Aston Hall.'

She gasped, made speechless by his audacity. Yet as soon as her gaze rose to meet his, she realised how wrongly she'd judged that audacity—his words weren't meant as an idle gallant's compliment, but as a confidence, a gift of unadorned honesty to her.

To *her.*

And if he'd never noticed her eyes were blue, how was it that she in turn had never noticed his were neither blue, nor green, nor brown, but a blending of all three that was as unusual and as complicated as the duke himself was. His life out of doors had carved little lines around those eyes, radiating outward like the rays a cartographer would draw around the sun, lines that became more pronounced when he smiled. He was smiling now, and she felt her own lips curl upwards in shy response.

Yet to her surprise, this time he was the one who looked away first, staring off past the gondolier and his sweeping single oar and towards the chilly grey canal.

'I met Lady Anne Hailey at a Twelfth Night ball,' he began, so softly that Jane had to lean closer to hear. 'I was down from school for the holidays, a cocky young whelp with a fearsome opinion of my own worth, while she was so young she'd not yet even been presented at Court. But she tamed me fast enough. She had red ribbons in her hair and freckles that she hated, and when she laughed I thought it was the merriest sound I'd ever heard. She'd no more use for the foolishness of the ball than I did, and she led me outside to see the moonlight on the fallen snow. She kissed me first that night, and in the summer, we were wed. She was my first love, aye, my duchess, and my only love, and then too soon, she was gone.'

He sighed, a little puff of old grief and warm memories in the chilly air. Wistfully Jane doubted he even recalled she was there with him, he was so lost in the past. Yet he had shared a part of himself with her that he kept buried from everyone else at Aston Hall, and the confidence touched her so deeply that she felt tears well up in her eyes. He'd trusted her with his duchess, and in return she could not keep back her own old sorrow.

'I was sixteen, and he was twenty-two,' she said, the long-buried story now coming out so fast that the words tumbled over one another in a tumbled rush. 'His name was George, George Lee, and he was a lieutenant in his Majesty's navy, visiting his uncle in our parish. And he was handsome, handsome as the day, with the sunlight on his gold lace and buttons. I'd walk with him through the orchard beneath the apple trees, and he told me of all the foreign places he'd seen and battles he'd fought. I'd never known anyone like him, and when he asked me to wait for him, I said yes.'

She'd never forget George. She never tasted apples without thinking of him, of how the boughs overhead had bowed beneath the weight of the ripening fruit above them, and how the heady sweet scent had filled the late-summer air. He'd let her see there was a world beyond that orchard, and taught her how to dream of it. And he'd kissed her, too, just the once beneath the apple trees, before he'd left.

'Did you love him, then?'

She blinked, like a drowsy sleeper wakened too soon.

'I did,' she said, sadly. 'I loved him, and he me. I

promised I'd wait for him. I would have done anything for him, anything at all.'

'And yet you are here.'

Jane shook her head, the old sorrow reduced by time to a dull ache, but an ache that had never quite abated. 'He sailed away, and though I waited, he never came back. His ship was lost with all hands off Gibraltar.'

Being a parish minister, her father had had much experience with bearing sorrowful tidings, and he'd waited until they were alone in their parlour before he'd showed her the paper from London with the news. She'd stared at him in shock, and refused to believe what he was so gently telling her. Instead she had snatched the paper from his hands and run to the orchard to read it for herself. Surely Father had misunderstood the news. Surely there had been survivors. But there had been no hope to be found in the tersely worded announcement from the naval office, and not even she could pretend her George would return. She'd dropped to her knees and wept until she'd no tears left, there among the last mouldering windfalls in the dry autumn grass.

'I trust you haven't shared that gloomy tale with my daughters,' the duke said solemnly, jarring her from her reverie. 'Young females can be melancholy enough without having their heads filled with stories of doomed lovers lost at sea.'

She stared at him, so wounded she could scarcely force the words from her mouth.

'How—how can you speak so, your Grace?' she stammered. 'How is my—my loss any less than your own?'

'Because Anne was my wife, my duchess, the mother of my children,' he said, as if this explained everything. 'I do not intend to belittle your grief, Miss Wood, but I don't believe our...ah...our losses are comparable.'

She shook her head, silently rejecting his hideous, selfish *belief.* How could she ever dream they'd something in common? He was her master, not her friend, her superior in every way. He certainly wasn't her confidant, and now she could not bear to be in his company another moment.

'Forgive me, your Grace, forgive me for everything.' She rose upright in the gondola, impulsive rather than wise, and the narrow boat pitched precipitously. Though she caught at the black-lacquered side to save herself, she refused to sit again, looking past the startled duke to the man at the oar.

'If you please, gondolier,' she called in Italian. 'Draw to the side, here, and put me out at once.'

The man nodded, doubtless deciding the English

lady was mad, and deftly steered the gondola to-wards the side of the canal.

The duke reached out to steady her, his fingers firm around her arm. 'Here now, Miss Wood, none of that. I won't have you tumbling over the side.'

She looked at him sharply, her hurt now flaring into anger. 'You needn't concern yourself, your Grace, not for me. My loss would not be comparable, would it?'

She jerked her arm free as the gondola slid closer to the walkway. She didn't wait for the gondolier to settle at a gate, but instead bunched her skirts in one hand and jumped towards the walkway. For one frozen second, she glimpsed the grey water lapping beneath her and the distance she needed to jump between the heaving boat and the walkway, and all too easily she imagined herself dropping down between the two, deep into the cold water never to rise. Then her shoes were scrabbling over the paving stones and she realised she'd landed.

She shook out her skirts and hurried away, praying he wouldn't follow as she ducked in a narrow alley between two houses.

'Miss Wood!' he shouted, his bluff English voice echoing against the ancient Venetian walls. 'Miss Wood, come back here at once!'

For the first time since she'd been in his Grace's

employ, she pretended not to hear him. Instead she quickened her steps and ducked into another alley, praying he wouldn't follow her. She needed to be alone, to recover control of her emotions, and, if she were honest, to recover her pride.

How had she let herself be such a fool where the duke was concerned? To him she was no more than another servant, and never would be otherwise, no matter that he'd noticed the colour of her eyes. When George had said such things to her, he'd meant it, but his Grace—no.

Furious with herself, Jane dashed the tears away from her eyes, and darted down yet another passage and over an arching bridge. In this impromptu escape, she had the advantage. She'd spent so much time in the last weeks exploring the city that she'd soon learned her way through the maze of inner courtyards and alleyways that existed inside the canals. Another right turn here and across the bridge over Rio del Palazzo, and she was in the Piazza San Marco, dominated by the glittering domes of the Basilica San Marco.

Crowned with statues of golden saints and horses, the ancient Byzantine cathedral was one of Jane's favourite places in Venice, and likely, too, the last place a staunchly Protestant Englishman like the duke would ever look for her. Here she'd be permitted to think of her lost love in peace, and she swallowed back a fresh surge of emotion. It was wrong, all of it, and tugging her hood lower over her face, she headed towards San Marco's welcoming steps.

On most days, the Piazza was thronged with people, Venetians as well as foreign visitors, but because of the cold, only a few hardy souls clustered beneath the arched passageway to the shops of the Procuratie Vecchie. Gusts of wind swept from the sea across the open square, swirling across the patterned paving stones and making the space so inhospitable that even the usual flocks of pigeons had gone into hiding.

Enough water had blown from the sea that wooden duckboards had been laid across the shuddering puddles, and cautiously Jane picked her way across the unsteady planks towards San Marco. Thanks to his Grace, the day had been humiliating enough already without soaking her boots or the hems of her skirts, and she chose her steps with care, her head bowed to concentrate on the duckboards.

She didn't see the man coming towards her, didn't see him at all until he'd grabbed her by the shoulders, and then—then it was too late.

Chapter Eight

'My dear friend!' exclaimed the man as he steadied Jane on the wobbling duckboard. 'I never thought to see you here!'

Startled, she looked up and gasped, nearly losing her footing on the board. 'Signor di Rossi!'

'You servant, Miss Wood.' He'd caught her easily, lightly, guiding her with his gloved hands on her shoulders as surely as if they were two circus performers dancing on the board together. 'There are few things more perilous than a quaking duckboard, eh?'

He smiled, his teasing as gentle as his support. His black beaver hat was drawn low over his forehead against the wind, and he paid no attention to how the lace on his neckcloth blew upwards to tickle the underside of his clean-shaven jaw. All he seemed to care for was the delight of finding her here, and saving her from a perilous puddle. It was the second time in the last hour that a man had reached out to steady her, but how differently the *signor's* hands felt upon her shoulders than the duke's possessive grasp!

'Thank you,' she said, taking his arm to let him guide her towards the drier side of the piazza. 'You cannot know how—how grateful I am.'

She hadn't meant to betray her feelings with that tiny catch in her words, but di Rossi heard it at once, his dark brows drawing together with concern.

'You are distraught, Miss Wood,' he said. 'No, no, do not deny it. From your voice, it is clear to me that you suffer.'

She shook her head, but he'd hear none of it.

'You're alone,' he said, swiftly glancing around her. 'That is not wise, Miss Wood.'

She tried to smile. 'You told me yourself that Venice was safe enough for travelling women by day.'

'When a lady is attentive to her surroundings, yes,' he said solemnly. 'Most days I would grant you that, Miss Wood. But not as you are today. No, not today.'

She looked away, ducking behind her cloak's hood. Long ago she'd learned to hide the private part of herself from others, to be unnoticed even as she stood in a crowded parlour; it was a necessary skill for governesses, as expected as a facility for French or geography. Yet today it seemed as if her practised governess's mask had vanished, leaving her more transparent and vulnerable than she'd felt in years.

'I—I wished to be alone,' she said, raising her chin in a brave if false show. 'It was by my choice that I came here.'

He raised a sceptical brow. 'Forgive me if I do not believe you, Miss Wood, and forgive me again if I bear you off to a warmer place so we might discern the truth together, yes?'

For once she didn't argue for her independence, but let him lead her meekly across the piazza, away from San Marco's and towards the row of chocolate shops that promised warm comfort. They were carried into the nearest shop on a final gust of wind, and shown at once to one of the intimate little half-rooms that were a feature of Venetian chocolate houses.

The first time Jane had come here with the *signor,* she'd been wary, not only because of the privacy of their table, hidden away behind a red curtain, but also for the sheer sensuous display: the plush-covered benches, the delicately wrought spoons and forks, the porcelain cups painted with twisting Turkish designs. But by the end of that first cup of chocolate—and the plate of fine-sliced ham that she'd been introduced to by di Rossi—she'd come to realise that dining like this was simply one more way that things were done differently in Venice than in London.

Now she drew off her cold-stiffened gloves and wrapped her fingers around the steaming cup as soon as it was set before her. Not only could she feel the warmth in her hands, but the bitter-sweet fragrance of the chocolate curled enticingly around her nose as well. She closed her eyes to enjoy it further, letting the sensations calm her. This was the kind of peace she'd tried to share with the duke when she'd shown him a Venetian breakfast this morning, and, oh, how wrongly he'd interpreted her offering!

'It is Aston who has vexed you, hasn't he?' di Rossi asked, his voice soft as a cat's purr. 'Doubtless he is the cause of your distress.'

Her eyes flew open. His dark eyes were so intent upon her that she almost felt his gaze upon her skin, as palpable as the warm porcelain in her hand.

'Tell me, *cara,*' he said, urging her to find solace in confidence. 'It will ease your unhappiness. Tell me all.'

She looked down at her cup and shook her head. Since she'd left home to take her first position at eighteen, she'd been on her own, and along the way she'd almost forgotten how to share her thoughts and worries with another. Governesses were supposed to be like that, pillars of well-starched strength to support the woes of their charges and offer endless consolation, but to neither seek nor expect any in return. Governesses weren't permitted to have inappropriate emotions or sorrows of their own. Even when her father had died, she'd taken only a week away from Aston Hall to tend to his last affairs, and when she'd returned, it had been as if she'd never left.

All of which was likely why his Grace had been able to disrupt her so thoroughly today, asking her about herself. Because his interest was so unexpected, she'd been unprepared to deflect it.

'You're silent.' Di Rossi sighed, and smiled without parting his lips. Their table was away from any windows, and though it was mid-day, the candlesticks were lit, and the pale golden light turned his face to ivory. 'To keep your suffering locked tight within your heart where it will only grow and fester—ah, that is not good.'

'I'm not suffering,' she said quickly, so quickly that the denial sounded false even to her own ears. 'Not at all. I was…*discomfited,* yes, but I was not suffering.'

He tipped his head to one side and waved his hand through the air with elegant dismissal. 'Forgive me if I do not believe you, *cara*. Philosophers claim that the eyes are the windows to the soul, and through yours I can see your pain.'

'You are mistaken, *signor*.' Swiftly she looked down at the steaming cup before her, fearing that she'd somehow betrayed herself.

'You need not deny it for my sake,' he said gently. 'You know you might confide in me.'

Again she shook her head, overwhelmed by his kindness. How was it that this man, who had only known her a handful of weeks, seemed to be more sensitive, more aware of her feelings, than the duke, in whose house she'd lived for years?

'Now these are exactly what you need,' di Rossi said as a waiter set a plate of sugar-dusted biscuits between them. He took one of the wafers and broke it in two, sending a dusting of sugar like snow across the table. 'There's nothing like pleasing the palate to help relieve the soul. Open, open that pretty mouth of yours, *cara*.'

He smiled and held the half-biscuit across the table to her like an offering. She could smell the browned butter of the fresh-baked sweet, so close beneath her nose, and the hint of the anise that flavoured it. She knew he expected her to play her part of the game, just as she had earlier with the duke. Instead she took the biscuit from di Rossi's fingers and slipped it into her mouth herself.

Surprised by her reaction, he sat back in his chair. 'So that is how it is to be, eh? As soon as you are again in the company of an Englishman, you are once again the properly suspicious Englishwoman?'

'The Duke of Aston is no ordinary Englishman,' Jane said defensively. 'He is a peer of the realm.'

'In your England, he is,' the *signor* said, giving his shoulders a shrug of indifference. 'But Venice is a republic, and titles hold no meaning or worth. Here, this fearsome peer of yours is simply one more gentleman.'

'That's not true,' Jane said swiftly. 'Not at all. His Grace remains his Grace, no matter what other places he might visit away from England.'

'So he shall for ever be a duke, a peer, your master, and you likewise are doomed to be no more than a governess in his employ?'

She hesitated. That was in fact what she believed, or rather, what she'd never questioned.

'It is,' she said finally. 'That is proper, the way it should be.'

He sighed, his dark eyes troubled as he studied her. 'You disappoint me, Miss Wood. I'd thought that Venice had changed you. I thought that you now saw yourself as a woman first, full of the loveliness and grace of a moonstruck Diana, and not some lowly drab of an English servant.'

'Signor di Rossi!' she exclaimed, startled. 'You should not say such things! It is—it's bold, and it's not right.'

'In Venice, it is.' He leaned forwards, his gaze intent on her face. 'You cannot chide me over this, *cara*. In Venice, beauty can be found everywhere one looks, from the flicker of morning light across the canal. Surely you have learned this since you have arrived here. Surely I've taught you that much in our rambles, yes?'

'Yes,' she admitted, and it was true. She loved to listen to him when he spoke to her like this, his voice as warm and golden as amber and his words flowing over her like poetry. No other man had ever spoken to her like this, describing everyday things as gloriously as if they were the treasures of some Oriental prince.

'I understand that much,' she said. 'But I am not—'

'Shush, shush, and listen,' he scolded. 'Venetian men are different from your English variety. In this city, beauty is a pleasure, to be enjoyed and relished, and we see no value in hiding our admiration, whether it is for a painting, a jewel, or a woman. And I see the beauty in you, Miss Wood.'

Jane flushed. Not again, she thought miserably—to be so thoughtlessly flattered by not one, but two, gentlemen in the span of a single day!

'Please, *signor,* I beg of you, no more,' she said swiftly. 'To speak of me in the same breath as such rare beauty, to pretend that my humble self belongs—'

'But you do,' he insisted, placing his hand over the breast of his waistcoat to swear the truth of his words. 'I would not say it now if it weren't so.'

'But idle flattery—'

'It is neither base flattery, nor idle,' he maintained. 'You may not believe yourself a conventional beauty, yet I see beauty in your face. You possess an inborn grace that few other women can claim, and it gives me pleasure simply to be in your company, so that I might admire you.'

'Please—please don't, *signor,*' Jane pleaded. 'It is not right for you to say such things to me. With a handful of careless words, you'll spoil our friendship.'

'Only if you insist on being a governess first, and a woman second,' he said. 'An *English* governess, quaking in the shadow of your fearsome duke.'

He leaned across the table towards her, resting

his hand beside hers. He was careful to make sure that their fingers did not touch, yet to her the intimacy was unmistakable and unbearable. Quickly she drew back her hand, folding her arms over her chest and tucking that same hand safely away.

'Your duke has done this to you, hasn't he?' he asked, his voice more regretful than angry. 'He reminded you of your place in England, and that you are his inferior. That is the reason you were alone in the Piazza, wasn't it?'

'I *am* a member of his Grace's household,' she said sadly. Di Rossi was right. Having his Grace here in Venice had put an end to the unreal fantasy of Venice. Seeing him was a sharp reminder that no matter how much she might have changed through this glorious experience, she'd now have to change back again. She *was* a governess first, and a woman second. What other choice did she have?

She bowed her head wearily. She felt more foolish now than wounded, her rational, sensible self once again subduing her sentimental heart. The duke had not meant to hurt her; she could understand that now. He was by nature a direct man, and he'd spoken directly. As dear as the memory of her long-lost sailor was to her, he had been her sweetheart and no more, while the duchess had been a much-loved wife and the mother of his two daughters.

'Englishmen have no appreciation, no regard, for women,' di Rossi was saying. 'This one is not worthy of your confidence, if he would treat you with such disdain.'

'But he didn't,' she said wistfully. His Grace hadn't treated her with disdain. He'd told her how her eyes were the colour of the lilacs at Aston Hall, as pretty a compliment as she could ever imagine because it was genuine.

Her eyes *were* a peculiar colour, not quite blue or grey, but something in between. Her father had always likened them to pewter, which had made her feel vaguely ashamed of the colour. Lilacs were much prettier, and the lilacs near the dovecote were the prettiest she'd ever seen. Most likely they were the prettiest that his Grace had seen, too, for he steadfastly believed that everything at Aston Hall was the best to be had anywhere in Creation. He'd smiled when he'd made his observation, and she smiled now as she recalled the interest and the kindness she'd seen in his own eyes as he'd listened to her.

And no disdain, not a morsel, for all that she'd bolted away from him in tears. Now she must be the one to put matters back to rights, and pray he'd forgive her.

'Forgive me, *signor*, but I must leave you,' she said, rising from the table. 'I thank you for your hospitality, but I must return at once to the Ca' Battista.'

'What is this, *cara?*' he asked with surprise as he rose with her. 'If I have misspoken, then I—'

'You haven't, *signor*, not at all,' she said. 'Rather, you said exactly what I needed to hear.'

Impulsively she reached for his hand and pressed it lightly, wanting him to understand how much she appreciated his concern. Then, before he could try to stop her, she hurried away, from him and from the sweet-smelling warmth of the chocolate shop, and back into the cold and towards the apology she must make.

'The lady has gone, *signor*?' The waiter frowned, standing expectantly beside the table with the pot of chocolate in his hand. 'She is finished?'

'So it would seem.' Di Rossi could still see Jane as she crossed the Piazza, her small figure bobbing resolutely along. She wouldn't come back to him, not now. He knew her well enough to realise that once she'd decided her mind, she wouldn't change it—another unpleasant English trait, really, that stubbornness of hers.

And here he'd been sure he'd had her. He'd been her rescuing knight, and there were few things that could push a virtuous woman towards sin more successfully than gratitude. She'd been poised, ripe for him, with those plump, unpainted lips of hers parted in breathy, innocent expectation as she'd hung on his words, until—

Until he'd said the wrong thing, and lost her.

A thousand saints in Heaven, he couldn't guess what it had been, though it wouldn't have any lasting effect on his seduction. This would only be a temporary hindrance in his plans, the kind of delay that a philosopher would say would sweeten the inevitable conquest. He'd send her a small token tomorrow and a prettily worded billet-doux, and she'd return to him.

But the presence of this English duke was a complication he hadn't counted upon. The man had power over Jane Wood, and clearly the conversation between them earlier in the day had gone far beyond what was customary for a governess and her master to have caused her such pain.

For a moment, di Rossi wondered if Aston had already claimed her maidenhead, and immediately discarded the notion. He was sure his little English dove was still a virgin: her air of innocence was unmistakable. The duke might desire her as well, but he hadn't taken her.

That, inevitably and most pleasurably, would fall to di Rossi, and with a smile of anticipation, he tossed a handful of coins on to the table, and left.

Chapter Nine

'You're not Miss Wood.' Richard set down the book he'd been pretending to read with a thump on the desk. 'Damnation, Wilson, where is she?'

'Beggin' pardon, your Grace, but how the devil should I know where's Miss Wood's taken herself?' Wilson set the tray with Richard's coffee on the desk beside him, managing to convey his cross-tempered indignation with every movement. 'The foreign lady what keeps this house—that Mrs Battista—says she'll send Miss Wood up directly when she returns.'

'*When* she returns,' muttered Richard darkly. 'More likely *if* she returns. I should never have let her go, not into this ridiculously confusing city. By now she could have drowned, or been ravished, or murdered outright by one of these rascally Venetians—'

'Beggin' pardon, your Grace, but Mrs Battista says

Venice is safe as can be during the day,' interrupted Wilson. 'Mrs Battista says Miss Wood knows her way about same as folks who've lived here all their lives, and that Miss Wood's likely looking about at old churches and such, same as she was with you. Mrs Battista says that she'll come back here whenever she's ready and—'

'No more "Mrs Battista", Wilson,' said Richard, turning away to stare out the window with the empty hope that he'd see Jane Wood returning. He didn't care how familiar she'd become with this city. She was a small, vulnerable Englishwoman alone among strangers, and his imagination was providing every manner of hideous perils for her to tumble into.

'Not another blessed word, mind?' he continued, clasping and unclasping his hands behind his back. 'It's only Miss Wood I care about, not the opinions of some foreign lady whom I can scarce understand.'

'Beggin' pardon, your Grace, but Mrs Battista's the housekeeper,' Wilson insisted, 'and housekeepers always have a rare way for knowing everything worth knowing.'

'Please do not speak so in the *signora*'s hearing, Mr Wilson,' Jane said. 'She is the owner of this venerable house, not its housekeeper, and her family is one of the most honourable of this region.'

At once Richard wheeled around. 'Miss Wood!'

'Yes, your Grace.' She bowed her head and curtsied, as calmly as if she'd just appeared in his drawing room at home and not from God only knew where here in Venice.

'You're safe?' he demanded. 'Unharmed?'

She looked up at him from beneath her lashes, without raising her chin. 'Yes, your Grace.'

'You are certain? No misadventures?' He was persisting beyond reason, but he couldn't help himself, not when he thought again of how much he'd feared for her. 'You understand that as long as you remain in my household, your welfare is my responsibility.'

'Yes, your Grace,' she said, slowly rising. 'I understand, and I am most grateful for it.'

'Yes.' Richard cleared his throat, now feeling vaguely foolish.

'Indeed, your Grace.' She nodded solemnly. 'Signora della Battista told me you wished to see me directly upon my return.'

'I did.' He waved his hand brusquely to send Wilson on his way, and cleared this throat again. 'Yes, I did.'

He wasn't exactly sure what he wanted to say to Miss Wood, but he did know he'd no wish to say it before gossipy Wilson. Her composure wasn't helping him, either. The dark wool of her cloak was dotted with spray from the canal, and the tiny dots of water caught the firelight like dozens of tiny jewels. Wispy ringlets of her dark hair had worked their way free of her cap, and they, too, sparkled with droplets around her face—she even had them, he realised, in her lashes. Her cheeks were rosy from the damp cold, her lips slightly parted and her breathing quick from the exertion of doubtless running up the stairs to join him.

She was, in short, dazzling.

When in blazes did she begin to look like this?

He knew he was staring at her—no, *gaping* at her like some sort of mooncalf boy, and like a mooncalf boy, the words he'd planned to say had fled completely from his head.

He wanted to tell her how she'd no right running off like she had, with neither warning nor leave from him. He didn't mean to scold her exactly, but rather to let her know how much he'd feared for her safety, the way he would for anyone in his employ. Yes, that was it. He'd always prided himself on being a responsible master to his staff, hadn't he?

Yet where Miss Wood was concerned, it might not be quite so simple. In her company this morning, he'd enjoyed himself more than he had in years, there in that gliding gondola. He'd lost himself in listening to the pleasing timbre of her voice, and seeing how brightly her eyes shone in the pale winter sunlight. She'd put him so at his ease that he'd spoken to her of his wife, of things he'd never spoken of to anyone else, and he'd enjoyed that, too, though in a bitter-sweet way. He'd even listened with fascination to her own tale of lost love, realising how she'd trusted him enough to tell it. Women didn't make confidences like that easily, especially women like Miss Wood. He wanted to hear more, which was part of the reason he'd been so stunned when she'd abandoned him in the boat. He'd tried to follow, but because she had had a head start, she'd soon disappeared, and he'd hadn't a prayer of finding her in this rabbit warren of a city.

He intended to tell her that, of course, and to explain how he'd never wished to offend or to wound her as he apparently had. He meant to apologise, too. He probably shouldn't confess that he'd no idea of how he'd misspoken, but he was still willing to take all the blame on himself. How could he do otherwise, considering her expression before she'd leaped from the gondola? For once, it seemed more important to make things right than to *be* right.

That was what he wished to tell Miss Wood now, and a great deal more besides. All this afternoon he'd planned his speech, rehearsing it a score of different ways in his head until he'd got it exactly right. Yet now, with her standing before him twinkling in the firelight, he couldn't remember one blasted word.

Fortunately, however, Miss Wood didn't seem to notice. Instead she was too intent on delivering a rehearsed speech of her own.

'Your Grace,' she began with a small, resolute shake of her head, 'pray forgive me for speaking first, but I wish to apologise for what I did earlier today.'

Mystified, Richard nodded and motioned for her to sit, an offer she either ignored or failed to notice. Ordinarily he would have sat regardless of whether she had or not, a prerogative of his rank. He was a duke, and dukes generally sat where and when they pleased.

Yet because he'd no wish to put any further distance between them, he, too, ignored the chair and remained standing, where he was certain not to miss every last emotion flicker through her blue eyes.

Yet there was also another reason, if he were honest with himself. By standing so evenly before her, he felt more her equal, less a duke and governess than simply a man and a woman—a man who was finding this particular woman more intriguingly attractive by the minute.

She took another breath to settle herself before she began, her breasts rising beneath the unadorned woollen gown.

'I must beg your forgiveness, your Grace,' she said, her words now coming in a rush. 'This morning you chose to confide in me, and I misunderstood the nature of your confidences. I fear that in that state of—of misunderstanding, I grew distraught, and acted on impulse and in haste, and fled the gondola without your leave.'

'You fled *me,* which is much more to the point,' he said gruffly. 'It didn't matter one way or the other to the gondola.'

She flushed, yet did not look away from him, a rare and enchanting mixture of vulnerability and resolve.

'Yes, your Grace,' she said. 'It did not matter to the gondola, but it did to me, which is no excuse for—'

'It did?' he asked, surprised beyond measure. And here he'd been thinking his attraction to her was a one-sided affair! 'It, ah, mattered to you?'

'Of course it did, your Grace,' she said, her voice shaking with a small wounded tremor that could have humbled a man twice the duke's size. 'You honoured me by telling me of her Grace, and I responded most inappropriately by speaking of a gentleman who was once dear to me. It was most grievously improper of me, I know, and I beg—'

'But it wasn't improper, or inappropriate,' he said. 'Not at all.'

'Forgive me, your Grace, but it most certainly was!' she exclaimed, her eyes widening with indignation. 'As you yourself have said, your Grace, I am a member of your household. It is my place, my duty, to put aside my own wishes and instead to obey yours, and I—'

'Dine with me,' he said. 'Now. I've kept the cook waiting long enough.'

'Yes, your Grace,' Jane said, already sinking into another curtsy of acquiescence. 'As you—'

'No, not because it pleases me, but because it pleases *you.*' Now the words came, though they certainly weren't the same ones he'd originally planned. 'I'd be honoured if you agree.'

She frowned. 'As we dined this morning, your Grace?'

'Not like that, no,' he said. 'That is, yes, to dine together at the same table as we did this morning, but in a different fashion, a different—oh, blast, I'm babbling like an idiot.'

'No, your Grace,' she said, a hint of amusement flickering through her eyes. 'Not at all.'

'Oh, yes, I am,' he said, shaking his head, 'and that's what I'm trying to explain. My daughters don't require a governess, and I don't require a guide or other contrivance meant to educate me further. At my age, I've likely learned as much as I ever will, and no amount of further lecturing from you, however informative and well meant, will change that, or me, either.'

She did not move, yet in some indecipherable way she seemed to wilt before his eyes. The tiny drops of water scattered over her had dissipated, too, and with it her fairy-like sparkle.

'I understand fully, your Grace,' she said softly. 'With my services no longer required, I will make arrangements to leave in the morning.'

Resigned to dismissal, she began to curtsy once again, until Richard seized her arm to stop her.

'Damnation, that's not what I intended at all!' he exclaimed. 'I meant that I don't need a nursery-maid. I'm not so old as that. I need company, feminine company.'

Her eyes widened, now sharp with outrage where they'd been soft, and she looked pointedly at his hand around her arm. 'This is Venice, your Grace.

You'll find a courtesan eager to oblige you waiting in nearly every doorway.'

'Surely you know me better than that, Miss Wood,' he said, his words clipped and his outrage now a match for hers. 'I wish *company,* not an amorous plaything who'll try to rob me blind. I want the company of an Englishwoman who'll accept me for what I am, and amuse me with her conversation.'

'You are still a duke, while I am a governess without a place.'

'Here I will be your host, and you my guest. We can put aside the rest.'

'You ask a great deal, your Grace,' she said warily.

'Not so much,' he said, all blunt honesty. 'I'm lonely, lass. I miss my girls.'

'So do I,' she said wistfully. 'But is that enough?'

'In Venice, it is,' he said. 'Mind you, here they put ham and chocolate together.'

She smiled, a wondrous, unexpected sight that pleased him no end. He released her arm, sliding his hand lightly down its length.

'I need someone I can talk to,' he said. 'Someone who'll listen to me, but who isn't afraid to speak her own thoughts in turn, or tell me when I'm being an ass. You'll do that, Miss Wood. I've no doubt of it.'

She looked up at his face. 'Your Grace, I have never in my life called anyone an "ass."'

'Then you have never been sufficiently provoked,' he said, teasing her. 'I must try my best, yes?'

He laughed and she laughed with him, shyly, but laughing still. It felt good, that shared laughter, something he'd been missing from his life for years and years. All that time, he'd believed he'd honoured his Anne by keeping to himself, with only her memory for company. He'd believed his heart had wanted nothing more. He'd been strong before everyone else, solitary in his grief and suffering, and admired by the world for his fortitude and courage.

But now, because of the laughter of a single small woman far from home, everything he'd believed in was changing. Though he'd never have expected it last night, this was what he wanted, what he needed. It was startling, even bewildering, and yet he couldn't deny that it somehow felt *right*, clear to his once-wounded heart.

He needed his daughters' governess. No, not quite—he needed Miss Jane Wood.

He let their mingled laughter fade, his expression turning solemn. 'You will join me, then?' he said, his voice more serious than he'd intended. 'We'll go below and dine together?'

'Yes.' She smiled shyly, just enough for him to realise how great a step this was for her. 'Because this is Venice, not Aston, and everything here is magic.'

Chapter Ten

Magic.

When Jane thought back to that first dinner alone with the duke, she couldn't recall exactly what Signora della Battista's excellent cook sent up to their table, or how much of it she actually ate. She couldn't have said if the *signora* herself stood by to explain the various dishes, as had been her habit on other nights, or whether she'd left them alone to discover the delicacies on their own.

What Jane did remember was entering the dining room with the table long enough to have seated a score of elegant Venetians. Tall gilded candelabras stood along the length, lighting the early dusk of the winter evening with long tapers in each dolphin-shaped branch. Fine linen, embroidered with gold and scarlet on the hems, dressed the table, and the silver and crystal gleamed by the candles' glow. The duke's place was laid at one end, and Jane's far down beyond the candelabras at the other, as was proper.

But the duke would have none of it.

'Here now, ma'am, this isn't what I ordered,' he said before they'd even entered the room. 'I don't want Miss Wood banished off to China like that. Put her chair next to mine, so we can be sociable, and dowse that blaze of candles. The ones before us are more than enough.'

In an instant the *signora's* servants had done as the duke had bid, and Jane found herself being seated on the corner of the table at the duke's elbow as a long-faced footman guided her chair.

'That's more to my liking.' The duke sighed with contentment as he settled in the tall-backed arm-chair. 'Now some wine, and we'll be happy as sheep in clover.'

At once another footman appeared to fill Jane's glass, or he would have, if she hadn't put her palm flat over the top of her glass to stop him.

'What is this, Miss Wood?' asked the duke, making a great show of his incredulity. 'You will not drink with me?'

'I'd shame myself for certain if I tried to keep pace with you, your Grace,' Jane said, still keeping her hand firmly in place. 'I've no gift for tippling.'

'No?' He worked his dark brows dramatically.

'Be truthful, now. I know I give leave for drinking in the servants' hall. I've seen the accounting.'

'Beer and ale, your Grace,' she said primly. 'None of the women drank it.'

'Then what of this long journey with my girls? Surely somewhere in all that wandering about France you acquired a taste for the grape?'

'What I acquired, your Grace, is an unshakeable knowledge of my own weakness where drink is concerned,' she said. 'I am a small woman. One glass is my limit, and no more.'

'Well, then, one glass it shall be.' Cheerfully he waved away her hand, and the dark red wine flowed into her glass. 'I've no wish to see you in your cups, Miss Wood, but it would seem that if we've this splendid vintage, then we should drink it.'

She smiled at him over the rim of the glass, recognising the challenge in his words. 'I vow I'll make this last until we rise from the table.'

He chuckled. 'I don't doubt that you will. Regardless of your size, you are a formidable woman, not to be crossed.'

That made her grin. 'Your daughters would agree.'

'Oh, I'm certain they would, just as I'm certain they tested you more times than we could count, the little devils.' He raised his own glass, holding it out towards hers. 'A toast. To Venice, and friendship.'

'To friends,' she echoed softly, and sipped from her glass. She wasn't sure what she'd expected when she'd agreed to dine with him, but so far the experience was most pleasant indeed.

'That's a good wine,' the duke said appreciatively. 'No wonder you've enjoyed yourself here, Miss Wood, with the *signora*'s cellar for company each night.'

'The wine here is well regarded, your Grace,' Jane said promptly, always ready to supply such information. 'Not exactly from Venice itself, to be sure, but from the region around us, called the Veneto. I believe we are drinking a Valpolicella ripasso, "robust and vigorous", as they say, and the Caesars—'

'Hush, hush, no more lectures,' the duke said. 'Not tonight, eh?'

'Oh, your Grace, forgive me,' she said ruefully. 'It's so much my habit, I can't help myself.'

'You should,' he said gently, his gaze so intent on her that she felt her cheeks warm. 'I'd much rather hear of you than a thousand dry old Caesars.'

She'd never had any man smile at her like that. She was most definitely flustered, yet it wasn't an unpleasant kind of fluster. She felt heated, and a little off balance, as if she might topple if she tried to stand. But what was strangest of all was how, when the duke looked at her, she almost felt…pretty.

'But gentlemen love the Caesars, your Grace,' she said, her voice sounding curiously breathy. 'Conquests, chariots, centurions! It's all a great deal more exciting than I am, your Grace.'

'Not to me.' The way he said it made her believe him, too. 'Tell me more of yourself.'

'But there's not much more to tell, your Grace,' she protested. 'Truly, there isn't.'

'Oh, come, come, come,' he said, coaxing her. He linked his fingers together on the table and leaned closer to her, lowering his voice as if they were con-spirators. 'You've had your swallow of wine. Hasn't that loosened your tongue sufficiently?'

She smiled, and shrugged from embarrassment. 'I assure you, your Grace, I've nothing to tell. My life has been most ordinary, or rather, it was until I came to Aston Hall.'

'Hah, now that's a fair start.' Impatiently he sat back in his chair to let the footman place a plate before him. With no regard for the cook's labours, he took up his fork and began to eat. 'Tell me all. What made you accept the place? What were your first impressions of us wicked old Farrens?'

'Not so wicked, your Grace, not by half,' she said. 'At least not the young ladies. They were a bit unruly when first I arrived, but that was soon corrected. They were the reason I took the post, too. Two small motherless girls! How could I have resisted?'

'I'd wager that their having a duke for a father didn't dissuade you,' he said, cutting the roasted pheasant on his plate with hearty enthusiasm. 'When I made it known it was time for the girls to shift from a nursemaid to a governess, why, I'd hoards of grim-faced women thumping at the gates.'

'Yet you chose me.' She smiled. 'I'd always wondered at that. I'd only had one other place in my references, and I was so young myself—'

'You're not exactly doddering now.'

'I'm twenty-nine,' she said evenly, not flinching from the horrible truth. Besides, he knew it already, so there wasn't much point in dissembling now. 'Which *is* doddering for a spinster governess.'

'Oh, bah.' He swept his hand through the air, dismissing every one of her twenty-eight years. 'Look at me. I'm—well, let us say that I am sufficiently advanced to have two wedded daughters, with a grandchild breeding. A grandchild, Miss Wood! Lord preserve me, if that doesn't make me a greybeard, fit only for a stool in the chimney corner, I don't know what does.'

'A greybeard!' scoffed Jane, chuckling at such a

preposterous notion. To see the duke here before her, more robustly virile than any man half his years—who would ever dare call him a greybeard grandfather? 'Oh, your Grace, you wrong yourself!'

'Then I've made my point, my dear Miss Wood,' he said, pausing to wave for more wine. 'If you cannot consider me old, than I can scarce feel the same of you, who are much younger than I. At least you are wise beyond your years, while I am foolishly beneath mine, and don't try to counter me on that, either.'

'Hush, your Grace, please!' she said, shocked by his familiarity, but also laughing so that she pressed her napkin to her cheek. She'd never imagined the stern Duke of Aston could speak so amusingly of himself, or that she would laugh with him, as if they were the oldest of friends.

'You laugh, Miss Wood,' he said, brandishing his fork for emphasis. 'But I did a wise thing in choosing you to guide my girls, perhaps the wisest I've ever done. I gambled, aye, but I won.'

'But why did you choose me from those hoards you claim were at your gate, your Grace?' she asked, for once giving in to curiosity. 'Why me, from so many others?'

'Because you'd written your letter of application in a neat, tidy hand,' he said evenly, sitting back as the footmen changed courses. 'Because I thought your name, "Jane Wood", sounded proper, as a good governess should.'

'Truly, your Grace?' She tried to keep the disappointment from her voice. 'My name?'

'Exactly.' He paused, looking down at the plate before him with scowling disappointment. 'Fish again!'

'Sardines, your Grace,' she said promptly. 'You'll find the sauce over them is very refined.'

'I hate fish,' he declared mournfully, still staring down at the neat row of sautéed sardines in their golden sauce on his plate. 'You'd think these Italians would sprout fins and gills themselves, for all the wretched fish they eat. What I'd give for a thick slice of roast beef and trimmings!'

'But you must grant it did appear a most delicious fish, your Grace,' Jane said quickly, raising her voice for the *signora*'s benefit, 'and the sauce was most cleverly wrought, unlike any to be found in all of London.'

'There you are, Miss Wood, tidying up after me again.' He winked, well aware of what she'd done. 'But that's the main reason I chose you for my girls. You wrote that you'd lost your own mother as a young lass, and you could understand their grief. I knew then you had a tender heart, full of kindness, and that was worth more than all the French lessons and other rubbish combined. A tender heart—aye, that was what I wished for, and you never did disappoint my daughters, or me.'

Startled tears sprung to Jane's eyes. 'Oh, your Grace, forgive me, pray, but that is most—most kind.'

He smiled warmly, and laid down his fork and knife. 'It's not empty kindness, my dear,' he said, covering her hand with his own. 'It's the truth.'

Overcome with emotion, Jane could only shake her head in disbelief, and gaze down at his hand over hers. His fingers were strong and thick and capable, nicked and lightly scarred from innumerable small accidents over time, the hands of a countryman rather than a gentlemen and more than a little at odds with the elegant Holland linen of his shirt's cuff. Her own smaller fingers were swallowed beneath, and yet she found his touch far from smothering.

She'd never realised he'd felt this way about her and how she'd taught and nurtured his daughters. She'd always thought she was beneath his notice, and here it seemed he'd been regarding her with approval before she'd arrived. She'd never known she'd been so appreciated. She'd never *guessed*.

But what had he guessed of her in return? Did he

somehow know how she'd been struck by his sheer physical presence and confidence from the very first time she'd stood in his presence? Had he caught her watching him whenever he'd paid his daily visit to the schoolroom, interrupting her lessons to laugh and play with his girls, his dogs jumping and barking gleefully along with him? Had he ever spied her high up at her window, watching him ride out on the huge bay gelding that only he could control?

He wasn't perfect, of course. Not even a duke was that. He blustered and stomped about, and behaved like any other man accustomed to having his own way. There'd been times when he'd disagreed with Jane, when they'd both grown angry with the other over something one of his girls had said or done or wished to do. But in the end they'd usually come to some manner of understanding, and not just because he was the father, either. Instead there had always been an unspoken agreement between his Grace and Jane that everything was for the sake of the girls, an agreement that both of them had tacitly respected and honoured. The young women the girls had become was proof enough that they'd succeeded.

Yet it was unbelievably, achingly strange for Jane to realise that those days were over for good, and that as soon as the duke returned to England, she'd shift her belongings to another house and another family. Most likely after that she'd never see him again. Did he ever guess how often she'd dreamed of him, the golden duke so far above her? Yet not once did she ever dream this: that she would sit beside his Grace in the glow of his smile.

'There, I didn't mean to make you sad.' He reached up with his thumb and swept away a single tear from her cheek. 'Was your fish even more wretched than mine?'

She sniffed, and tried to smile through the after-effects of that single wayward tear.

He saw it for the miserable attempt that it was, and gently turned her hand over in his, threading his fingers into hers. 'If you must be too shy to speak of yourself, then we'll talk of something I know we've in common—the girls. Now I've read their letters as well as yours, but I'd rather hear the tale of your journey told by you. Play the part of a bard for me, Miss Wood, and spin me the story of the odyssey you three took across the Continent.'

She caught a tremulous breath. 'Oh, your Grace, we've been travelling for months and months. I can't conceive of how long the telling would take!'

'I've time.' His voice rumbled low and encouraging, enough to send a shiver of pleasure down her spine. 'I want to learn everything, as if I'd gone with you. Begin at the beginning, on that gloomy day you sailed on the packet from England for Calais.'

'It *was* a gloomy day, your Grace,' Jane agreed, remembering. 'The rain kept off, but the wind was stiff, and the Channel so rough that the packet was pitching even at her moorings. The young ladies were both in a foul humour, too, and distraught over having to say farewell to you, though they'd no wish to admit it.'

'I was scarcely better,' the duke admitted. 'I'd never intended to send both of them abroad—recall the tour was first to be for Mary alone—but then I'd lost my temper with Diana, and as much as forced her to go, too. There was no turning back from that. To lose them both—'

'But you didn't lose them, your Grace,' Jane protested. 'They're both thriving and happy.'

'I've lost them to other men, which to a foolish old father is a sorrowful day indeed.' He sighed, and smiled wistfully. 'How I fussed and feared for the three of you! Do you know I remained on the dock even after the packet's sails and pennant were gone from my sight, as if I could have willed you safely to the other shore?'

'Not so foolish, not at all.' She curled her fingers into his, seeking to comfort him as he'd comforted her. She liked how their hands fit improbably together, large against small, their palms pressed one to the other in unexpected intimacy. 'The weather made our crossing a miserable one, but the packet's master assured us we were never in any real danger. The real peril came once we'd landed, your Grace, when the French officials swept down upon us like vultures ready to prey upon our sickly English personages.'

He shifted his chair closer to hers. 'Go on, Miss Wood. Tell me everything.'

'Yes, your Grace.' She took another sip of her wine and a deep breath, and launched into recounting the tour of France and Italy that she'd made with his two daughters. It had been a journey filled with adventures and experiences, wondrous sights seen and mishaps barely avoided. The duke had been wise to ask Jane to speak of this rather than herself, for once she'd begun, the story seemed to tell itself. Without Jane quite knowing how or when, the duke had begun calling her by her given name, and when she'd shyly noticed, he'd given her leave to put aside his title, and call him Richard.

Before they'd realised the time, it was well past midnight and into the hours of earliest morning. Jane had finished her single glass of red Valpolicella, and at the *signora's* suggestion, they'd proceeded to a sparkling white wine that sent bubbles up Jane's nose, but had made her story-telling all the easier. Not that she'd needed such help. Her words had flowed of their own volition, and the warm laughter she had shared with Richard had been so full of magic that she could scarce believe it.

'But Lady Diana always preferred to view historical sites by moonlight,' she was saying. Because of Richard's frequent interruptions, she'd only finished telling of the first fortnight of their journey, yet she was secretly pleased. The more untold stories that remained would only mean more nights like this one. 'She claimed they were more romantic that way, and therefore more interesting and tolerable to her.'

'Did you agree?' Richard asked. 'Did the moonlight improve the old churches and such?'

She frowned a fraction. 'What, by making it more interesting and tolerable to Diana?'

'More romantic,' he said. 'Were those old ruins more romantic to you?'

'To Diana, they certainly were. She was born with a romantic, sentimental temperament,' Jane said. 'But to me, it seemed more of an inconvenience, traipsing about in the dark when good Christian folk should more properly be asleep in their beds.'

'Moonlight an inconvenience?' teased Richard.

'Jane, Jane, Jane! What a wicked governess thing to say!'

'Well, it was inconvenient,' she protested, though laughing as she spoke. It was impossible to remain stern and proper with him resting his chin on his hand to study her more closely. 'The guides expected to be paid double for their pains. We needed extra wraps against the damp and chill, and boys to carry lanterns to light our way so we wouldn't stumble or fall, and—'

'Enough of this.' He caught her hand and pulled her to her feet, pulling her after him across the room. 'You're coming with me.'

'What are you doing?' she exclaimed, instinctively pulling back and trying to break away. 'Where are we going? Richard, please, *please!*'

He was much larger and stronger, and no matter how hard she tried to stop, he still pulled her along, into the hall. The single footman who remained to tend to them was caught dozing on the bench, and he stumbled to his feet, clumsy with sleep.

'Fetch Miss Wood's cloak, and my coat,' Richard ordered. 'My man will know which ones. Go on now, move your feet.'

'What are you plotting?' Jane demanded. 'We can't go out of doors now. It's the middle of the night. No respectable people will be about at this hour!'

'So I've heard,' Richard said. 'I suppose that will make us either heartily disrespectable, or merely English—equal sins, I'd wager.'

'Richard, we can't—'

'We can, and we will,' he said, grinning down at her. 'There are precious few times when I have the chance to prove the scholarly Miss Wood is wrong, and now that I have one, I'm not about to abandon it. Ah, here are our things. On with your cloak. I don't want you complaining of the cold.'

'I don't complain,' she said, reluctantly letting the duke settle her cloak on her shoulders. 'I never have, nor will I begin tonight. Or I won't unless you tell me what manner of preposterous nonsense you are—'

'This is the way to the back garden, isn't it? I've seen it from my windows.'

'The steps are there, through that door,' she said. 'But I still don't see how—'

'You will.' He pushed open the garden door, and led her outside. The air was cold and sharp, the night still as the city around them slept. 'Where's the nearest bridge?'

In the quiet, Jane automatically lowered her voice

to a whisper. 'There's a small one over the next *rio,*
on the other side of that courtyard.'

'Show me,' he said, letting her lead him. 'Take
me there. This town's the very devil of a place to
learn for an outsider. One wrong turn and you're
bobbing like a cork.'

That was true enough, and even with the wrought-
iron lanterns that every house kept lit outside the
doorway, Jane chose her path carefully, leading
Richard through the courtyards and narrow passages that she'd learned since she'd been here.

It wasn't far to her favourite bridge. Fashioned
of white stone that seemed almost luminous in the
moonlight, this bridge was arched in the centre
to permit gondolas to glide beneath, with steps
that followed the curve of the crest. As Venetian
bridges went, this wasn't a particularly noteworthy
one, being only a hundred or so years old. It wasn't
sought after by visiting tourists, or documented in
paintings by Canaletto. But for Richard, it was apparently exactly the bridge he wished most to see.

'This will do most splendidly,' he said with satisfaction as he guided Jane up the steps to the centre
of the bridge. With his hand on the small of Jane's
back, he gently turned her around so she faced towards the mouth of the *rio,* where it emptied in the

Grand Canal. Unruffled by any traffic at this hour, the waters were so calm that both the moon and the stars reflected on the glassy surface.

Jane breathed deeply of the salty air that came straight from the sea, mingled with the oddly exotic, spicy scent that always seemed to linger in the air here, like a carry-over from the glorious old days of trade with Turkey and China. Behind her she felt Richard's hand move from her back to settle at her waist, holding her lightly, gently, almost as if he feared she would topple over the rail.

None of it seemed real to Jane, not the moonlight, or the water lapping at this spun-sugar bridge, or Richard's hand at her waist. It was all magic, the sweet, heady spell of Venice, full of temptation she knew she should resist.

Yet for once in her life, she'd no wish to be good, and do what she should. As inexperienced as she was, she could guess what was coming. The duke had made that clear enough, and she, just as clearly, had not rebuffed him as perhaps she should. But this once, she wanted to follow temptation, not reason.

And this once, in Venice, she'd let herself be tempted by love.

Chapter Eleven

It had been a long time since Richard Farren had held a woman in his arms like this. To be sure, there was little similarity between holding his long-lost wife Anne and Jane Wood. Anne had been tall and lissome with a dancer's grace, while Jane was small and slight and restrained.

For more than ten years, he'd believed that there could never be another woman who could rival Anne in his heart and in the faces of their two daughters, and he believed it still. He'd long ago reconciled himself to having no son of his own. His brother Peter had sired sons as readily as he had done daughters, and Richard knew the title and estate would remain in the family, and in excellent hands, too. Peter would see to that. No matter that a widowed peer in his prime was regarded as an abomination to unmarried ladies and a waste to their mothers. Richard had held firm against their attacks, and was sure he'd missed nothing.

But now, here in Venice, Jane Wood had come creeping into his affection, too, in a way he'd never sought and certainly hadn't expected. He'd wager she hadn't, either. She hadn't the guile for that, which was much of her charm for him. There was even more charm in how devoted she remained to his daughters, speaking of them with more unabashed love and regard than many women showed to their own children.

But there was much more to Jane than that, of course. She was thoughtful, almost solemn, and he'd always liked that about her. Straightforward and direct, that was Jane's way, yet when she looked up at him and blushed, she became the loveliest woman imaginable. Strange how he'd never seen it at Aston Hall. Strange how it had taken the damp air of this place to clear his head where she was concerned. She'd never replace his wife in his heart, no. But he was beginning to realise that his heart might be big enough to include a place for Jane, too.

He tightened his arm around her waist, drawing her closer. He felt the soft curve between her waist and hips beneath the rough wool of her cloak, and felt, too, how neatly she fit against him. She must have felt it as well, for she slipped her hands lightly over his, almost as if she feared he'd take his away.

'Your hands are cold, Jane,' he said. 'Like ice.'

'I'm sorry,' she said, quickly lifting her hands away. 'But they didn't bring my gloves with my cloak.'

'I'll warm them.' He covered her hands in his own, and as he did, he couldn't miss the unconscious small shiver of pleasure that rippled through her. 'That's better, isn't it?'

'It is.' She smiled, tipping her head to look back over her shoulder at him. 'You make a most excellent handwarmer.'

'I only want to please you, sweet.' He gazed past her, at the houses and canal before him. He'd brought Jane here meaning to tease her more about not finding Venice romantic by moonlight, the way he was certain his daughter Diana would. If Jane had even tried to be her usual practical self in the face of this, then he'd intended to make a jest of it.

But as he stood here in the moonlight with her in his arms on this wedding cake of a bridge, he felt himself tripped by his own amusing snare, and it wasn't just the fault of all that excellent Italian wine he'd drunk, either. Damnation, if this wasn't the most romantic place he'd ever seen, with Jane herself the centrepiece.

'You have pleased me,' she said softly, 'by insisting we come here. I'd never have come here by myself, you know. Have you ever seen anything more beautiful in all your days?'

'Or nights,' he said. 'I suspect it's something better viewed in company, eh?'

'Oh, yes,' she said. 'Especially if the company is so—so agreeable.'

She turned in his arms so she was facing him, her expression becoming oddly solemn as she leaned back into the crook of his arm. With great daring she rested her hands on his chest with her fingers fanned apart.

'Now,' she said, her voice a breathy whisper, 'now I suppose you shall try to kiss me.'

He smiled. 'Would that please you, too, Jane?'

'Yes,' she said slowly, thoughtfully. 'Yes, I believe it would.'

'I could kiss you,' he said, lowering his mouth over hers, the fragrance of her skin mingling with the saltiness of the air around them. 'I can.'

'No,' she said suddenly, ducking her head away at the last moment. 'No, Richard, please.'

Disappointment welled up within him. 'If you're going to bring up some damned nonsense about you having been my daughters' governess, and therefore can't—'

'No!' She shook her head fiercely, slipping her hands around his shoulders to draw his face down to hers. 'No nonsense. I only wished to kiss you before you kissed me.'

Instinctively her mouth found his, turning the exact distance for their lips to meet and meld, and for Richard to forget any idea whatsoever of protesting how she'd foxed him. He forgot, and instead realised everything that was fine about kissing her: how eagerly she sighed as her lips parted for him, how warm her mouth could be, how she seemed to melt against him, as if making her body touch his in as many ways as she could, how she tasted and smelled and felt and kissed him in return.

It was as if he were a young man again, stealing away with his first lass. They kissed, and everything in life seemed once again possible, as long as she was there to share it with him. He'd forgotten the magic of kissing a woman, of discovering how sweet and soft and welcoming her mouth could be. He curled his arm around her waist, lifting her up more tightly against him. She seemed small, as light as a will-o'-the-wisp, and as warm to hold as a kitten. With a little moan of startled pleasure, her lips slipped apart for him, and hungrily he deepened the kiss, desire drumming deep in his belly with the taste of her. Her response was rarer for being unexpected and eager, and he could feel the bliss vibrate through them both like a live spark.

He kissed her long and hard, her hands pressed flat against his chest in confused delight. He liked that, for it meant he was the first man to draw this response from her, the first to kiss her with such urgency. He could taste her surprise in the way she fluttered beneath him, yet he could also tell the exact moment when that surprise gave way to eagerness and to pleasure all her own, when her lips began to respond to his, when the resistance in her body lessened and her hands curled round his back, and when, most of all, he realised he'd forgotten everything and everyone else except the woman in his arms.

'Ah, Jane, Jane,' he murmured, threading his fingers into her hair to hold her face before him. Lightly he feathered kisses over her cheeks, along the curve of her jaw and throat that he knew would be most sensitive. 'My own sweet Jane.'

With a shuddering sigh, she gently twisted her face away from his lips, drawing far enough away from him to study his face. Her lips were wet and parted, her breathing rapid, leaving no doubt in his mind that she'd relished their kiss as much as he. Yet in the moonlight her eyes were enormous with uncertainty, their confusion punctuated by the spiky shadows of her lashes falling across her cheeks.

'What next, Richard?' she asked softly. 'What next?'

'Next?' he repeated. 'Why, I suppose we shall go back and rouse the *signora's* cook for an early breakfast. Unless, that is, you wish to kiss me again.'

She smiled, her pale face full of a sadness he didn't understand. 'The *signora's* cook will be happy to oblige you, I am sure. He'll even brew that dreadful coffee of yours.'

'No more, Jane,' he said gruffly. 'It was only a kiss, a single kiss. If you never wish to kiss me again, well, then, you needn't. But considering how there's only two weeks before—'

'Don't plan, I beg you!' she cried plaintively. 'All my life I've planned, and prepared, and arranged, trying to make a tidy order of everything. For now, for this once, I wished to live upon my impulse, my whims, alone, without any arrangements or planning. For once, here in Venice where there'd be no consequences, I wanted to be free.'

'Oh, Jane,' he said softly, stroking her cheek with thumb. 'There are always consequences in life, even in Venice.'

'As soon as I kissed you, I realised that,' she said.

'I wanted to kiss you as if it didn't matter, but it did. It *does*.'

She pulled free of him and turned towards the rail of the bridge. The hood of her cloak had fallen back and she'd lost her customary linen cap, leaving her hair loose and beguilingly unruly. He wondered if she'd turned to hide a tear from him. He'd understand if she had. He knew all too well the melancholy of loneliness.

'Moonlight changes everything, doesn't it?' She gazed out over the water as if seeing everything for the first time. 'Everything's different. Nothing's the same.'

He came to stand behind her, his hands on her shoulders. The moon was setting and the stars disappearing with it, and to the east the first glow of dawn was beginning to show in the fading night sky.

'The world never does stand still, Jane, whether we wish it to or not,' he said, his voice more poignant than he'd intended. 'Sometimes that can be for the best.'

He'd not intended to think of Anne now, of all times, but he had. Yet it wasn't with the old grief, the old sorrow. Instead he had the oddest sensation of letting go, not of Anne's memory, but of the hard grief that had kept his heart a prisoner for so long.

Could a single kiss have done that? he marveled. Could Jane truly have worked such a miracle without even realising it?

Now Jane nodded without looking back at him, then tipped her head to one side to rub her cheek against the back of his hand.

'Everything does change,' she said softly. 'We'll have at least a fortnight here before the young ladies and their husbands join us.'

'Two weeks.' He kissed her cheek, whispering close to her ear. 'I'll treasure every minute, Jane, and squander not a single one.'

She touched her fingers to where he'd kissed her cheek, as if to hold the kiss there.

'Every minute, one by one by one,' she said softly, and at last turned back to face Richard. 'For truth to tell, what else do we have?'

She stretched up on her toes and kissed his cheek as he had kissed hers, then brushed her lips across his, sweetly, in a way that made Richard long for more. He was relieved to see that if there had been an unshed tear or two glistening in her eyes, they were gone now.

But instead of another kiss, a Venetian rooster in some nearby courtyard seized the silent opportunity to crow and announce the coming day.

Jane laughed, and Richard couldn't help but laugh with her.

'I promise to cherish even that moment,' she said, 'and that particular cock's crow, however inopportune they may be.'

'Then we'll agree together on that,' he said, his spirits rising again. He took her hand and tucked it into the crook of his arm. 'Now come. I do believe that rooster was calling us to breakfast, eh?'

Chapter Twelve

By moonlight, it had all made perfect, even logical, sense. But by the time the first rays of the morning sun were creeping into Jane's bedchamber—and Jane herself finally creeping into her bed—all sense of logic was gone, let alone perfection.

Her conscience in turmoil, Jane could not begin to sleep, no matter how exhausted she was. Instead she lay curled in her bed beneath the feather-filled coverlet, watching the dappled reflections of the water dance across the ceiling overhead and trying to determine exactly what had happened last night with Richard.

Richard. How easy it had been to slip into addressing him with such familiarity! A week ago she'd been living in dread of the almighty Duke of Aston, and his judgement of her and her actions. Now, after one night and two glasses of wine, she was not only calling him by his given name, but kissing him. *Kissing* him! Oh, preserve her, what folly and foolishness had she committed in that siren moonlight!

She groaned, and pressed her face into the pillow. Nothing good would come of this—this flirtation last night. Nothing. She'd resolved to be less reserved while she was here in Venice, and to try to enjoy herself more fully. Not wanton, of course, but a bit more adventurous. Where would be the harm in that?

But she'd never meant to behave so foolishly in Richard's company. She'd acted boldly, without shame, announcing she'd kiss him and then doing so, like any practised harlot. Worst of all, she'd enjoyed doing it, more than she'd enjoyed herself in—oh, in her entire life, if she were honest. She'd enjoyed his company, his conversation, their dinner, and then she'd enjoyed walking out in the moonlight with him, and his embrace, and every word of the sweet nonsense he'd told her.

She groaned again at the memory. What demon had possessed her and urged her to act in such a brazen fashion? It was entirely her fault, of course. She'd no doubt of that. How could it be otherwise, when the Duke of Aston was such a paragon?

In all her days at Aston Hall, the duke had never so much as pinched the bottom of a parlour maid.

There was a certain bewilderment among the staff that their duke had kept so faithful to the duchess's memory and hadn't remarried, or even been tempted beyond a dance or two at a county ball. The footmen and grooms in particular couldn't believe that a gentleman as fine and rich as their master didn't keep a mistress in London, the way other peers did. Wilson assured them he didn't, and Wilson would know.

But now she had come along and somehow bewitched their saintly duke into kissing her beneath the Venetian moon. He had drunk considerably more of the *signora's* Valpolicella than she, which might account for how susceptible he'd been to the lure of the moonlight. Yes, that must have been it, the wine and the moonlight besides. She wasn't so foolish as to believe it had been her dubious charms that had lured him to misbehave with her. He had been in his cups, and she had been willing.

Was he now feeling the same remorse? Was he also tossing and turning with shame over this dreadful misstep, wishing with all his heart that it could be undone? Surely dallying with a woman from his household must be a dreadful burden to a man who behaved as honourably as the duke.

And how would he treat her when they met again? Would he pretend nothing had happened?

Would he apologise? Or would he dismiss her as a loathsome wanton, and finally cast her out in this foreign city as she'd been expecting him to do ever since he'd arrived?

Yet as tormented as Jane felt herself to be, she still had stayed awake for the entire night and more, and even the most guilty conscience needed rest. Finally she had fallen asleep, and so deeply that it took Signora della Batista's determined thumping on her bedchamber door to finally rouse her.

'Miss, miss, miss!' the *signora* was calling on the other side of the panelled door. 'Hurry, miss, and waken! Make haste, if you please. His Grace grows weary of waiting!'

'His Grace!' cried Jane, her voice thick with sleep. 'One moment, *signora,* one moment.'

At once she rolled from her bed, dragging the coverlet with her, and tried to hurry across the long room to answer. With fumbling fingers, Jane unlatched the door, and the *signora* herself swept inside, bearing a tray with a steaming teapot and a plate of biscuits.

'It is late, Miss Wood,' she scolded, setting the tray on the table by the window. 'Only the infirm and the debauched are abed at this hour.'

'I am sorry, *signora,*' Jane said, yawning as she

stood at the door with the coverlet as a makeshift cloak around her shoulders. She knew she should be rushing to dress and not keeping the duke waiting, but she was having a dreadful time waking. 'I was very late coming to bed.'

The *signora* clicked her tongue with contempt. '*Very* late,' she muttered in Italian. She touched her fingers to the handle of the teapot, judged it too hot to lift, and bunched her skirts in her hand to protect her fingers. 'Very late, or very early, and with the man you said was your master. My cook could tell the hour you went to bed.'

'His Grace *was* my master, *signora*,' Jane said. 'Because his daughters have wed, I am no longer in his service.'

'As you say, miss,' the *signora* said, pouring the fragrant tea and arching one of her neatly plucked brows to signal her scepticism. 'As you say.'

Jane noticed that she had brought not one, but two cups with the teapot, and was briskly filling them both. 'Only one cup, please, *signora*. There's no need for—'

'Good day, my dear Jane, and good morning,' declared Richard, suddenly appearing to push his way past the door. 'Or perhaps I should be saying "good afternoon", given that it's almost mid-day. Rouse yourself, sweet, else our entire day will be lost.'

She stared at him, stunned into silence. While she felt grey, dishevelled and raspy with lack of sleep, he seemed so fresh as to almost be spritely, his cheeks ruddy and newly shaved, his eyes cheerfully bright, and his linen immaculate. Painfully aware of her own sorry state, she clutched the coverlet more tightly around her shoulders.

'Come, come, Jane, enough of this lolling about abed,' he said in the same booming voice he used when riding to hounds. 'I asked the good *signora* here to fetch you tea, the same as at home. That's sure to fortify you better than that sweetling chocolate. Drink up and make ready for the day's adventures, or what's left of the day, at any rate.'

'Forgive me, your Grace, but I'd believed you'd no further interest in seeing Venice's sites,' she said, crossing the floor with the coverlet trailing behind her like a train. 'I'd not expected you to wish to go about so soon after retiring.'

'Hah, you believe I must still be drunk from last night,' he said almost gleefully as he popped one of the biscuits into his mouth. 'I'm as sober as a curate on the Sabbath, my dear. It will take more than that Italian grape to set me back.'

The *signora* snorted, not hiding her disgust as she made a perfunctory curtsy. 'If you do not need me any further, your Grace.'

'Thank you, *signora,* you may leave us.' He nodded as the *signora* left, not quite waiting for permission. He helped himself to one of the two cups of tea and sat in an overstuffed armchair. 'Fah, this is a strange brew! I had the *signora* offer up tea, figuring it would be a comfort for you, but this is no proper English tea.'

'There is no such thing as "proper English tea", your Grace,' Jane said tartly, 'because tea doesn't come from England, but from China. Nor can I conceive of why I should be in need of "comforting", whether from tea or otherwise.'

He spread his hands, unperturbed. 'You have always been a creature of predictable habit, Jane, a most admirable quality. You did not come down to breakfast at your usual hour. The *signora* said you were still in your bed. What else was I to think, but that you were indisposed?'

'You might have thought the truth, your Grace,' she said, coming to stand beside his chair. 'That I was very late in going to bed, and thus I would be equally late in rising from it.'

'Oh, Jane, enough.' He set the dish of tea down on the table, and gently prised her hand free from the coverlet, taking her fingers in his own. 'No more of these practised school-room recitals, I beg you.'

That was wounding. 'Forgive me, your Grace, but I do not understand.'

'You should,' he said with a sigh. 'Last night we agreed to take each day as it came in turn, without worry or concern. To my mind, looking back over one's shoulder to try to re-order the days that are done does not seem to be in the spirit of that agreement. Where's the use in it, I ask you?'

'I wasn't attempting to re-order the past.' She tried to pull her hand free, but he held it firm, leaving her to feel embarrassed and foolish. She was all too aware of his gaze upon her, and how her feet were bare and her body covered only by her night shift and the coverlet, and anywhere in England this would have been the most scandalous situation imaginable. 'Not at all, your Grace. Rather I was merely—'

'No more of that, either,' he said gently. 'I want you to call me by my name, not my title.'

'I thought that was a folly from last night,' she said, choosing her words with care.

'A folly?' he repeated with patent disbelief. 'A *folly*?'

'Yes,' she said as firmly as she could. 'A folly seems as appropriate a term as any.'

Now that the moonlight had been replaced with the harsher reality of the mid-day sun, she'd let him change his mind if he wished it. Really, she expected it. All she asked in return was to be permitted to save her own pride—and her heart—in the process.

Which was, of course, most difficult while he was holding her hand and gazing up at her with such a show of good humour and, yes, of affection, too.

She made herself look slightly to the left of his face and away from his eyes, his lovely, lovely eyes, so full of kindness.

'I will not hold you accountable for things said or done last night, your Grace,' she said, purposefully keeping her manner formal. 'I understand that it was a jest. I know you meant to prove to me how sentimental a place Venice can be, and that you did not intend to—'

'I meant every word,' he interrupted. 'It wasn't a jest. Every word. All of it. I meant it, Jane, and you can't make me take any of it back.'

'You do?' Her voice squeaked upwards with surprise, and two words were the sum of what she could manage. Perhaps she had misunderstood. Perhaps he didn't mean to turn her out after all. And perhaps, perhaps, her heart would be safe. 'You would—you would honour such a statement?'

'I would,' he said, 'and I'll swear to it in any fashion you please. I like your company. I like your conversation. I like listening to you, and teasing you and kissing you. I liked that very much. But most of all, Jane, I like you. Not as my daughters' governess, but as a woman. There, I can speak no more plainly than that.'

'No,' she said, her voice quaking. In all the time she'd thrashed about last night and this morning, she'd never imagined him saying this. 'I do not suppose you can.'

'I can't, so don't hope that I will. I haven't your way with words, you know. They're not my friends, the way they seem to be with you.'

'Oh, but that's not true!' she exclaimed. 'I think you speak beautifully!'

'Be that as it may.' He sighed, and looked up at her beneath his brows. 'At least this time you appear to have heard what I've said, so I won't have to repeat myself again.'

'No, no,' she said slowly, trying to accept the magnitude of what he'd just told her. This time, there was no moonlight or wine. If he spoke this way to her when she was in such slovenly disarray, why, then he *must* mean it. 'That won't be necessary.'

'Thank the heavens for small favours.' He took her hand and pressed it briefly to his lips, his gaze never leaving her face. 'You do realise, Jane, that, after the sort of speech I made to you, it's considered customary for the other party to make some sort of reply in kind.'

'In kind?' she said, puzzled.

'Do you in turn like me, Jane?' he demanded, a demand that was endlessly sweetened by the gruff, unvarnished beseeching in his voice. 'Do you find me tolerable company? Or am I nothing more than a hoary old tyrant, and was last night the most tedious and dreary of your entire life?'

'Tedious?' she exclaimed, horrified that he'd so wrongly misconstrued her response. 'Nothing could be further from the truth! Last night was more beautiful, more perfect, than ever I could dream, and to call yourself a hoary old tyrant—that is simply not true!'

'No?' He smiled slyly up at her. 'My dear, you give me hope.'

'Hope!' she cried indignantly. Now she did pull her hand free, and with it give his shoulder an impatient small shove. 'Hope? I should offer you a great deal more than that hope if you weren't so—so—'

She broke off abruptly, sputtering as she realised that all of the conclusions she might have used to complete that sentence were not suited for polite conversation. Richard might claim that words were her friends, but at this moment, she felt as if they'd betrayed her.

'If I weren't what?' he asked. 'Don't leave me dangling like a villain from the gallows, Jane. If I weren't what?'

His smile had become more amused than plaintive, and that was his undoing. She'd already learned how swiftly he could slip into teasing, and she'd no doubt he was teasing her now. She was not in the humour for teasing, not from him, not from anyone. If he wished to hear the words she'd held back, well then, he'd hear them now.

'If you were not so *provoking*,' she said with an extra furious poke at his shoulder for emphasis, 'or so *irritating*, or so righteously puffed with your own—'

But before she could finish, he'd grabbed her by the wrist and pulled her over the cushioned arm of the chair and into his lap. She yelped with surprised protest, and he drew her closer, the coverlet slipping from her body as she struggled. His arm circled neatly around her waist, drawing her closer, and she realised he meant to kiss her.

Again.

But this kiss would be a far different creature from what they'd shared before. Last night there'd been the excuse of the wine and the moonlit bridge, and here in the chilly late-morning light of her bedchamber there'd be neither. Last night she'd been wrapped in many layers of warm clothing: a heavy cloak, plus a thick knitted tippet, a woollen gown, boned linen stays, a quilted petticoat and a shift. She'd been protected by her clothes, like armour on a warrior, and when Richard had held her, the embrace had been genteelly muffled by her dress and his as well.

There was no such protection now. With the coverlet crumpled on the floor, Richard was holding her close with only her night shift over her body, the thinnest layer of linen so thriftily worn that it had become nearly translucent. Through it she could feel the muscles of Richard's arm around her waist, the buttons of his shirt and waistcoat and his chest beneath pressing against her breasts, the legs sprawled over his and her bottom nestled against his, well, his *lap;* she could scarce make herself so much as put a word to that large manly part of him that was clearly lurking there. She was as good—or as bad—as naked and tumbled across him, and she felt shamed as well as embarrassed.

Shamed, and embarrassed, and yet oddly excited, too. Her heart raced with anticipation, not dread, and she realised to her surprise that her ungainly position was making her long to kiss Richard more, not less. She also realised she was tempting fate by tempting him like this. She knew the nature of that fate—she'd spent most of her life cautioning her young female charges against such perils, to little avail—though she'd little experience of her own. But now, with Richard, she could think of nothing else.

She stopped struggling, and instead went still. Slowly she brought his hand to her lips and kissed it, the same way he'd kissed hers, and looked up through her lashes to see his reaction.

It was an admirable reaction, too, well worth watching. The bluster left his face, and the teasing, too. His eyes filled with wonder and pleasure, and something darker, rougher, more excitingly male.

'Ah, lass, you've a warm nature,' he said gruffly, his breath quickening as he turned his hand to cup her cheek, caressing the side of her throat with his thumb.

'There's no fault to a warm nature on a cold day,' she said, turning her head to rub against his thumb like a little cat. 'I'd venture yours is warm as well. And it is January.'

'Aye, it is.' he said. 'But I vow you won't be burned by me, lass, even on this cold January day.'

'Not burned, Richard, never that,' she said, again echoing his gesture by touching her palm to his cheek, cradling his jaw as she threaded her fingers into his waving gold hair. 'But I do need warming.

We both do. We both could use the merry sun of my Venice to chase away the English chill from our souls.'

She meant it, too. Their pasts, their lost loves, the careful respectable shells that both of them had constructed around their hearts needed to be melted if either of them was ever to love again. And with each other, perhaps it was still possible.

'Ahh, my Jane,' he said, his voice so full of emotion that she knew he understood. 'And you said you'd no gift for words!'

She wasn't sure if she kissed him then, or if he was the one who kissed her first, but when their lips did meet it seemed the most natural, the most perfect thing in the world. This time, she wasn't startled; this time she knew what to expect, what to anticipate, what to do.

Eagerly she answered his kiss, slanting her lips to accommodate his. Letting him coax hers apart, she relished the exciting sensation of having his tongue play against hers, the feel and the taste of him. She'd teased him about how they'd both needed warming, but there was nothing cold about how he kissed her, or the desire she felt simmering between them, the same as it had the first time he'd kissed her last night on the bridge.

But while she'd thought she known what to expect,

she soon learned that, however passionate, that first kiss had been only the beginning. He had more to offer her, and much, much more for them to claim together. Emotions and weariness and denial, too, had worn away at her earlier misgivings to a degree that she hadn't realised until she felt his hand upon her hip, his fingers spread to caress her.

He shifted beneath her, making her aware of the hard heat of his arousal. He tugged the front of her night dress down and she arched against him, giving her wordless permission for him to slip his hand inside her shift to the bare skin beneath. She wriggled, weakly trying to protest more because she knew she should rather than from any real wish for him to stop.

How could she, when what he was doing was building such a delicious tension in her body, when every bit of it was what she wanted, what she craved, because *he* was the one doing it?

'Oh, Richard, please,' she whispered breathlessly, not even sure what she was asking for. 'Please, oh, please.'

But instead of kissing her again, as she'd wished, he groaned, and drew back. 'You are right, Jane. Damnation, but you are right.'

With the greatest care, he set her back on her feet.

He reached down for the discarded coverlet, and slipped it over her shoulders, covering her entirely.

'What are you doing?' she asked, bewildered. 'If I have displeased you, why, then I beg—'

'You pleased me too much,' he said heavily. 'I am the one who must apologise, Jane, for abusing your sweet nature in such a barbarous fashion.'

'But it wasn't barbarous,' she said, daring to lay her hand on his arm as she searched his face. 'It was fine, and good and honourable, such as you are yourself, Richard, and exactly what I wished.'

'Then all the better that we stopped, and acted upon reason rather that passion alone,' he said, with such deliberation that she realised he was convincing himself, too. 'I've no wish to sully my regard for you, Jane. Not like that.'

She looked away so he wouldn't see the tears of disappointment that stung her eyes.

'Jane.' He caught her arm, and turned her back towards him so she couldn't hide. 'Jane, my own. Mark what I said. Not now, here, with you tumbled like a tavern chit in my lap. That was all.'

She raised her chin. 'I don't wish to be so honourable that you won't kiss me.'

He laughed softly, breaking the tension between them. 'A lack of desire is not the problem, Jane, not, I'd wager, for either of us. Rather I wish us both to be certain of our regard, and not act in regrettable haste.'

'I wouldn't regret it,' she said wistfully. 'Not with you.'

'Damnation, Jane, don't tempt me again,' he said, and circled his arms loosely around her shoulders. 'I want you to be sure of me first.'

She tried to smile up at him. 'We haven't much time for such decisions, Richard.'

'We've time enough, and more,' he said, and kissed lightly on her forehead. 'And more.'

But though Jane smiled in return, her heart wasn't nearly as sure. Two weeks or less, a fortnight, a handful of days and nights—how could that be enough for what he was asking?

Day by day, she told herself fiercely, and slipped her arms around his waist as if she'd never let him go. *Day by day by day.*

Chapter Thirteen

'So what is it you'd like to see this day, Richard?' Jane asked as soon as the gondolier pushed them free of the steps before Ca' Battista. 'Shall we visit the Doge's Palace, or view the mosaics at the Basilica San Marco? You can't return to London without having seen San Marco, you know.'

'We'll save those for another day,' Richard said cheerfully. He knew exactly what she was doing, hiding behind her efficient-governess mask so that she didn't have to acknowledge what had happened earlier in her bedchamber.

'I'd rather visit something less taxing than a palace, or a whatever-that-was.'

'A basilica,' she answered promptly, the way she always offered her endless bits of information. 'That's what the Roman church here in Venice calls its cathedrals, in the fashion of the Eastern Orthodox Christians. If you wish something less taxing, I suppose we could visit the Accademia di Belle Arti, to see the pictures.'

'You know I haven't much of an eye for pictures.' Richard smiled down at her, nestled beside him in the gondola. She was bundled against the winter afternoon, a woolly shawl of some sort wrapped beneath the hood of her cloak and around her face. Her eyes were bright and her nose and cheeks already pink from the cold, and whatever ill effects had come from lack of sleep seemed to have disappeared.

He'd like to think that kissing her had helped her recovery, too. He hadn't gone to her rooms intending to haul her into his lap like that, and he regretted behaving like a drunken soldier. That wasn't the way he ordinarily was with women, especially not a woman as respectable as Jane Wood.

Yet there was something about her that seemed to spark him in a way that he'd almost forgotten. She'd said she'd wished to warm him clear to his English soul, and, oh, how she'd done that. She'd set a righteous fire in his blood, and he'd wager she felt the same for him, for all that he was just as certain she was a maid. She'd none of the tedious skittishness of young girls, but there was still an innocence to her that he found enchanting, and tempting, too.

No, he'd not come to her rooms intending to

behave dishonourably, any more than he'd come to Venice intending to begin an intrigue, or a friendship, or whatever it might be with his daughters' governess. But it had happened, and though he was glad that it had, the real challenge now would be what happened next between them.

For *them*—how many years had passed since he'd been a part of a 'them'?

'Of course you have an eye for pictures,' she said, scandalised. 'Only a blind man doesn't. Taste can be taught and acquired, of course, but anyone can see a picture hung before them, and decide whether it pleases them or not. Why, Aston Hall is full of excellent pictures!'

'My grandfather's,' Richard admitted. 'They came with the place. Except for the portraits by Ramsey of the girls and Anne in the parlour. I paid for those. Oh, and the pictures of my chestnut hunters that that fellow Stubbs did for me, over the chimney-piece in the library. You could say I had an eye for those, couldn't you?'

'I suppose I must.' Jane sighed mightily. 'But to compare the portraits of *horses* with what we might see at the Accademia, where the masterpieces of Titian, Bellini and Tintoretto are!'

'I like my horse pictures,' Richard said defensively.

'I liked the horses, too. That's one of the faults of Venice, you know. There aren't any horses.'

'That's because the Venetians believe horses bring bad luck,' Jane said. 'Historically, invaders from the north always came on horseback to attack the city, and thus horses aren't particularly welcome. Excepting those huge gilded-bronze ones on the top of the basilica. Those were political plunder, seized centuries ago from the Hippodrome in Constantinople—'

'Here we are,' Richard said, already beginning to rise as the gondolier deftly guided them to the side. 'Here now, let me help you ashore.'

Jane scanned the buildings along the water and frowned. 'Are you certain? This is the Rio di San Salvador, isn't it? An ancient neighbourhood, to be sure, but not one of an artistic note, Richard. There's nothing here but costly shops.'

'Exactly,' he said, not waiting any longer to claim her hand. 'It's called the Mercerie, and we're bound for the Merceria dell'Orologio. Signora della Battista assured me this was the proper place for quality shops.'

'Shops,' she repeated with a sigh of resignation. 'Shops.'

She stepped up to the paved walkway, waiting while he paid the gondolier. He liked having her there with him, and not just because she was a handsome young woman, either. He felt comfortably at ease with her, without either of them putting on airs, as if they already were the oldest of friends. She was excellent company, even when she rattled on and on about the Venetian horses. In fact, it had occurred to him that her impromptu lessons might actually be her way of teasing him, and he'd always had a weakness for clever, pretty women.

'Yes, shops,' he said as he rejoined her. 'I thought this might be a good day to buy some things to have for the girls when they arrive. A few little baubles to show them their old father hadn't forgotten them, eh?'

She slipped her hand into the crook of his arm without him asking, and that pleased him, too.

'You spoil the young ladies outrageously,' she said, though not with disapproval. 'They will remember you well enough without showering them with gifts. Besides, anything you purchase in these shops will sorely tax even your pockets.'

'My pockets are prodigiously deep where my girls are concerned,' he said, patting her hand fondly as they began walking. He'd come here with another purpose, too, though he meant to keep that to himself a bit longer. 'The *signora* told me that only Paris could rival these streets for ladies' goods.'

Richard did, in fact, spoil his daughters, and he'd never returned to Aston Hall from London empty-handed. As a result, he was more familiar than most gentlemen with the best ladies' shops in town, and they with him, and he was curious to see how the Venetian shops here in the Mercerie would compare.

From the curving bay windows alone, he could at once tell the differences. Clearly the wealthy Venetian ladies, even now bustling from shop to shop with their servants in tow, favoured the same rich luxury in their dress and ornament that seemed to permeate the entire city. Or rather, not Venetian ladies; though he'd say nothing to Jane, he suspected that most of the beautiful women here in this street were the courtesans for which the city was so famous, all of them eager to spend the largesse of their keepers.

While there'd be no mistaking his sensibly dressed Jane for any of the gaudy birds around them, Richard still took care to keep her protectively on his arm as they wandered through the crowded alleys and narrow streets from one shop window to another, with Jane marvelling and gasping with wonder. The goldsmiths' displays featured pearls and precious stones in elaborately wrought pieces, the shoemakers' delicate slippers of gilded kidskin with scarlet heels. The perfumeries wafted their rare fragrances into the air. There was even one shop that specialised in the oversize hats the Venetian ladies used to keep from the sun as they entertained on their rooftops, and another entirely devoted to the spangled costumes for *Carnevale,* and the curious white-and-black half-masks that were popular year round with both gentlemen and ladies alike.

'I've never seen so many fine things gathered in so many shops, and I can't begin to guess at what the keeps will ask,' Jane warned.

'Then it's past time we entered one of them and found out for ourselves,' Richard said heartily. 'Besides, I can feel how cold your little fingers are inside those pitiful gloves of yours. Best I take you inside before you turn into an icicle yourself.'

'Oh, Richard, please,' she scoffed, wrinkling her cold-reddened nose. 'You worry entirely too much about how cold I am.'

'Why shouldn't I?' he said, guiding her towards the nearest shop, where a bowing clerk was already holding the door open for them. 'Considering how agreeably you warm us both, I'd be a fool not to.'

'You're a wicked gentleman, your Grace,' she scolded with mock sternness as she slipped back her hood. 'Possibly the wickedest gentleman I've ever had the honour to, ah, to warm.'

He laughed with her, and was laughing still when the shop's owner stepped forwards, bowing so low over his bent leg that the tail of his beribboned queue flipped forwards over his head. Clearly the man must have overhead Jane use his title, thought Richard with wry amusement. No matter how much the Venetians pretended to scorn nobility for the sake of their dear republic, they still flocked to scrape over foreign titles like ravens in a cornfield after harvest.

'We are deeply honoured by your custom, your Grace,' the man said in careful, accented English. 'We are the humble servants to the desires of your Grace and her Grace.'

Beside Richard, Jane caught her breath. 'Thank you, *signor*,' she said swiftly in Italian, determined not to let the man's error stand, or to take advantage of it. 'But I am only his Grace's friend, not wife.'

'A thousand apologies!' the owner stammered and flushed a mortified purple. 'I did not know, *signora*, I did not understand, I did not—'

'Please, it's of no consequence,' Jane said, her kindness intended to ease the man's shame. 'I'd rather you tell me more of this lady's pocket-glass.'

She pointed to an arrangement of engraved sterling and tortoise-shell combs, brushes and other pieces for an elegant dressing-table, and at once the relieved owner launched into a torrent of description of the mirror's virtues.

'What all is the fellow saying?' Richard whispered in English, uneasy with a conversation that he could barely follow. 'You haven't bartered your soul away for some bauble, have you?'

'Oh, no,' she answered, nodding encouragingly at the owner as he brought out more combs from behind the counter. 'I offered him yours in return for that hairbrush.'

'Indeed.' He studied the brush, running his fingers lightly over the polished silver oval on the handle left plain for the new owner's monogram to be engraved. 'Diana would like this, I think. Ever since she learned her letters, she's fancied things with her initials on them.'

He remembered how, as a golden-haired little girl, Diana would climb on his knee to reach his desk, and with the greatest concentration and a wobbling pen spell out her name.

'Yes,' he said softly. 'This for Diana. Engraved with her mark, of course.'

'That's a lovely, thoughtful gift, Richard,' Jane said, and from the look in her eyes he was sure she understood its significance to him. 'Each time she brushes her hair, she'll think of you.'

With a touch of the old melancholy, he smiled at how transparent his thoughts must be to her. 'Tell the fellow that I'll take the entire lot if he can have it ready by next week.'

'All of it?' Jane asked with surprise. Hoping to tempt them to a larger purchase, the shop's owner had been arranging other pieces that matched the brush across a length of black velvet spread over the counter, at least a dozen pieces to the full ensemble. 'It's very dear, you know, even for your generous spirit. It could well cost you your soul by the time the final reckoning's done.'

'Not too dear for my daughter,' he said firmly. 'Make sure he has the proper letters engraved—DF for Diana Farren. Then we'll find something for Mary, too—perhaps those cameos we saw in the other window.'

'Oh, Richard.' She lay her hand over his. 'Remember Diana's wed now, and you must make the gift proper for a new bride. It's her new initials that should be engraved—DFR, with the R for Randolph.'

'I hadn't forgotten,' he said automatically, but the truth was that he *had* forgotten, or more precisely, he'd chosen to forget. He felt like a doddering fool before Jane. 'Damnation, Jane. Have the whole blasted alphabet engraved on the thing for all I care.'

'But you do care, Richard, and so will Diana,' Jane said. 'It worried her greatly that you would be angry and refuse to accept his lordship as her husband. But in the end she trusted that you loved her enough to forgive her, and in time would come to respect and to love Lord Anthony as a son.'

'I've never met the man, Jane,' Richard grumbled, admitting only the least troubling of his concerns. 'How can I respect the rascal after he seduced my daughter?'

'You will meet him soon enough,' Jane said, the pressure of her hand over his increasing for emphasis. 'And you'll like him, too, I am sure.'

'You're always sure of everything, Jane,' he said gruffly. She knew his girls so well, better, really, than he did himself.

'Oh, hardly,' she said, and smiled. 'They say that girls will give their hearts to men who in some fashion remind them of their fathers, and I do believe both the young ladies found men with a share of your best qualities. Not all of them, mind you, but a share.'

The owner hovered over the counter, waiting to learn the fate of the dressing set. Richard sighed, and glanced down at all the silver and tortoise shell.

'Tell him I'll take the whole set,' Richard said, 'and that he should mark it with my daughter's new monogram. That's a fit gift for a new bride, eh?'

'Yes.' Jane reached up and kissed his cheek, quickly, so that he'd know how she'd felt, but so that it wouldn't cause a fuss in the shop. 'And thank you.'

'Thank you, my dear,' he said, and, throwing restraint to the winds, kissed her in return. Not on the cheek, but on the mouth, and he didn't care who saw it.

'Richard!' she exclaimed afterwards, her voice squeaking upwards. Her cheeks were flushed, but from the pleasure of kissing him rather than embarrassment, and he decided she'd never looked more charming to him. 'You surprise me!'

'Then we're even,' he said, 'considering how often you do the same to me. Now let's find something for my Mary, and then, if you'll guide me, a few small things for those young rogues they wed.'

Chapter Fourteen

It took them the rest of the afternoon and visits to a half-dozen more shops before they were done, yet Richard couldn't recall having enjoyed himself more thoroughly. It was all due to Jane, and he'd give her full credit for it. Jane's company, Jane's humour, Jane's taste, Jane's thoughtfulness when it came to helping him choose gifts for his daughters, and his new sons-in-law as well.

For Mary, who loved old things and the antique world as much as Jane did herself, they found a gold necklace and earrings set with classical cameos. For Mary's husband John, who was a collector and connoisseur of fine paintings and art, a small bronze statue of a plunging horse. And for Diana's Anthony, who liked to ride and hunt, an elegant fowling piece with a stock of curly maple, inlaid with a pattern of brass-wire flourishes.

By the time they were done, the short winter day

had faded into early twilight. The shopkeepers had lit the lanterns outside their doors, and the bow windows themselves, lit from within, seemed to glow like larger lanterns themselves. Unlike in England, where most shops closed in the late afternoon, the narrow streets of the Mercerie remained crowded, the patrons merry and laughing, the way it seemed Venetians did most everything.

'We should return home soon,' Jane said, looking up beyond the overhanging rooftops to the narrow slip of starlit night beyond. 'Signora della Battista will wonder what's become of us.'

'Let her wonder,' Richard said. 'We've one more stop to make.'

He'd purposefully saved the best for last, or so he hoped it would be for Jane. It certainly would be for him.

The furrier's shop offered countless suggestions for a wealthy lady to keep away the damp chill of the canals, from squirrel-trimmed slippers to a magnificent gold-embroidered cloak lined completely in sable, worthy of the Doge himself.

'I hope the young ladies have one of these as they travel,' Jane said as she stroked the soft fur lining a rich carriage blanket. 'This, and a box of coals at their feet and their husbands beside them. What a luxurious way to keep oneself warm!'

But Richard had happily found a clerk who spoke enough English to make himself understood. The woman had nodded and disappeared into the back room to hunt for his request.

'What now, Richard?' Jane asked as she joined him. 'Surely even you have reached the limit of your generosity for one day.'

'Not quite,' he said as the clerk retuned with a flat box, draped over with a linen cloth. She set the box on the counter and lifted the cloth with a theatrical flair.

'That's it,' Richard said, smiling with approval as the woman lifted a barrel-shaped muff from the box. 'That's it exactly. What do you think, Jane?'

'I think it's very beautiful,' she said, her voice full of admiration and a bit of awe.

All the better for his surprise, thought Richard, his anticipation growing. 'Go ahead and slip your hands inside,' he urged. 'Try it.'

She hesitated only an instant before taking the muff from the clerk and putting her own hands inside. It wasn't as outrageously oversize as some of the muffs he'd seen on fashionable ladies strolling in the London parks. Instead this one was exactly the right size to cover a lady's hands and forearms, and made of a dark, elegant, silky fur that put velvet to shame. It was quietly luxurious and in exquisite, elegant taste, the perfect choice for a woman who was herself quietly elegant.

Her hands buried deep inside the muff, Jane grinned, and rubbed her cheek against the soft fur with such unabashed pleasure that Richard couldn't help but smile in return.

'What fur is it?' he asked the clerk, but without looking away from Jane's delighted face. 'What beast, eh?'

'*Castoro della Nuova Francia,* your Grace,' the woman said. 'Very fine, very elegant. *Bellissima!*'

'That's beaver,' Jane said, ever helpful. 'From the wilderness of New France.'

'But doesn't it sound better in their lingo?' Richard said, teasing. '*Castoro della Nuova Francia!* Rather like that *calamari* of theirs. Sounds delicious, until you learn they're trying to feed you some infernal squid.'

She narrowed his eyes, now recognising his jesting. 'You ate it, Richard, and enjoyed every morsel, so please don't pretend you didn't.'

He laughed. 'You still haven't told me if you like the muff.'

'I do.' She sighed, reluctantly pulling her hands free of the muff to return it to the shop clerk. 'Whichever of the young ladies receives it will be pleased indeed.'

'It's not for either of my girls,' he said softly. 'It's for you, Jane. To keep you warm.'

She gasped, and stared down at the muff. 'But—but—oh, Richard, this is too much!'

'Not for you,' he said, taking her into his arms. 'Never too much for my own dear Jane.'

Overwhelmed with emotion, she buried her face against Richard's shoulder, the muff still clutched tightly in one hand. Yet without a word from her, he knew he'd never in his life made anyone happier with a gift, nor himself so happy in return.

'The lady's satisfied,' he said over Jane's quaking shoulders to the clerk. 'We'll take it.'

It was late, very late, by the time Jane and Richard finished their supper and returned to the Ca' Batistta, with Richard's arm around Jane's waist and her own arms cradling the lovely new muff. It had instantly become her most precious possession, and not because of its intrinsic value, either. Though Jane appreciated things of beauty and artistry, she didn't value them for their cost.

No, for her the little muff was worth treasuring because it had come from Richard, his first gift to her, and one chosen with much care and significance special to her. No matter what else happened between them, she knew she'd always have this token from him. Each time she slipped her hands into the silky interior, she'd remember how they jested about keeping one another warm, and how, too, they'd acted upon those jests. But most of all she'd remember Richard, and how, for these handful of bright winter days in Venice, he'd made her feel like the most special woman under heaven.

'Damnation, but it's as cold in here as it is on the water,' Richard was saying as the porter shut the door behind them. 'Don't know why the good *signora* doesn't have one of those *kachelofens* here in her front hall, just to be more welcoming.'

Jane smiled, not because the notion of *kachelofens* here at the foot of the stairs was so preposterous, but because she was so happy. She pressed more closely into Richard's arm, relishing the warmth of his body against hers.

Belatedly one of the *signora*'s footmen came hurrying down the steps to greet them. The man's livery coat was buttoned crookedly and his wig askew, proof enough that she and Richard had once again been out late enough to disturb the house's routine.

'Good evening, your Grace, Miss Wood,' he said in stiff, newly learned English. 'Please to dine now, yes? To table, yes?'

'No, no, we're still stuffed as peahens from supper,' Richard said, patting the front of his waistcoat by way of demonstration. 'Please, Jane, help me. Tell the poor fellow we've no need of anything more this night, and that he should pack off to his bed.'

Quickly Jane did exactly that in Italian, adding her own apology for keeping the staff awake. Relieved, the footman nodded, stifling a yawn.

'The *signora* had us bank the fires for the night in your rooms, miss,' he said. 'If you wish me to build the fire in his Grace's bedchamber, I would be happy to—'

'Thank you, no,' said Jane, her cheeks flaming. She told herself that the man was merely being practical, especially as a Venetian, and acting on what he saw without judging her, yet she couldn't help but feel shamed by his offer. Building the fire back to life for them in Richard's bedchamber could only mean one thing. As much as she was coming to care for Richard, she wasn't ready to share his bed. She thought of it, thought of it often; she couldn't deny it. But she still wasn't sure she'd take such a momentous step, no matter how dear Richard was to her. Two weeks—oh, two weeks couldn't possibly be enough time to make that decision.

'Thank you, that won't be necessary,' she said,

nodding to the footman to dismiss him. 'You may go.'

'What's the fellow about, Jane?' Richard asked suspiciously. '"Camera da letto" means bedchamber. What is he asking you?'

'Only if we wished to have the fires fanned in our rooms before we went to sleep,' she said, very nearly the truth, but far enough from it that she flushed again with guilty misery. She glanced at the footman again. 'Thank you, you may go.'

'This came for you, Miss Wood, while you were out.' The footman handed her a sealed letter on a small charger, bowed. 'Good night, Your Grace, Miss Wood.'

'What the devil is that, Jane?' Richard asked jovially as the footman left them. 'You're not receiving billets-doux from another, are you?'

'It's from Signor Rinaldini di Rossi,' she said, 'and it most assuredly will not be a billet-doux. He is a worthy gentleman of this place, much respected for his collection of pictures and his knowledge of Old Master painters. You should recognise his name. We brought a letter of introduction to him.'

'Potter assembled those letters, not I,' Richard admitted. 'He made all the arrangements for your tour. I wouldn't know di Rossi from Adam himself. A collector of pictures—a dry old stick, then?'

'He's a model Venetian gentleman, full of charm and grace,' Jane said absently, scanning the *signor*'s impeccably composed letter. 'Oh, how kind of him! He's inviting me to come to the theatre as his guest.'

'I've a better notion,' Richard said easily. 'Come to the theatre with me as my guest, and then you can introduce this charming gentleman to me in between acts.'

She looked up, startled. His expression hadn't outwardly changed, his half-smile still reflecting his enjoyment in their day together. But there was a new resolve to his eyes that she hadn't seen before, a hint of steely forcefulness that was new to her. It took her only a moment to realise what it meant, but when she did, she grinned with giddy wonder in return.

'You're jealous,' she said softly. 'You, Richard, are jealous of a man you never so much as guessed existed not five minutes ago.'

'I am jealous, yes,' he said, circling her waist with his arm.

'You've no reason to be,' she said, delighting in the novelty of her situation. This was an entirely new experience for her. No other gentleman in her life had ever cared enough for her to be jealous, yet it wasn't the power of it that she enjoyed, but the caring. 'Signor di Rossi has been an excellent guide and friend to me while I have been here, alone in a foreign city.'

'And no more?' asked Richard, exaggerating his question to soften his concern, but Jane wasn't fooled. He cared, cared desperately.

'No,' she said, and she meant it. There had been times when di Rossi's interest had seemed more intense than was perhaps necessary, enough that she had felt discomfited by it. But now, reconsidering, she believed it had been nothing more than the difference between the customs of their two nations, the difference between what was proper address for a Venetian gentleman and what was expected by an English gentlewoman. Truly, she doubted di Rossi meant any more than that, and never the way that Richard so clearly did now.

'No,' she repeated with more emphasis, wanting to reassure him. She rested her hands on his shoulders, loving the strength she felt in his broad muscles and bones. 'This invitation is no more than a cordial offer between acquaintances.'

'Good.' He relaxed, and smiled, the tension easing in him beneath her palms. 'Can you fault me for wanting to keep you all to myself, Jane?'

'No,' she whispered, daring for the first time to

speak the truth of her heart, 'because that is how I wish to keep you as well.'

'Then you'll have your wish,' he said, and when he kissed her, she knew that he meant every word.

Chapter Fifteen

As was usual at the Teatro San Samuele, the orchestra began dolefully playing the first overtures to a half-empty house. It didn't matter that nearly every ticket had been sold, as was also usual as well. No one of any importance ever arrived before the first act was done, and some not until the second.

Which made di Rossi's appearance, sitting alone in his box, all the more painful for him to bear.

He sat to the back of the box, away from the bright chandeliers that were meant to light the ladies and their jewels, more important than anything that might happen on the stage. He had not yet shed his dark cloak, and, as was customary for Venetian gentleman who preferred fashionable anonymity for evening, he'd kept his black cocked hat and his white half-mask tied over his face, too. He'd look no different from scores of others, always the point of such dress, even if there were anyone here to see him in the first place. But here di Rossi was, and here he was determined to stay, waiting for the appearance of his little English governess.

Idly he watched the boxes around him slowly begin to fill. He'd come early because he'd suspected that Jane Wood, too, would arrive then. Promptness, however unnecessary, struck him as an English trait, especially for an oafish English duke.

He sighed, more resigned than impatient. He would wait here as long as was necessary, until Miss Wood and her noble master deigned to show themselves in the box across from his. He had never expected this duke to debase himself to this extent, choosing to appear so publicly with his daughters' governess. For a nobleman to be seen at the theatre with a mistress or other famous beauty would be one thing, but to go about with one of his own household on his arm was unfathomable. Female servants could provide a certain amusement, but they were no more than a passing novelty, to be soon replaced and forgotten, not honoured with public favour and regard. Perhaps such arrangements were common in England, but here in Venice, it was simply ridiculous.

Of course, di Rossi realised the irony of such a judgement, when he himself had been hoping to accompany the governess himself to this same play. But the sweet-faced governess was not a member of *his* household, and therefore fair game—a nicety, yes, but a one of the ways in which he differed from the duke. He trusted there were a good many more.

Di Rossi had yet to view the Englishman, let alone make his acquaintance, but he was already certain he'd find him wanting. While the poor tender creature must be dazzled, even besotted, by her master's attention, di Rossi was quite sure he could make her see every one of the duke's imperfections, especially when compared to di Rossi himself. Truly, what better way than this for her to observe the two of them side by side, here at the theatre?

With a weary sigh, di Rossi brushed an infinitesimal speck of lint from his sleeve. This intrusion by the duke had presented an unexpected delay in his seduction, but that was all it was: a delay. The first fury he'd felt when he'd received her rejection to his invitation earlier today had passed. He smiled, considering all the delicious possibilities ahead, much like a gourmet pausing at the doorway of a sumptuous feast. Philosophers claimed that anticipation, coupled with perseverance, only served to crown the ultimate achievement. If that were true, then the sensual rapture he'd find when at last he claimed the maidenhead of the virtuous Miss Wood would make for a rare conquest indeed.

Ahh, then—then the waiting would be worth every minute.

'Our box must be along here, Richard,' Jane said eagerly as the usher led them along the curving row of panelled doors. 'Oh, I hope we're not too late!'

'It's a playhouse, sweet,' Richard said. 'Plays and players never begin on time. You know that.'

'How could I, when this is the first play I've ever attended?' she asked. 'That is, the first in a proper theatre. I'd hoped to go in Paris with the young ladies, but we were there in the wrong season. In Rome, we attended the opera, but never the theatre. I've seen the travelling companies when they put on a play in the ballroom at the inn in Aston, but I've never attended one like this.'

'None?' he asked, surprised. 'Surely in London—'

'But I've only been to London twice in my life,' she said, 'and even then not for play-going, but to attend to my father's business affairs.'

'Not after that?' he asked. 'Not once for pleasure?'

She shrugged shyly, and rubbed her new muff against her cheek.

'I've always stayed at Aston with the young ladies,' she said. 'You were quite firm in your determination that they remain in the country until they were ready to be presented. Not that I'm complaining, mind—for I do believe the young ladies were much better served by remaining at home—only explaining why this truly is my first play.'

'Then I hope this night will meet your expectations.' He squeezed her hand gently. She might not have been complaining, but he none the less felt guilty for all the amusements she'd missed in London because of her loyalty to his wishes. He knew he didn't owe her anything for any of the past necessities of her life; to be honest, compared to the lives of many women left without means, Jane had provided well for herself. Yet he couldn't help but want to make things better for her, and show her whatever she'd missed, even spoil her. 'No, I'll hope this exceeds them, and proves better than whatever you've imagined.'

'Oh, I am certain of that,' she said fervently. 'How could it not?'

Richard laughed. 'I suppose that will depend on what exactly you've imagined.'

The usher finally stopped before a door, unlocked it and, with a flourishing bow, opened it for them to enter. She hurried inside while Richard pressed a coin into the usher's hand. When he joined her, she was standing at the very front of the box with her hands pressed together in wonder.

'Look, Richard,' she whispered over the music. *'Look.'*

He didn't know how exactly she had imagined the theatre would be, but even he would grant that this one was a fine sight to see, a fine sight indeed. All the boxes of the Teatro San Samuele were so elaborately carved and decorated that they appeared to undulate around the inside of the theatre. The woodwork was painted a creamy white with painted garlands of flowers, and picked out with gold. More gold covered the arches that supported the ceiling, which in turn was painted a midnight blue, and spangled with glittering stars like the sky overhead. Everything was lit by long tapers, perhaps four feet high, held out from the boxes by curving wrought-iron supports.

'Isn't it the most beautiful place?' Jane sighed, her eyes as wide as a child's. 'Truly you can see the exuberance of the Venetian spirit evident in the basilica, here transformed into secular display.'

'Jane, Jane,' he said softly. 'Can't you just say it looks like a fairy bower or some such?'

She turned back to him and grinned. 'Very well, then. It's as pretty as the queen of the fairies on midsummer night. Will that do?'

'Scamp,' he said. 'Here now, Miss Fairy Queen, come light on your throne beside me.'

She laughed and sat in the chair he'd offered, perching on the very edge so she could still lean forwards to watch everything on the stage, and in the theatre around them.

'I've always heard that the most interesting performers are to be found in the audience, not the actors or actresses,' she said, 'and surely here in Venice that would seem true. Oh, goodness, I've never seen such jewels and gowns!'

But Richard was admiring the neat line of her back and the curve of her hips as she leaned forwards. Among so many peacocks, her untrimmed dark-blue worsted gown seemed like the plainest of serviceable plumage. It suited her, though, just as the neatly twisted coil of her hair suited her, too, and yet he couldn't help but imagine her beauty displayed to a better advantage in a gown that flattered her figure, rather than shrouding it away.

'We should have bought you some finery, too, Jane,' he said. 'You could have chosen whatever you pleased from the shops yesterday, you know.'

She twisted around to look at him. 'That would be generous of you, Richard, as you always are,' she said slowly. 'But what would be the purpose?'

'Why, to please you,' he said, for to him it seemed

an obvious answer. 'I'm not ashamed of you as you are, so don't go thinking of that. I thought you'd like a bit of finery of your own. Every female likes a new gown, at least all the ones in my family do.'

She shook her head. 'For the young ladies, yes, that is true, but not for me. Not for a governess.'

'But you're no longer my daughters' governess,' he protested. 'Tonight you're with me, as my friend.'

'That I am,' she agreed. Her smile was gentle and bitter-sweet, as if she understood what he never would. 'Goodness, look at that lady with the small dog in her lap! I vow I've never seen so small a dog with such outsized ears.'

Purposefully she turned her back to him, and on his offer of new clothes. So much for day by day, he thought glumly, at least by his lights. If this was her version of it, then he'd no choice but to agree.

'Who sees the dog, when the lady's hiding behind one of those infernal masks,' he grumbled, venting his disappointment on the unknown lady three boxes away. 'God only knows why anyone wears those ridiculous things.'

'It's the custom of Venice,' Jane said, 'to play at masquerade every night and hide one's true identity. And, of course, it's the beginning of Carnevale, and then everyone wears fanciful costumes and no one is who they seem.'

Richard grunted, still unhappy. 'Queer sort of custom.'

'But one that's said to be most useful for conducting intrigues,' Jane said earnestly. 'Those, too, are much the custom here.'

'Most likely you're right,' Richard said. He slipped his arm around her shoulders to draw her closer against him; she could hardly protest about that. 'Though you and I aren't husband and wife, we're not hiding ourselves behind long-nosed masks.'

'No,' Jane admitted. 'But then, we're English, as everyone has most likely guessed as well.'

'A good thing, too.' He pulled her closer still, and with a contented sigh, she nestled her head against his shoulder. 'Rule Britannia.'

'And God save the King,' she said, laughing softly, her hand curling around his arm. 'Huzzah, huzzah.'

As if arranged, the orchestra began a loud trumpet fanfare, and a handsome actor in a purple cape appeared, bowing grandly, and began to speak the prologue of the play. The rest of the audience, who naturally could understand him with ease, laughed appreciatively at his jests, and applauded when he was joined on the stage by two actresses, one a fair young maiden, and an older one clearly meant to stand in the way of young love.

Richard sighed. Although he didn't understand more than a word or two, he'd no doubt it was all exactly the same nonsense that Drury Lane trotted out every Season. Yet for Jane's sake, he'd manfully suffer through far worse than this, and take his own private enjoyment from simply having her beside him. After all, where else could he be and have her head resting on his shoulder and his arm around her waist?

'Richard,' she whispered at the end of the scene, 'tell me true. This play makes no sense to you, does it?'

'None at all,' he confessed. 'But so long as you're finding pleasure in it, why then—'

'I cannot decipher any of it, either,' she confessed. 'Oh, Richard, I feel so foolish after begging to come tonight, but the accents are far beyond me.'

'You didn't beg, sweet,' he said. 'I offered to bring you. But there's no need to feel foolish. There are, you know, other ways to entertain ourselves here at a playhouse, ways that are common enough.'

She tipped her head warily to one side. 'I won't throw fruit at the poor players, if that's what you'll suggest.'

He laughed, and took her hand as he led her to the last row of chairs. 'Here, come with me to the back of the box.'

'But we can't see anything from back there,' she protested, even as she willingly joined him.

'No, and no one will be able to see us, either,' he said. 'Consider the other boxes around us, and how few of those gentlemen and ladies you were regarding a few moments ago remain in their places to the front.'

'Where have they gone, I wonder?' she asked innocently. 'Surely they would not have left, given that the play's scarce begun.'

'They've not come to the playhouse for the play, Jane,' he said. 'They're here to make agreeable use of these pleasing shadows here to the back of their boxes.'

She realised the truth and her eyes widened, and to his relief, she laughed, gleefully covering her mouth with her hand. 'All those erring wives and husbands! Oh, Richard, how wicked of them!'

'Wicked of us, too,' he said, 'if you wish it.'

He smiled slowly, challenging her. Over these last days, he'd learned exactly how brave Miss Jane Wood could be, and how, for all her outward primness, she didn't like to back down. He was counting on that now.

'Day by day, Janie,' he said, his voice a rough whisper of enticement. 'But only if you wish it that way.'

She lowered her eyes, an unexpectedly seductive glance.

'I wish it,' she said. 'And you do, too, you wicked rogue.'

To his delight, she bunched her skirts in her hands and clambered on to his lap, finally looping her arms around his shoulders.

'Why, Miss Wood,' he teased. 'whatever has come over you?'

'You, Richard,' she whispered shyly, slanting her face as she tipped her mouth to his. 'Only you.'

There was nothing shy about how she kissed him then, or how he kissed her back. Richard felt as if he spent most of his nights alone and just as much of his days remembering how much he enjoyed kissing Jane, yet in all that remembering, he'd never come close to getting it right, not by half. The reality of her in his arms was that far beyond his imagining.

Her small, round body was soft and yielding, filling his hands with the vibrancy of her flesh beneath that grey wool in a way he'd never thought possible in a woman. He eased his hand from her waist higher, along her ribs to the curving swell of her breast. She caught her breath but did not flinch, and he took that as permission to push aside her white linen kerchief and slip his hand within. Her skin was warm and impossibly soft, and as he filled his palm with her breast, she trembled, and sighed her contentment.

Was there any better way to choose life over a fading memory of lost love, or to be reminded of the boundless joys of one over the sorrowful finality of the other?

Her lips were eager, her mouth wet and hot, and, when she shifted on his lap, her bottom pressed so enticingly against him that he groaned and could quite happily forget everything else except having her in his arms.

Well, not precisely all. She'd called him a wicked rogue to tease him. Had she any notion of how apt that description was? His body was reminding him of what exactly he wanted to do with her, of how this was Venice and a darkened theatre box and no one would notice or care if he were to unfasten the fall of his breeches and shove aside her petticoats and—

'*Per favore, signor!*' The porter rapped on the door of the box with a furious intensity. 'Your Grace, if you please, at once, at once!'

'What the devil?' muttered Richard, unwilling to be interrupted by anything short of out-and-out disaster. 'That fellow can go straight to blazes for all I—'

'But it must be important,' Jane said, already

slipping from his lap to smooth her gown. 'They wouldn't disturb us otherwise. What if something serious has occurred?'

'Very well.' With a grunt of resignation, he rose and unlatched the box's door. 'What is it, sirrah? Speak, you impudent rascal, spit it out!'

The porter puffed out his chest with indignant self-importance. 'Your servant waits below with a message of great importance.'

Richard scowled. 'Which servant? What's his name? By God, if it's—'

'Oh, Richard,' Jane said anxiously beside him. 'What if it's word from the young ladies? What if something grievous has happened?'

He couldn't ignore the possibility. 'Very well, then,' he said. 'Send the man up.'

The porter bowed. 'I am sorry, *signor,* but your servant has no ticket, and cannot be admitted.'

'Damanation, I can't see—'

'We'll go, Richard,' Jane said, reaching for her cloak and muff. 'There's no use in lingering if it's important.'

'I'm not sure it is.' Richard sighed impatiently. 'You wait here, Jane, and I'll be back directly, once I've settled this.'

'Are you sure, Richard?' she asked, resting her hand on his arm.

Her eyes were full of beseeching concern for his welfare, yet also trust that he'd resolve whatever nonsense this interruption was. Could there be anything more guaranteed to swell his affection for her?

'Only a moment, sweet, I vow.' He bent and quickly kissed her again. 'With you waiting for me, that will be all it takes.'

Chapter Sixteen

With a sigh, Jane returned to the chair she'd been sharing with Richard, or, more accurately, the chair on which Richard had been sitting, with her on top of him. He'd assured her that he wouldn't be away long, and she'd no reason to doubt him.

And yet she missed him as much as if he'd gone off to sea on a voyage of years' duration, not answered an errand that would take ten minutes at most. It made her feel a bit foolish, too, like one of her overly romantic young charges, but she couldn't help it. What she felt when Richard kissed her was beyond anything she'd ever experienced. As much as she prized her education, she'd no words at all fit for describing it, and when he'd caressed her breast, why, she'd thought she'd perish from delight.

She'd arched against him, shamelessly pushing her breast against his hand to seek more of the pleasure his touch brought. Her nipple had tightened and grown more sensitive and somehow warmer, and that glow had then spread through her whole body, centring curiously between her legs. Self-consciously she'd pressed her legs together, and discovered that the pleasurable warmth only increased, and the more she restlessly shifted her limbs, rubbing herself against him, the more the warmth grew, stealing away her breath and her senses, too. It had been most…remarkable.

She took the muff from the chair beside her and cradled it in her arms, brushing her cheek against the silky fur as she thought of the man who'd given it to her. The play on the stage before her was forgotten, the orchestra's music unheard.

Day by day, day by day—they'd each promised to follow that, without regrets. Yet those same days were passing so quickly, as fast as sand slipping through the waist of an hourglass, and she couldn't bear to think of all the other days that would follow in her life without Richard Farren in them.

She heard the door behind her open, and she turned and rose at once with anticipation, expecting Richard's return. But standing there in the doorway, lit from behind by the brightness of the hall, wasn't Richard, but Signor di Rossi, dressed all in black like the night.

'Ah, *cara mia,* here you are at last,' he exclaimed,

his cloak swirling around him as he closed the box's door. He tossed aside his hat and the white half-mask, and bowed deeply to her, the silver scabbard of his dress sword glinting beneath his cloak. 'I cannot tell you how I've missed you.'

He seized her hand before she'd realised what he was doing, and pressed his lips to the back of it. She gasped, astounded by his audacity, and more than a little frightened by it, too.

'*Signor,* please, you forget yourself!' she exclaimed. She jerked her hand free and whipped it behind her back, as if to keep it beyond his temptation.

'How can I not forget myself when it is you I cannot put from my mind?' he asked, pressing his hand over his heart. 'Ah, Miss Wood! How grieved I was to receive your letter, and its unhappy contents! To learn that your—your *master* chose to exert his lordly English will over you, and forbid you from my company at the exact moment when we—'

'But that is not true, *signor.*' She was startled and confused by his impetuous manner, so much so that she wondered if he were drunk. 'You're most grievously mistaken. His Grace hasn't forbidden me anything.'

'Forgive me, Miss Wood, but I cannot believe that,' he said, his elegantly accented voice filled with sorrow. 'What I do believe is that you and I are friends, and must keep no secrets between us. Is that not so, Miss Wood?'

'It is, yes,' she said carefully, unwilling to agree to more than she intended. 'You have been wondrous kind to me as a stranger in your city, and for that I shall be always grateful. But our friendship is also one of short duration, *signor,* and therefore perhaps open to a misinterpretation.'

His hand closed into a fist over his heart, as if to contain his anguish. 'How have I misunderstood? Did you not come to me when you feared for your welfare at this man's hands?'

'I was not so much fearful as uncertain.'

'It is the same,' he declared firmly. 'The English duke made you unhappy.'

'I never said that, *signor!*'

'But you did, *cara mia,*' he insisted. 'Not in words, perhaps, but surely in your tears. I saw them in your eyes, you know. Can you deny your unhappiness when I found you wandering in the Piazza San Marco?'

Jane winced, remembering. 'At that time, I was unhappy, yes. But my unhappiness was more my own fault than any suffering caused by his Grace.'

'Do not excuse him, Miss Wood!' he said fervently. 'He showed neither regard nor respect for you as a woman, nor has he—'

'*Signor,* please.' Why didn't Richard return? What servant's errand could have kept him away so long? 'I must ask you to stop. Nothing will be achieved by pursuing this conversation further.'

'Nothing, and everything,' di Rossi said, his voice dropping lower. 'I know in my heart you wished to join me here tonight, alone in my company. I know he forced you to write that letter rejecting me. That they were not your words, but his.'

Jane's gaze darted past him to the door, willing Richard to return. 'I expect his Grace at any moment, *signor,* and I am sure he will be honoured to make your acquaintance.'

'I care only for you, Jane Wood, not for him,' he said, as if she'd not spoken at all. 'Come with me, *cara mia,* before he returns.'

'Forgive me for speaking plain, *signor,* but it's not appropriate for you to call me *"cara",*' she said, an edge of panic beginning to undermine her firmness. Now she recalled how forward he'd been in the chocolate shop, lavishing her with compliments that she'd not wanted. At the time, she'd been so preoccupied with Richard that she'd let it pass, leaving her to wonder if he'd taken her lack of protest as encouragement. 'Our friendship is based entirely on an appreciation of art. I've never pretended anything beyond that. For you to believe I sought such attention would be most ungentlemanly of you.'

In the half-light of the box, di Rossi's eyes were nearly as black as his clothing.

'Then you have never met a true gentleman,' he said, sweeping his hand through the air with an elegant flourish. 'Permit me to show you how a *gentleman* admires a woman. Let me introduce you to the rarest of raptures, and let us discover together joy such as you've never imagined.'

He took another step closer, and Jane scuttled backwards, knocking over one of the chairs before she braced herself behind another.

'There will be no such discoveries made with you, Signor di Rossi!' she exclaimed warmly. 'Pray recall who *you* are, sir, and who *I* am, and—'

The door flew open, and Richard loomed in the sudden splash of light from the hall like an oversized silhouette.

'I tell you, Jane, you will not believe the nonsense I've had to endure for—what the devil is this? Who are you, sir?' He gaze shifted from Jane to di Rossi, and back again. 'Jane, what's this about?'

Relief swept over Jane. Her first response was to throw herself into Richard's arms, but almost instantly she realised the folly of so open a display.

She'd no wish for di Rossi to see the intimacy that had risen up between her and Richard and to spread the news wickedly as gossip about Venice, not if she hoped to find a new place as a governess here. Given the Venetian's unexpected misunderstanding of their own relationship, she could only imagine how wrongly—and hatefully—he'd interpret any sign of open affection between her and Richard.

But that wasn't the only worry that raced through her thoughts in that half-second. First came the sword that di Rossi wore beneath his cloak, second was Richard's notoriously quick temper when he believed he'd been wronged, and third determining how best to keep both under control.

So instead of giving way to her fears and sinking tearfully into the reassuring comfort of Richard's embrace, she drew herself up straight, her hands clasped before her to personify capability and calm, and pretended that nothing, absolutely nothing, was wrong.

Only she would know that her hands were trembling.

'Be at ease, your Grace,' she said, curtsying to him in the old way. 'There's nothing amiss. This is the Venetian gentleman of whom I have spoken to you, the gentleman who has been so very helpful to me in my visit to this place.'

'Helpful, you say,' Richard muttered sceptically, his gaze raking up and down di Rossi. 'To you, eh?'

'Anything to please a lady, *signor*,' di Rossi said. He drew himself up very straight to try to lessen the differences in their heights. 'Though perhaps that is something an Englishman would not understand.'

Richard's answer came as an ominous, wordless rumble, like some great, cross beast roused from his sleep. In return di Rossi's right hand was hovering near to where his cloak masked the hilt of his sword, and at once Jane stepped between the two men to make a proper introduction.

'Your Grace, may I present Signor Giovanni Rinaldini di Rossi, an esteemed gentleman of this city,' she said swiftly, relieved that she'd been able to recall the *signor*'s entire name. '*Signor*, his Grace the Duke of Aston.'

Di Rossi made one of his most elegant bows, low over his leg, yet taking care, too, to flick his black cloak to one side to show his sword.

Richard, being Richard, made only another grumbling growl of acknowledgement.

'Signor di Rossi came to our box to pay his compliments to you, your Grace,' Jane prompted, feeling every bit the governess forcing good manners upon two balky charges. 'Signor di Rossi was expressing his hope that his Grace was enjoying the play.'

'It's rubbish,' Richard said curtly. 'Rubbish and nonsense.'

'Your Grace!' Jane exclaimed with dismay. 'That's hardly—'

'He is entitled to his opinion, Miss Wood,' di Rossi said, adding a disdainful sniff for emphasis. 'Most likely an English duke has been entitled to whatever he pleases his entire life, yes?'

'Damn your impertinence, sir!' Richard thundered, so loudly that Jane was sure the very actors on the stage must have heard him. 'No Englishman should stand for such slander from a foreigner, nor should I—'

'Nor should you, indeed, your Grace, since we are leaving.' She snatched up her belongings and took Richard's arm to try to steer him away, no easy feat when he seemed so stubbornly determined to stand his ground. 'Pray recall that you'd already decided the play was not to your taste.'

Richard frowned down at her. 'You are certain you wish to leave, Jane?'

'I am, your Grace,' she said, exerting as much pressure as she could on his arm, for all that it felt as if she were trying to lead a bull. 'Please excuse us, *signor,* and a good evening to you.'

'A good evening to you as well, Miss Wood,' he said, bowing again. He began to reach one more time for her hand, but Jane ducked behind Richard, leaving di Rossi to scowl at her, too.

'Your Grace,' she said, urging Richard forwards before he noticed the other man's attentions. She smiled up at him, silently pleading as hard as she could. 'If you please, your Grace.'

To her amazement, it worked.

'Very well,' Richard said gruffly, and without acknowledging di Rossi any further, he walked with Jane through the theatre and outside, to where a line of gondolas for hire waited. Not expecting any custom until the performance was done, the gondoliers had gathered to smoke their pipes and pass a bottle at the far end of the piazza. As soon as Richard's imposing figure appeared, one of the men hurried forwards, and within minutes of having left the box, they were gliding safely along the canal, and away from Signor di Rossi and his silver-hilted sword.

Jane knew she should be relieved, even blessed, to have escaped such a scene. Without much more tinder, matters between the two men could have sparked and flared into a quarrel, a scuffle, a fight, and a tragedy. She'd done the proper thing by re-moving Richard when she had and she knew it. Yet since they'd left the box, Richard in turn had not spoken a word to her.

Not one single word.

She sighed forlornly, wondering if she dared to take his hand. He was sitting as far apart from her as was possible on the gondola's narrow seat, and he was staring steadfastly out across the starlit water. She knew he wasn't *seeing* it; he was clearly too angry still for that. What she wasn't sure of was if that anger was somehow directed at her.

'I trust the message that came for you wasn't of importance?' she cautiously asked. It would be eas-iest to let him stew, but his silence was so painful for her that she'd rather risk having him rage at her than endure it any longer. 'It wasn't—'

'There was no damned message,' he said with blistering disgust. 'No message, and no messenger. The whole business was trumpery and lies, con-trived to make me go traipsing downstairs and up again on a fool's errand.'

'But who would contrive such a wicked trick?'

'I do not know, Jane,' he said curtly. 'But damna-tion, when I return and find you with that—'

'You cannot believe that I bid Signor di Rossi there!' she cried, shocked. 'That I would send you away to invite him to me in your stead! That you would believe such shameless duplicity of me, and that you would dare to believe—'

'I don't know what I believe,' he said. He sighed, almost a groan. 'What I saw was that fellow forcing himself on you, and such dread on your sweet face that I was ready to throttle him on the spot. Yet when you spoke, it was as if you were asking us both to a dish of tea. What was I to make of that, Jane? What was I to think?'

'What you must think is the truth,' she said fervently. 'I'd thought the *signor* was an acquaintance, even a friend, after the kindness he has shown me. But no friend would ever treat me as he did this night. I have never been so happy to see you as I was when you returned, and save me from—oh, Heaven deliver me, I've no notion of what wickedness he'd plotted.'

'Then why didn't you tell me?' Richard demanded. 'I would have taken the bastard's own sword and run him straight through!'

'Oh, Richard, that is exactly why I didn't,' she said softly, finally reaching for his hand. 'I didn't want swords or pistols on my behalf. I know your temper well, and know that you will often act from justness and noble intents, rather than from common sense. Italian gentlemen who wear swords are likewise eager for an excuse to draw and use them, and I couldn't bear to have you risk harm for me, not for a moment.'

'Do you doubt my skill, Jane?' he asked, squaring his shoulders and his jaw, ready for any combatants, even in the gondola. 'I'll have you know that I'm still regarded as a swordsman of the first order, as I'll defy any Italian popinjay to discover at his own hazard.'

'I don't doubt your skill in anything,' Jane said quickly. 'But what would it have achieved, I ask you? The di Rossis are a powerful, ancient family in Venice, and for you to challenge one so publicly would have brought us both nothing but ill fortune.'

'Di Rossis, hah,' Richard scoffed, bristling with bravado. 'The Farrens are double their match! I'd like to show them what English steel can do.'

'Richard, that's exactly why I said nothing to you,' she said. *'Exactly.'*

Without thinking, she'd slipped into her governess's voice, but she couldn't help it. Perhaps that was what Richard needed to hear, anyway, and she plunged on ahead.

'It wouldn't matter if the Farrens are ten times the men the di Rossis are, Richard,' she said. 'You are English. You're foreigners to them, and they'll always take their own side over yours.'

His dark brows came together, a rebellious glower in the night. 'You're English, too, if you recall.'

'I haven't forgotten,' she said. 'But I'm not being traitorous, Richard. It would be the same for any Venetian who dared cause trouble in London. I've heard that the Doge's prison is so cruel and fearsome that it can make a Turk shudder, and I've no wish for either of us to learn for certain. What must I say to make you understand that, Richard? What must I *do*?'

'Don't leave me,' he said, his bluster gone and his voice turning raw with emotion. 'When I saw you with di Rossi, I thought I'd lost you.'

'Richard.' To her own surprise, she felt tears sting her eyes, the same tears she'd kept back earlier and now, with no reason to keep back any longer, began to slip down her cheeks. Embarrassed, she fumbled beneath her cloak for her pocket and her handkerchief inside. 'I won't leave you, not for the *signor*— I vow I'll never see him again—nor any other man, and you are the—the greatest ninny in the world if you dare believe otherwise.'

'There now, don't cry.' He slipped his arm around her shoulders, and she let herself curl against his chest. 'Nothing gained by that.'

'No.' She tried to snuffle back the tears with a shuddering sigh, and miraculously he produced a handkerchief of his own: clean, pressed, and smelling dearly of him. 'No.'

She shook the handkerchief open, the flutter of white linen enough to startle a small flock of pigeons nesting beneath the curving eaves of a nearby house. With a flurry of silvery wings, the birds flapped and wheeled over their heads in the night sky, and together Jane and Richard looked up to watch.

'My mother died of smallpox when I was away at school,' he said softly, as if speaking more to the pigeons than to Jane. 'I was blessed with my wife for scarce five years, and now my daughters have left me as well, off to lives and husbands of their own. I'm always the one left behind. I've no reason to make any claim on you, Jane, none at all, yet somehow I've come to believe you'd be the one who stayed. Hah, there's your great ninny for you, isn't it?'

'I'll stay,' she said, letting her tears fall where they pleased as she slipped her arms into his coat and around his waist. 'If you're to be a ninny, then I'll be one at your side, the ninniest ninnies in all of Venice.'

'Then you are a ninny,' he said solemnly as

he tipped her face up to kiss. 'What a pair we make, eh?'

Oh, aye, what a pair, thought Jane as he kissed her, as fine a pair as could be found in Venice.

Yet still their days together were slipping away, and in her heart she knew there was no way to stop them.

'Miss Wood received my gift?' Di Rossi looked down at the small package sitting alone and unwanted in the middle of the salver in the footman's hand. Since his unfortunate meeting with Jane Wood at the theatre three nights ago, he had sent a package like this one—an elegantly worded apology, full of charm and contrition, and a small but costly token. A perfectly contrived offering, truly, and yet all of them had been treated like this one, and returned unopened. 'Are you certain it was delivered directly to her?'

'Yes, *signor*,' the servant answered. 'The messenger delivered it and waited for the reply, as you wished. The woman of the house took it away to Miss Wood, and brought it back almost at once. She said it was Miss Wood's wish that it be returned directly to you, *signor*.'

For a moment, di Rossi remained silent, his expression unchanging while he considered how best to respond.

How to respond: oh, yes, that was a quandary. He'd admit that he'd erred with Jane Wood, that he'd frightened her with his display of passionate regard. He'd underestimated her pathetically English sense of decorum, and that, too, was his own fault.

And yet, in the curious way of desire, that same decorum had made him want her all the more. Clearly she and her buffoonish duke had been engaged in amorous play when he'd had them interrupted and the duke sent away. Di Rossi had seen it at once in her face: the dreaminess of her eyes, the flush of her cheek, the reddened fullness of her lips were all signs of arousal that he recognised, even if she did not. She'd wanted to be possessed; he'd seen that in her eyes, too. If he'd had only a minute more alone with her, he felt certain he would have had her. The little fool—didn't she realise yet that he was the one destined for her maidenhead?

Of course in time he'd make her see her errors, and punish her accordingly. That would be pleasurable, too. Seduction, correction, complete conquest and subjection. How much he'd enjoy educating his little governess, and his lips twitched with anticipation. But before he could begin his delicious course, he needed to remove her from the influence of that fool of a duke. The time for subtleties and wooing gifts was done. Di Rossi knew now he must act decisively, even boldly.

And then, at last, she would be his.

'Shall I put this with the others, *signor?*' the waiting footman asked. 'Shall I—?'

'Insolent.' He swiftly struck the footman, hitting his cheek so hard with his fist that the man staggered backwards. The salver flew from his hands and clanked across the floor, the little package flying. At once the footman scrambled back to his feet and retrieved the package and the salver.

'Yes, *signor,*' he said, as if nothing had happened, as if the angry red handprint on his face meant nothing, too. 'Forgive me my insolence, *signor.*'

Slowly di Rossi smiled. He had trained his staff with such careful discipline, and how beautifully they responded to him now.

And soon, very soon, his little English governess would do so as well.

Chapter Seventeen

For the next five days, Jane and Richard behaved as any other affluent English visitors to Venice. They dutifully viewed the paintings they were supposed to view, and marvelled at the galleries and churches and palaces at which one came to Venice to marvel. For Jane, the paintings and gold-flecked mosaics were a rare joy, especially as she saw them all with her hand linked through Richard's substantial arm. She tried her best to interest him in the paintings, too, and to make his eyes see the same wondrous glory that her own did.

But though Richard never begrudged her their time in the galleries, it was clear that his pleasure was only in hers. Jane recognised the signs all too well, having had her share of uninterested pupils in her schoolroom. The expression that never changed, the slightly parted lips, the gaze that remained as blank as a fresh-washed slate—each told her that no matter how manfully Richard resolved for her sake to be edified and enlightened by the great art works before him, he was more truthfully being bored.

Yet still her heart swelled because she realised how hard he was trying to please her, no matter that the pleasing went against all his own wishes. For years she'd been a part of his household, where everything was done to keep the duke happy, and now here she was, with that self-same duke doing his best on her behalf, and, truly, she could scarce believe it. What else could she do but try to be as agreeable to him? If he wanted to devote their mornings to sites of Jane's choosing, then she in turn would make certain that the afternoons were given over to Richard's.

Besides, the entertainments Richard found for them were fun, more fun, if she were honest, than most of the ancient palazzos and churches. On the first afternoon, they watched a regatta from a bridge, and waved little flags like the children around them. And like the children, too, they cheered their favourites, especially when the competition between the gondoliers become so fierce that several indignantly knocked one another into the chilly water of the canals.

Afterwards they sat close together on a nearby

bench and ate *frittole,* the sweet puffs of dough fried freshly to order in special pans set on tripods over open fires. As insubstantial as a breeze, the *frittole* were dusted with clouds of fine sugar from a polished canister, and heaped with spoonfuls of the bright green pine nuts. To educate Richard in this delicacy, she drew off her gloves and fed the nuts to him with her fingers, one kernel at a time, and laughed with delight as he'd licked the powdered sugar from her fingertips.

To Jane's amazement and more than a little dismay, Richard had also developed a ghoulish fascination with the saintly relics that were so revered in Venice. They traipsed past the holy remains of Santa Lucia and San Zaccheria, of Santi Cosma and Damiano, as well as the foot of Santa Maria of Egypt, the thigh bones of Santa Ursula, and the arms of Santa Cecelia. What interest could be found in the mummified bodies of poor martyred saints was beyond Jane, even if they were housed in beautifully crafted and gilded reliquaries. She still shivered when she thought of what lay within, while Richard taxed the limits of his Italian by asking gory details of the ageing priests who served as guides.

Far more cheerful were the amusements connected to Carnevale. At the suggestion of Signora della Battista, Jane and Richard explored the entertainments set up for Carnivale along the Riva degli Schiavoni. To Jane it was much like the travelling circus that stopped in Aston each summer before harvest—except, of course, everything was strung along the canal beneath a brilliant Mediterranean sky.

There were performers of every kind, to please every audience, from shivering small hounds in ruffled petticoats and collars who danced on their hind legs, to rope dancers in bright satins who skipped with ease on the swaying rope stretched between houses. There were mandolin players and ballad singers, jugglers and mountebanks, games of skill and games of chance, and even a fortune teller who promised to tell their future, whispering it like a precious secret down a long silver tube.

'Your fortune, kind sir, pretty lady, your fortune for a *soldi!*' the old woman called. 'Will you prosper, sir? Will your lot be sorrow or joy? I hide nothing, kind sir, the truth as I see it!'

'Don't you wish to hear your fortune, Janie?' Richard asked, pausing before the striped awning that sheltered the fortune teller. 'Draw off your glove and show her your hand, and learn when a long-lost pirate uncle will leave you a chest full of gold and pearls.'

'Thank you, no,' Jane said, hanging back. The old

woman made her strangely uneasy; with a scarlet Turkish turban on her head, she sat on a small stool with her gnarled hands flat on her knees, swaying back and forth as if the blown by the awful knowledge she claimed to see.

'It's a lark,' Richard said without any of Jane's reluctance. 'You know it's rubbish and invention. Likely she tells the same tale to everyone.'

'Then what is the purpose?' Jane asked. 'For all the truth that will come of it, you might as well toss your coins into the canal.'

'Only truth, kind sir, only truth!' the fortune teller called, sensing Richard's interest. 'Will your ventures succeed? Will your health flourish, sir, or are your best days done? Surely a fine, brave, strong sir needs to know! How many more handsome sons will you sire with your pretty lady-wife, sir? That is the proof of a man's mettle, his fire! How many more boys will come to bring glory to your name and your house, sir? How many?'

Jane caught her breath, and looked sharply up to Richard. He was smiling still, but his smile was now fixed and joyless, and the bright good humour seemed to have drained from his eyes.

She understood, for she felt much the same. To be mistaken for his wife, his perfect duchess, to be taunted about the sons that Fate would never grant her the joy of bearing—oh, it was too cruel, and made miserably worse for being so unthinking.

'I told you it was all rubbish,' she said, tugging on his arm to lead him away. 'Nothing but emptiness and lies.'

'Rubbish, aye,' he said, and as he turned his back on the fortune teller, he forced himself to laugh. 'We've no need to hear any more of that, Jane, do we?'

'None,' she said as firmly as she could, and they moved along to a booth where a pair of marionette donkeys were cavorting for a crowd of laughing children.

But Richard's earlier delight in the Carnevale amusements was gone, and by now Jane understood that no amount of cajoling by her would alter his humour. Only time seemed to do that, and it was best if she simply let him make peace with himself however he needed to. That was a fine line for anyone to tread, to realise the difference between sympathetic concern and meddlesome prying, and just like the rope dancers over their heads, Jane had always aimed for the steadying balance.

'Perhaps it's time to return to the Ca' Battista,' she said, leaning her head against his shoulder. 'I'm weary of so much Carnevale, and likely so are you.'

'Soon,' he said, glancing down the next narrow street. 'There's a *malvasie* shop, sweet. Let's stop for a glass, and then we'll head back to our lodgings.'

Jane nodded and followed him. On his first day in Venice, Richard had discovered *malvasia,* a sweet, delicate wine made from tiny Greek grapes, and though it seemed completely at odds with his usual plain and sturdy tastes, he now made sure they stopped by a *malvasie* shop whenever they were out. Like a native, he'd tried and considered all the varieties—*cipro, malaga, eleatico, scopulo, samos*—before he'd finally settled on *garba,* with its hint of almonds and herbs, as his favourite.

If a small glass of *garba* would make Richard feel better, than Jane would happily join him, even if most *malvasie* shops were a bit too close to low English rum shops for a lady. This one was much like all the others they'd visited: a single narrow room with whitewashed walls, rough benches and small tables, and sailors and gondoliers far outnumbering the gentlemen. In London, she'd never venture into such a place, but this was Venice, the familiar rules of propriety didn't seem to count, and besides, she was with Richard.

The shop's keeper instantly recognised Richard as a foreign gentleman of importance, and found them two seats at a table near the window. Just as quickly came the round tray with two small glasses, filled with the golden liquor.

'To the King,' Richard said solemnly as he raised the little glass, dwarfed in his fingers. 'To the King, and Carnevale.'

'To the King,' Jane echoed. She sipped from her glass, while Richard emptied his in a single long swallow. At once the keeper himself refilled the glass, but Richard didn't drink it, instead holding it up to the window to let the sunlight pass through. He studied it like that, twisting and turning the glass in his hand.

'Your *garba* could be any strong water, couldn't it?' Jane said softly. 'Brandy, or Madeira, or Scottish whisky, even a common ale. To glance at the glass like this, one would never know how special it is.'

'Now that would be a pity,' he said, 'and a waste as well. You can never judge any wine by sight alone. Only an abstemious fool would do that.'

'True enough,' she said softly. 'Just as that fortune teller could tell nothing of you or your love for your daughters by her casual appraisal alone. She couldn't know of her Grace, or your loss.'

'My loyal Janie.' His smile was lopsided and bitter-sweet. 'I've long ago made my peace with the notion that God saw fit to grant me daughters, not sons. My brother's boy is a good lad, and will make a fine duke after I'm gone.'

She rested her hand on his arm, all the affection she'd dare show in so public a place as the *malvasie*. 'I'm glad of that, for your sake.'

He sighed, still studying the glass in his hand. 'No, Jane, I'm the fool. That woman on the street only made me see it, whether I wished to or not. I've felt like a young man here in Venice, Jane, a cub without a care in the world. It took that woman to clear my eyes. I didn't have to give her a penny, yet she told me the truth.'

'That's nonsense, Richard,' Jane said quickly. 'What the fortune teller said hadn't a grain of truth in it. Most likely she says the same nonsense to every man who passes by. Her prattle is only idle flattery, or so she believes it to be.'

But Richard shook his head, unconvinced. 'No, pet, she was right. My best days are behind me. I've outlived my wife, and my daughters are wed and making a grandfather of me. I've made a righteous old ass of myself by traipsing about with you, as if a pretty young woman on my arm will drag me from my dotage.'

'But you are not old, Richard, not at all!' she exclaimed, scandalised. 'What made you think such a thing, even for a moment?'

He looked away from her, out the window, as if he were being noble and resigned, instead of simply self-indulgent and wounded. 'Don't coddle me any longer, Jane. I know I'm at least ten years your senior.'

'What does that matter?' she cried. 'At least it doesn't matter to *me!*'

'How can it not?' He waved his hand impatiently through the air. 'Be reasonable, Jane. You are still a young woman, while I am—'

'No more, Richard,' she said fiercely. 'Not a word more!'

And before he could say another ridiculous word, she slid from her chair and took his face in her hands and kissed him, kissed him to stop the foolishness that he was saying, kissed him to make him believe the truth, kissed him long and well and without regard for all the other men in the room who'd stopped their talk to turn and gape and grin.

It worked, or at least so far as she'd managed to stop his morose self-pity. Instead, when they finally ended the kiss, he looked at her with a kind of dazed content, his smile spreading slowly over his face.

'Why, Janie,' he said, 'that I did not expect.'

'You should,' she said promptly. 'Leastways you

should have if you weren't occupied with feeling so woefully sorry for yourself.'

'No, sweet, tell me,' he said, his voice low an urgent. 'Did you mean that? Are you sure?'

She gave a quick little nod to her head, smoothing out her skirts. 'I meant it, yes. I wouldn't have done it otherwise.'

Slowly his mouth curved into a grin. 'My own Jane.'

She smiled, too happy to say more. But now she was also aware of how her impulsiveness had made them the centre of attraction in the *malvasie* shop, how all around them were men craning their necks for more and grinning like a pack of wolfish hounds. It was unsettling, that much attention, and she felt her face grow hot with self-consciousness. Men never looked at her like that. Most times, men never so much as noticed she was in the room, she was that invisible.

But Richard—oh, Richard could look at her like this for the rest of her life, and she wouldn't mind in the least.

'Jane, Jane,' he said again, raising her hand to kiss it. 'My own sweet Jane. Are you taking notice of how I'm not feeling sorry for myself now?'

'Everyone else certainly has,' she said with a shy

shrug of her shoulders. 'But I must say that I've noticed, too.'

'Well, now, that's a good thing,' he said, and winked wickedly. 'A fine thing for us both, eh?'

'Richard, please,' she said. 'Everyone is watching.'

'Let them watch,' he declared. 'And recall, my dear, that you're the one who drew their eyes to us in the first place.'

'Richard, please,' she said again, though more softly this time.

'You have restored me, Jane,' he said. 'I cannot put it any other way. You have restored me in a fashion I'd never thought possible.'

Emptying the second glass of *garba* in a single swallow, he thumped the glass on the table with hearty satisfaction and rose to his feet. Then, in a final show of bravado, he finished Jane's wine as well, and when he set that one down, too, the men in the shop cheered their approval.

'Perhaps it is the *malvasia,* Richard, that has improved your humour,' Jane said over the men's roaring, 'and not me at all.'

'There's one way to know for certain, isn't there?' he said. 'Here, let me thank these good fellows for their support. Some gestures are always the same, no matter the country.'

He reached into the pocket of his waistcoat and

drew out several coins. With a nod of acknowledgement, he tossed the coins to the keeper, who caught
them easily, and bowed his gratitude with a court-
ier's sweeping grace. At once the rest of the house
understood. Every hat was raised from every head,
and every man bowed, sending Richard and Jane
into the street with a chorus of *'grazie, grazie.'*

'Heavens, Richard, you've made scores of new
friends,' Jane said, looking back over her shoulder as the door closed after them. 'Did you leave
enough for the entire house to drink?'

'I did,' he said. 'They deserved it. Now up you
go.'

With both hands he caught her around the waist
and lifted her up to second step in a nearby doorway. She yelped with surprise, and instinctively
grabbed his shoulders, her muff sliding down her
arm.

'What are you doing?' she demanded breathlessly. It was an odd feeling, standing here on the
step where for once she'd look down on him. 'Let
me go free, Richard, this isn't—'

'I love you,' he said. 'There, I've spoken it plain.
I love you.'

She gasped, all words gone, and her thoughts as
well.

He smiled crookedly, his hair tossing beneath the

brim of his hat, and to Jane he'd never looked more handsome.

'It's been a long time since I've said that,' he said, 'but I haven't forgotten how. I only had to find the right woman to say it to. I love you, Jane.'

Still she was too overwhelmed to reply, tears of joy smarting her eyes.

'You kissed me, and I knew for certain,' he said. 'I knew this was right. For us, Jane, yes?'

'Yes,' she whispered, and pulled him close. 'Oh, Richard, I love you, too!'

She kissed him again, and pledged her love again to him that way, for that was in fact what she'd been doing when she'd kissed him in the window of the *malvasie* shop. She just hadn't dared to speak the words aloud.

But now—now she didn't care who knew, because Richard felt the same for her. *I love you*— could there be any more joyful words to hear, or to speak?

'I love you,' she whispered again, unable to resist the magic words. 'Oh, Richard, you cannot know how much!'

'I can, because I feel the same.' He chuckled, turning her gently in his arms so she faced the *malvasie* shop they'd just left. 'And so, I'm guessing, do they.'

The men had spilled out of the shop to watch them, along the steps and into the street. Some still had the glasses that Richard had paid for in their hands, and as soon as they saw that Richard and Jane had noticed them, they raised those glasses and tossed their hats in raucous salute.

She should have been shamed, even mortified, by so public a tribute. Surely the Jane from the old days of Aston would have felt that way. But this was Venice, and because of Richard, she'd never be the same again.

She laughed with giddy delight, and boldly pulled Richard's hat from his head and stuffed it jauntily on her own.

'I love you, Richard!' she crowed. 'I love you, oh, more than anything, and I don't care who in the world knows it!'

The longer Richard was in Venice with Jane, the more he appreciated gondolas as a form of transportation. They were fast and they were quiet, so long as one didn't get a gondolier who wished to test his English in conversation. But best of all, in Richard's opinion, was how the narrow bench of a gondola made for such cosy proximity for the passengers. He liked having Jane snug beneath the robe beside him, having her small, curvy body pressed next to his in an unavoidable intimacy that was at once public, yet private, too and he smiled down at her now, nestled beside him with her head against his shoulder as they glided back to the Ca' Battista.

He loved her, but infinitely better, she loved him.

How wonderfully perfect that sounded! When Anne had died, he'd been certain he'd never love again, or that there wasn't another woman in the world who could rival his wife's memory. For years Jane had been right beneath his nose, and he'd not noticed her. It had taken the gaudy spell of this place and the chance to be alone with her that had made him realise how special she was, and would always be. If Anne had been his youthful first love, then Jane must have been destined to be the love that would last him the rest of his days.

He wasn't a perfect man, not by half, and he didn't know what he'd done to deserve such a reward. Jane *understood* him. It was as simple, and as complicated, as that. She was brave and fair and passionate and, best of all, she could make him laugh, and what more, really, could a man ever want?

The gondola nudged the landing and the gondolier pulled the boat steady. With agile grace, Jane stepped out, holding her skirts to one side the way the Venetian ladies did. She was practical, his Jane, and if a new skill was necessary, she was quick to learn it, easily and without fuss: a rare and charming quality in any woman.

She skipped up the steps to the house, and turned to grin at him. He clambered from the gondola and in two steps was at her side. Before she could protest, he'd settled his hat back on to her head where she'd put it earlier. When she looked up at him, the oversized crown slid low over her eyes, and as she pushed it up, she laughed, and he laughed with her, and so much for the practical, capable governess.

It was nothing, really, a bit of foolish play between the two of them, and yet that single moment seemed to show exactly why he'd come to love her so much in so short a time. He wasn't yet sure what would happen next between them—he was still letting the notion of being in love, new as it was, settle on to them both—but he was confident that the most difficult challenge was now behind them, and only the brightest of shared futures lay before.

Or would, at least, once he'd caught her again.

Dancing beyond his reach and laughing still, she fled through the door that the porter held open. Richard followed, into the hall and across the polished marble floor. Her laughter echoed against the painted columns as she grabbed her skirts and tried to escape, running up the staircase two steps at a time and squarely into the chest of Richard's secretary Potter. Potter fell backwards and sat hard on the step with Jane atop him, the letters and papers he'd been carrying scattering around him like startled hens.

'Oh, Mr Potter, forgive me!' Jane exclaimed, clearly mortified as she rose and helped the startled secretary back to his feet. 'I am so very sorry, sir, I didn't intend—'

'No matter, Miss Wood, no matter.' He glanced pointedly at Richard's hat on her head, then bowed to Richard as Jane began to collect the letters scattered over the steps.

'Your Grace,' Potter began, 'you've returned at a most opportune time. We have just received a large parcel of letters, your Grace, from England and elsewhere, that will require your attention.'

'More correctly my drudgery and toil,' Richard said with a resigned sigh. Of course he'd have to set aside time to tend to all those letters and queries with Potter. If these letters had followed him clear to Italy, then they must indeed contain matters of importance that could not be ignored, either to his finances, his properties or his seat in the House of Lords. No wonder Potter was beaming in anticipation. 'Very well, Potter, bring on the righteous affairs of business.'

'It's not all business, Richard,' Jane said as she slipped her finger through the seal of one of the letters. 'This one's addressed to me, writ in Lady Mary's hand.'

'Mary?' At once Richard forgot Potter and his business. 'How is she? How fares Diana? Is there any word on her health, her babe?'

Swiftly Jane scanned the page. The cocked hat slipped unnoticed from her head, and still she read, turning the page over to read the reverse as well.

'What is it, Jane?' Richard demanded, his concern growing by the second. Here he and Jane had been frolicking about Venice without a care, while any manner of disaster could have befallen his girls. 'What has happened?'

'They are well, both of them, and their husbands, too.' Finally Jane looked up, her expression impossible to read. 'They will be joining us here in Venice by the end of this week.'

Chapter Eighteen

Jane woke early the next morning, dressed and read beside the window while she waited to hear Richard come thumping down the stairs from his quarters to breakfast. Since the first morning when she'd taught him the delights of starting the day with steamed chocolate and ham, breakfasting together had become a pleasing habit for them. They'd sit close in the tiny, opulent room to the back of the house, enjoying both the warmth from the *kachelofen* and each other's company as they planned the day ahead.

But this morning she waited for his familiar footsteps, and waited more. Again and again she checked her little travelling watch, unclipping it from the chain at her waist to hold it to her ear and make certain it was running properly. It was nearly eleven now. Richard was by habit an early riser, and this wasn't like him to stay abed so late. She hoped he hadn't been taken ill during the night; he'd seemed positively boisterous last evening at supper, thrilled by the prospect of seeing his girls once again.

Finally her growling, empty stomach could bear no more. She closed her book, and climbed the stairs to Richard's quarters. She'd not ventured there since that first night, when she'd gone in her nightclothes to give Richard his daughters' letters to read. Strange to realise how that one impulsive gesture, born as it had been of desperation, had led to so much more between them. Certainly now when she tapped on the door, she did so with much more confidence, and far less trepidation.

'Richard?' she called softly, not wanting to wake him if by some chance he slept still. 'Are you risen yet?'

'Jane!' He threw open the door himself, just as he'd done on that earlier night. 'Good morning, my dear.'

But now he was completely dressed, a cup of black coffee in his hand, and there was nothing at all sleepy about him. Beyond his shoulder she could see Mr Potter and another man, some sort of local clerk from his sombre dress, clearly waiting for Richard to return to his now-empty armchair. They sat at a large table covered with Mr Potter's letters and it was obvious that the three men had been deep in their labours. Likewise, too, from the plates scattered across the sideboard, they'd already eaten their breakfast some time before, with Richard still lingering over his beloved coffee when she'd interrupted.

'Forgive me, your Grace,' she murmured self-consciously, reverting to the old formality before the others. 'I didn't realise you were occupied. I won't bother you further.'

'But you're not bothering me, not in the least.' He glanced back at the other men, then stepped into the hall with Jane, closing the door part way to give them more privacy. 'I've a thousand things to tend to, Janie. I've let matters slide a bit while I've been here, and now old Potter's determined to sit on my back today until I'm done. I let you sleep.'

She tried to smile and make a jest of it. 'You know I never sleep late. Farmer's hours, that's what I keep, the same as you do.'

'Ah, true, true.' He was smiling, too, but Jane still had the uncomfortable feeling that his thoughts were more with the men and the letters on the other side of the door than with her.

'Will you be occupied the entire day?' she asked. 'Should I make my own plans?'

Relief swept over his face. 'That would likely be for the best, yes. I'm sorry, Jane, but—'

'Don't concern yourself, Richard,' Jane said swiftly, though of course she'd rather wished he had. 'I amused myself perfectly well before you arrived.'

'You did indeed.' He sighed, preoccupied, and looked back into the room. 'I'd left so much undone after that infernal long voyage, you see, and now it's past time I settled it all. What's the way the sailors say it? "Clear the decks for action." That's it. With the girls coming, I need to clear my own decks, so I can give myself over to them with a clear conscience.'

She nodded wistfully, understanding more than he realised. The time he'd spent with her this week had been charming, yes, but now it had faded into a pleasing interlude that had kept him from his ducal responsibilities. And of course the arrival of his daughters must take precedence. He hadn't seen them since last summer, and they'd always been at the centre of his life.

But Jane understood. She'd been the one who'd heard of *love,* and opened her heart. It wasn't his fault. He hadn't promised anything more to her. He'd a life beyond her, and obligations that didn't include her. Together it made him the honourable gentleman that he was, the one that she loved, that she'd always loved.

Oh, yes, she understood it all.

'Very well, then,' she said as briskly as she could. If he'd once again become the Duke of Aston, then she'd again be Miss Wood. 'You clear your decks, and I'll look after myself. Perhaps I'll return to San Marco, to view the mosaics again.'

'That's it,' he said heartily. 'You go about as if I weren't even here.'

'That I will,' she said. 'Good day to you, Richard.'

Then she turned away towards the stairs before he could see the disappointment in her face, and before he'd a chance to bid her farewell without a kiss.

She understood everything.

'Hah, that was close, wasn't it?' Richard said, his smile broad and gleeful as he closed the door. 'I'd never thought she'd come here to beard me in my den. But I'll have the last surprise, won't I? Where's that confounded hen-tailor?'

'Here, your Grace.' His manservant Wilson ushered the wide-eyed mantua-maker and her two assistants out from the bedchamber where they'd been hidden away. 'Fearing for their lives, they were, though, your Grace. They thought you'd taken 'em prisoner.'

'That's preposterous,' Richard said. 'No one's made a prisoner in a bedchamber. Leastwise not *my* bedchamber. Does she have the goods with her?'

'Oh, aye, she brought it,' Wilson said. 'And a sight it is, too.'

After a bit of arm-waving pantomime, the mantua-maker nodded vigorously and clapped her hands together for her assistants to obey. The older one darted back into the bedchamber, and returned with a stunningly elaborate Carnevale costume draped over her arm, while the second assistant followed with the matching headdress and cloak.

'Dear me,' Potter said faintly. 'I know it's your intention to surprise Miss Wood, your Grace, but I've never imagined the lady in any garb so—so—'

'Gaudy,' Wilson said with relish. 'It do be gaudy, don't it?'

'It is.' Richard's grin widened. 'But won't she look fine in it?'

'Indeed, your Grace,' Potter said carefully. 'I didn't intend to find fault with your choice, if you please.'

'No, what you intended to say was that you can't conceive of Miss Wood dressed in all those ribbons and spangles,' Richard said with unabashed pleasure. 'Likely she wouldn't conceive of it, either. But this gown's special, and she'll see it at once. This is Venice in the proverbial nutshell, done up with silver ribbons.'

'It is, your Grace?' asked Potter, ever doubtful.

'It is,' Richard said with approval, running his hand lightly over the pink satin skirts. He couldn't wait to see Jane rigged out like this, in bright silk that fit her instead of those wretched drab gowns she always wore. 'You see, Potter, Miss Wood's enchanted with the "spirit" of Venice, all the pictures and fripperies and customs of this place. Loves them, she does, and who am I to argue with that?'

Potter shook his head, unconvinced. 'But if the gown were more in keeping with her usual quiet tastes, then perhaps she'd find more use to it than this one.'

'Hang the use, Potter,' Richard said. 'Miss Wood's spent her whole life thinking like that, and it's high time she had her share of frivolity. She'd refuse a sensible gown outright, as not being proper or she being unworthy, or some other rubbish. But this one—*this* she'll have to accept. I'm giving her the chance to *be* part of Venice, at least for a night.'

'Miss Wood will be grateful, I am sure,' Potter

said finally. 'Not many masters are as thoughtful as you are, your Grace.'

Richard grunted. Of course Potter thought he was daft, and why shouldn't he? Potter was his secretary, not a conjurer. He'd no notion of how much Jane meant to him, or how much he loved her, or, for that matter, that she loved him in return. To Potter Jane was still simply Miss Wood, governess to his Grace's daughters, and nothing beyond that. That the Duke of Aston would fall in love with a governess would be inconceivable to a man like Potter, just as it would be inconceivable to most every other person in Richard's acquaintance. The only ones sure to share his joy would be Mary and Diana.

As for the others, Richard didn't care. Jane had made him happy in a way he thought he'd never be happy again, and he wasn't going to give that up now. Instead he'd do whatever he could to make her equally happy, beginning with this extravagant Carnivale costume.

He flicked one of the tiny silver bells stitched to the sleeves and chuckled. Jane was the best woman in the world for surprising, for she never seemed to expect anything for herself. He'd wager her reaction would be even better than when he'd given her the fur muff, and when she actually wore the entire costume with the mask and cloak tonight, when he would take her to the Ridotto—why, he couldn't wait.

Jane, his Janie. For what more, really, could he want?

Jane trudged over the last bridge, returning to the Ca' Battista through the back way rather than by the canal. She'd told herself that she'd walk as much as possible today because the weather had been so fine, warm and bright and almost with the softness of spring in the air, and Jane prided herself on having learned Venice well enough to do so. Yet with every step, she'd known the truth: she'd avoided the canals because the gondolas reminded her of Richard, of sitting side by side, snug and cosy beneath a robe as they'd glided along the water.

The whole day she'd done her best to forget Richard. She'd gone to places she hadn't gone with him and she'd resolutely sought to entertain only herself. It should have been easy, for she'd had a lifetime of being on her own, and less than a fortnight with Richard Farren. But everything in Venice seemed to betray her best intentions, for everything was now inexorably linked with him.

She walked past the shops and remembered

how much he'd enjoyed surprising her with the fur muff.

She made a shortcut down a narrow alley, and thought she heard his good-natured laughter echoing back and forth between the ancient walls.

She stopped for chocolate, and she thought of how she'd taught him to sip it with Venetian discernment.

She visited the Basilica of San Marco, and she'd found herself drawn back to the reliquaries that had so fascinated him.

She walked across the piazza, and remembered how he'd made her laugh by fitting his feet to the herringbone pattern of the paving stones and lurched along with a cockeyed gait.

No wonder she'd never be able to remember Venice again without remembering Richard as well. And yet, though her heart would ache from such bitter -sweet memories, she knew, too, she'd not wish it any other way.

Now she let herself into the house by the back door, wearily pushing back her hood as she passed the kitchen and the servants already busy with their preparations for the evening meal. She wondered if Richard would be joining her to dine, or if he'd still be at work on those countless papers and letters. She could dine alone in her rooms if he was; she'd done it enough times before, and heaven knew she'd do it again.

'Miss Wood!' Signora della Battista swept down the hall towards her. 'At last you have returned! You have kept the duke waiting. He has been quite mad from it, demanding of us all to tell the instant you returned.'

'I am sorry for that, *signora,*' Jane said, wishing her heart didn't race with joy at being missed by Richard. 'I'll go up to him directly.'

Jane hurried up the three flights of stairs, pulling off her gloves and tucking them inside her muff, but not pausing at her own rooms before she went to his. This time, the door was open, and as soon as she appeared in the doorway, Richard himself rushed forward to welcome her.

'Where the devil have you been, Janie?' he demanded, folding her into his arms. 'I would have sent the watch after you long ago, if there'd been a watch in this place to send.'

'I was safe enough, Richard,' she protested. It was easy to make such a protest from the sanctuary of his embrace, and how she'd missed it! 'I've told you that before.'

'No place is safe for respectable women,' he said sternly, hugging her as if he'd never wish to release her again. 'How was I to know where you were?

What if that ne'er-do-well di Rossi had snatched you up off the street, eh? I might never have seen you again.'

'I'm sure the *signor* has already forgotten me, and moved his interest to another lady.' Finally she disentangled herself from him, smoothing her skirts. 'At least he's stopped sending his messages and attentions, and that is perfectly, perfectly fine with me.'

'With me as well,' Richard declared. 'If the rascal went straight to blazes, he couldn't please me more.'

He was studying her, stroking his upper lip in a curious way, as if he were trying to hide his smile. She'd been so pleased by his welcome that she only now noticed there were others in the room with them: Mr Potter and Wilson, same as this morning, plus two tradeswomen, watching wide-eyed from the bench beside the door.

Self-consciously Jane took another step apart from Richard, clasping her hands at her waist. She didn't know how much Potter and Wilson knew of her attachment to Richard, or what they'd make of these obvious signs of affection between the duke and his daughters' governess.

For that matter, she wasn't entirely sure herself of Richard's intentions towards her.

'I passed the day visiting the sights, your Grace,' she said, reverting to the old formality, just to be safe. 'It was a pleasant day to be about, sunny and mild. If we felt such a day in Kent, we'd call it spring.'

'I didn't feel a bit of it, boxed up in here all the day long,' he said. 'But you can tell me more over supper.'

She smiled: so they would be dining together after all. 'When I passed through the kitchen, I saw the cook making—'

'But we're not dining here,' he said. 'I've made other arrangements. And I should warn you, Jane, I'm wicked hungry.'

'Then I'll go down to my rooms to dress at once,' she said happily. 'It won't take but a moment for me to ready myself.'

'There's no need for you to leave,' Richard said. 'There's a gown laid out for you on the bed in the other chamber.'

'Oh, your Grace,' Jane began to protest. 'Thank you, but no. I told you before that I haven't a need for fancy dress.'

'Tonight you do,' he said, his grin spreading wide. 'We're going to the Ridotto, you and I, and I'm told we wouldn't be admitted unless we come in Carnevale garb.'

'Masquerade costumes? For us?' she asked, bewildered.

'Yes, yes,' he said triumphantly, taking her by the hand to lead her into the other room. 'Here you are. A handsome turnout, isn't it?'

Jane stared at the costume on the bed, once again made speechless by both his gift and his generosity. This was no tawdry, casual costume, meant for one night's wear and no more. This was an exquisitely fashioned gown of salmon-pink silk satin, pieced with silvery white in a fanciful interpretation of traditional diamond-patterned motley. Bright green ribbons crossed the patches, and each diamond was centred by a shimmering cluster of sequins, and the gown itself was stylishly cut with a narrow pointed waist and a full skirt.

But the gown was only the beginning. With it came matching satin slippers and pink thread stockings, and gloves, as well as the dark, hooded cloak, small black three-cornered hat, white mask and black veil that would provide the complete anonymity that the Ridotto required of its high-bred patrons.

'Do you like it, Janie?' Richard asked. 'You'll be Columbina, the "little dove", while I'll be your rascally partner, Arlecchino. You've always wished to do everything as a true Venetian would while you are here, and by God, I can't think of a better way than this.'

'You're right,' she said softly, reaching out to touch the lavish costume. She'd never had anything half so fine of her own, and if it had been an ordinary gown, she would have had to refuse it, on principle's sake. But the fact that it was a costume, and a costume meant only for Carnevale at that, was different. 'I suppose there's no harm from wearing it this once.'

'No harm,' Richard declared, 'but a great deal of amusement for us both. At least that's my intent.'

'To be sure,' she said, still hesitant. She could already tell just by looking that the costume was going to be shockingly immodest by English standards. 'But I've never worn such attire, not once, and I don't—'

'Then we shall be equal,' he said, 'for I've never rigged myself out in diamond-patterned pantaloons, either. Come now, Jane, be daring. We swore we'd both try different things here in Venice. What could be more different than this?'

'And we will be wearing masks,' she said thoughtfully, then grinned, her decision made. 'Very well, then. This night I shall be Columbina to your Arlecchino, and no one will ever guess who we are.'

'Swathed in all this, your own father wouldn't know you.' He kissed her impulsively before all the others, though no one other than Jane herself seemed surprised. 'These ladies will help you to dress, and I believe the *signora* has already sent for some fellow to arrange your hair.'

Before Jane quite realised what was happening, she was whisked back to her rooms downstairs and promptly undressed by the mantua-maker and her assistant. Jane had always dressed herself, without the assistance of a lady's maid or even a sister, and she found having these two women fussing and clucking over her disconcerting, even embarrassing.

Yet before long she realised that where this costume was concerned, she did need their help. Instead of the comfortably raised waist of her usual gowns and the short buckram stays she wore beneath them, Columbina's costume was old-fashioned, with a long, narrow, pointed waist that required equally old-fashioned stays that Jane couldn't possibly lace up the back by herself. They tugged and pulled the laces taut, squeezing her waist so tightly with the whalebones that she gasped.

'Goodness,' she said breathlessly, holding on to the bedpost to steady herself, as the women had advised, 'perhaps the size has been misjudged?'

But the women only smiled and nodded, and draped her dressing gown around her shoulders just as the *signora* introduced the man who'd come to dress her hair. Wearing a preposterously high wig that was, in Jane's estimation, little recommendation for his skills, he briskly set about brushing out her hair and then twisting and pinning it into an arrangement that felt strangely unfamiliar. The *signora* herself produced pots of rouge and other colours, and sat before her with a brush in hand.

'Thank you, no,' Jane said firmly. 'I do not paint.'

The *signora* drew back. 'In Venice, all women paint, to improve their beauty, especially for the Ridotto.'

At once Jane thought of the courtesans. 'But I'm not Venetian, *signora*. I'm English.'

'*That*'s true enough,' she said with irritation. 'But his Grace has implored that for tonight you be arrayed as a Venetian lady, and no true Venetian lady would go to the Ridotto with a bare face. It would be as shocking as if she were to appear in her shift alone.'

Jane sighed. 'Very well, then. But only a little.'

Patiently Jane waited for the *signora* and the hairdresser to finish with her, and at last the two women slipped the pink-and-white satin gown around her and laced it tightly up the back.

'*Bellissima, bellissima!*' exclaimed the *signora*, beaming with approval. 'Go to the glass, miss, and see how beautiful you are!'

Jane smiled politely, recognising the *signora*'s compliment for the dutiful flattery it was, and went across the bedchamber to the tall looking-glass as she'd been bidden.

And gasped with shock.

She hadn't need of a mask for disguise tonight, for no one would ever recognise her, not like this. She scarcely recognised herself. Her pale eyes gleamed with bewitching ardour and her cheeks glowed rosy pink, her waist seemed impossibly small, and her breasts—oh, my, she'd never seen her humble bosom presented like this, supported by the stays and bared by the low neckline of the gown. At once her hands moved to cover herself, fluttering over the unfamiliar expanse of skin.

'Do not be so modest,' the *signora* scolded gently. 'You are a beautiful woman, Miss Wood, not a little girl from the schoolroom. You should be proud of the prize of your beauty.'

'But—but this is not me,' Jane said, still staring at her reflection with dismay. 'Not at all.'

'It is,' insisted the *signora*. 'We women are not

all one thing, you know. We have as many facets to us as a well-cut diamond, yes? In spite of how you choose to hide your beauty, his Grace has fallen in love with you. Now, dressed like this, he will desire you as well.'

Her cheeks blushing nearly as pink as the ribbons on her costume, Jane thought of how Richard seemed to be both loving and desiring her perfectly well without any of this…this *display*—not, of course, that she'd tell that to Signora della Battista. But her words were enough to plant a niggling seed of doubt—what if this was how Richard preferred her?

'Forgive me, *signora,* but I do not believe it is appropriate dress for me,' she said, turning away from the looking glass. 'I cannot—Richard!'

He was standing in the door to the room, already in his long cloak for evening. She could just glimpse his costume beneath, a full shirt and loose-fitting trousers like a sailor's, only patterned with black-and-white diamonds. His face was so full of open admiration that that first seed of doubt grew.

'Why, Janie,' he said softly, 'look at you.'

She wasn't looking at herself, but how he was looking at *her*, full of unabashed desire, just as the *signora* had predicted. No man had ever regarded her like this, and she wasn't at all sure what to make of it.

The *signora* smiled, and bowed, and ushered the others from the room, closing the door gently behind her.

'What is wrong, Jane?' Richard asked as soon as they were alone. 'What's upset you?'

Jane tried to smile, not wishing to spoil the evening. 'Nothing is wrong.'

'Oh, nothing at all,' he said, 'which is why you look as if you're going to weep at any moment. I know you better than that, Jane. What's amiss? Is it the costume?'

She turned away from him, her bell-shaped skirts swinging around her ankles in an unfamiliar fashion, and unhappily looked again towards her reflection in the glass.

'You have been most generous to provide such a costly costume for me,' she began, 'and I will grant that it's very beautiful, but I do not—that is, I cannot—oh, Richard, is this how you wish me always to appear? Is that why you gave me this gown? Because it pleases you to see me dressed like this?'

'Like Columbina?' he asked, mystified.

'No, no, like *this*,' she said, helplessly spreading her hands on either side of her tight-laced body. 'I don't feel like myself at all, Richard, all pink and white like an iced confection, and so *uncovered*.'

'Not at all, Jane,' he said gruffly, coming to stand behind her. 'You would be beautiful to me in the plainest gown imaginable. What I'd hoped was that these fripperies would make you see for yourself how beautiful you are.'

What Jane saw was her nose redden and her eyes grow too bright as he slipped his arms around her waist.

'But I'm not beautiful, Richard,' she protested. 'I never have been.'

'I say you are,' he insisted, holding her close with her back to his chest. 'It's my turn to play the tutor now, sweet. Look at yourself as you are. Forget whatever notion you have of what you should be. See yourself as I see you.'

'I do not believe that—'

'Hush,' he said softly, 'and look. *Look*. You've a mouth that's made for smiling, and for kissing, too, ripe and full the way I like. Your skin puts me to mind of peaches in the summer, rosy gold and like velvet to my touch. You're not some haughty beauty, Jane, but a kind one, full of warmth and gentleness.'

She studied herself as he'd bidden, and tried to see herself as he described. She'd grant that she did look different here in Venice to what she had in Aston, though she'd assumed that was Venice's magic, not her own. Haughty she'd never be, but she'd never thought of being a warm and gentle beauty, either, and as for having a mouth that was ripe for kissing…

'Look, Jane,' he continued, settling his hands around her waist. 'You don't need this lacing, not for me, because I know already how small and sweet your body is, and how when I hold you, I don't want ever to let you go.'

He drew her back against his chest, her small satin-clad figure in sharp, shocking contrast against his black cloak. He kissed the side of her throat, and she tipped her head wantonly back against his shoulder, reaching up to touch his jaw.

'You're in love, Jane,' he whispered fiercely, turning his head to kiss her palm. 'Look, and see for yourself. You're in love with me, and I'm in love with you. That's the truth, and nothing in the world is more beautiful than that, eh?'

'Oh, Richard,' she whispered, still staring at their reflection. The desire she'd seen in his eyes earlier was still there, every bit as potent as before, and matched now by the desire she saw in her own eyes, too. But there was more to their joined image, much more, because that heady desire was matched by love. She couldn't miss it in the way he was kissing her, or in the tenderness with which he held her, or even in his voice. He wanted her not because of how she was dressed, but because he loved her, and she loved him.

And he was right: in some unfathomable way, love *had* made her beautiful.

Overwhelmed, she twisted around in his embrace to face him. How could he keep doing this to her, this great gruff gentleman, surprising her when she least expected it? How did he always know exactly what to do and say to make her love him all the more?

'Happier now?' he asked.

'Don't be foolish,' she whispered, laying her hand on his cheek. 'I'm always happy with you.'

'That's not quite true,' he teased wryly. 'But I'm willing to pretend it is.'

'Here,' she said, stretching up against him. 'Will you believe me now?'

She kissed him quickly, surprising herself by her own playful daring. Perhaps it was the costume that was making her so bold, claiming the spirit of flirtatious Columbina for her own, or perhaps it was simply being in Richard's arms like this.

'I'll believe whatever you say, Columbina,' he

said, pulling her closer to kiss her more thoroughly. 'Especially when you persuade me like that.'

But though she could taste the hunger in his kiss—a hunger that mirrored her own—she could also tell he was holding back, reluctant to lose himself too thoroughly in the heat that glowed between them, and when at last he broke away with a heavy sigh, she understood. He'd gone through a great deal of effort arranging this evening for them, and she'd no wish to spoil it by dawdling, even if the dawdling was as pleasurable as this.

'Later, Arlecchino,' she whispered breathlessly, using the name of his costume's character. She pressed her fingertips across his lips. 'Then we shall find happiness together.'

He clasped her wrist, holding her hand against his lips to kiss her palm, nipping lightly at the tender flesh in a way that made her shiver with delight.

'Later,' he said softly, his eyes dark with longing as he met her gaze. 'I won't forget, Columbina. Later.'

Chapter Nineteen

To Richard, the Ridotto seemed to be only one more example of Venetian peculiarity. In London, there were plenty of gaming houses and clubs, each operated with more or less corruption. The house generally won and the players generally lost, and anyone who wasn't careful could lose all he owned at the turn of a card. But most gentlemen—and a few ladies, too—who played did so only for amusement, and the better gaming houses were pleasant enough establishments for that. He'd two or three favourites that he visited with friends when the House was in session and he was in London, but he wasn't cursed with a gambler's nature, and he'd never won or lost any substantial amount.

But in Venice, the Ridotto wasn't a separate establishment, but rooms in a nobleman's house—the Palazzo di Dandolo—that the fellow had decided to make public, with the government claiming a portion of all the winnings as a sort of tax. The gaming was supposed to be restricted to aristocrats and others who could afford it; to protect their identities, the Ridotto enforced strict rules of dress, including masks, hats, veils and cloaks.

It seemed to Richard to be the damnedest thing, dressing up like an All Saints' Day ghoul to play bassett or faro, and he'd been warned that there were as many rascals as nobles hidden behind the masks, and that for every true lady, there were two courtesans. He'd thought twice about taking Jane into such a place, but the Ridotto at Carnevale was supposed to one of the most memorable sights to experience in Venice. Finally he'd decided it would do Jane good to see something of the city beyond old churches and picture galleries, and he'd accepted the invitation he'd been sent when he'd first arrived.

But now, as he and Jane joined the other costumed revellers who crowded the Campo San Moise outside the palazzo, his misgivings vanished. Though he couldn't begin to see her face beneath the mask and veil her costume required, he could hear her delighted chuckle, and knew from the way she squeezed his hand that she was thoroughly enjoying the spectacle around her.

'Have you ever seen so much fancy dress,

Richard?' she asked. 'It's as if a flock of bright birds has landed.'

'Righteous large birds,' he said, laughing, for they did all look like birds. It wasn't so much the bright silk of the fancy dress, but the half-masks that nearly everyone was wearing. The mask's long noses were designed to make breathing and drinking possible, but they also resembled birds' beaks. Combined with the cloaks that fluttered like so many wings, it didn't take much fancying to imagine the crowd around them as a jumble of noisy parrots, just as Jane had said.

She laughed with him now, a sound he found even more merry than the hurdy-gurdy player who'd turned the steps of a nearby church into a musician's gallery. A few couples danced on the pavement before him in an impromptu ball, and impulsively Richard seized Jane by the waist and joined them.

'Richard!' she exclaimed with surprise, then fell into step with him, laughing breathlessly as she did. As dances went, there wasn't much finesse to their performance, and Richard doubted they were even doing the proper steps to fit the music, but he didn't care. For joy and exuberance, it couldn't be beat, and he was sure his Jane felt the same, her skirts twirling above her neat little ankles and her hand holding tight to his. The sight of her in the close-fitting Carnevale costume had stunned him; he'd intended the costume to please her, but he'd been astonished by the pleasure it had given him, too. He'd never seen her look so charmingly alluring except on that first night when she'd appeared at his bedchamber door in her nightshift. A very different impression, to be sure, but the effect on him had been the same.

He'd wanted her, wanted her so badly that he'd shocked himself. He'd been hard in an instant. The first time, he'd been appalled because he'd felt such desire for his daughters' governess. Tonight he'd been equally horrified because it was Jane, his Janie, a woman he'd come to love and respect and outright *enjoy* more than any other since his wife.

Yet when he'd seen her standing before the glass in that cunning little costume, her breasts displayed as if begging for his caress, his one overwhelmingly male thought had been to toss her back upon her own bed and make love to her. It had seemed a shame to cover her up so completely in the required cloak, veil and hat, but Richard had to grant these Venetians did have an eye for beguilement. Though half of Jane's face was hidden by the mask, the sheer black veil that fell nearly to her waist seemed magically to reveal more than it hid, giving her smile a delicious air of mystery, and making that shadowed glimpse of her breasts even more tempting as she danced with him.

But all too soon, the song came to an end, and Jane made him a charmingly foolish curtsy. She laughed, out of breath, and pressed her hand to her side.

'Listen to me,' she said, laughing still. 'I'm laced so tight that I'm winded and wheezing like an old bellows!'

Before Richard could answer, another man dressed in the same black cloak, mask and black hat came forwards to take her hand, making some sort of bold declaration to Jane that Richard didn't like at all.

'Here now, none of your impertinence,' he said curtly, stepping between Jane and the stranger. 'The lady's with me.'

The man shrugged and backed away, and pranced off to find another partner.

'All the man wished was to dance, Richard,' Jane said, taking Richard by the arm. 'He meant no harm.'

'You don't know what the rascal meant.' Richard was glad that beneath his cloak he wore his sword, as he always did when they went out at night. He knew Jane didn't like it, but it was better to be careful than not, especially in a city like Venice. He'd been warned by many friends that all this gaiety could hide a great many villains, and as much as he wanted her to enjoy herself, he was also determined to keep her safe. Who knew how many poor sots were robbed each night and tossed into the canals to drift out to sea? 'The fellow could have intended all manner of mischief towards you.'

'Whatever he wished is of no importance now,' she said winningly, her veiled smile still visible to him by the lanterns' light. 'The only intentions that concern me are yours. Do you mean all manner of mischief, too?'

'Only if it involves you, my dear,' he said gruffly. He wished he'd the grace to play the gallant to match these gaudy costumes.

She lifted the veil below her mask and reached up to kiss him swiftly, surprising him.

'I'll consider that a promise,' she whispered close to his ear, and then laughed sheepishly at her own audacity. 'I fear I'm not terribly good at being bold. Does that sound like Columbina?'

'What it sounds like is very charming, and very wicked,' he said, relaxing enough to laugh with her. The kiss might have disarmed him, yes, but he'd also taken notice of the quick glimpse of her corseted breasts when she'd raised her veil. She was doing a much better job of being bold than she realised.

'Come, Columbina,' he said, tucking her little hand into his arm. 'The sooner I take you inside, the better.'

She laughed again, and together they made their way through the costumed crowds to the tall double-doors of the Palazzo di Dandolo. On account of the masks, no one was recognised as either a noble or a commoner by their face or person, but as soon as Richard presented their tickets, they were immediately ushered inside. The palazzo's front hall was like all others in Venice—grand with gold-leaf stars on the ceiling, painted panels on the walls and tall columns of bright polychrome marble—but also burdened with a chill damp that no fire could ever ease. Footmen bowed them towards the staircase that led to the Ridotto itself, another wide room with a high, beamed ceiling. Eight-armed chandeliers of polished brass with glittering spun-glass drops hung low on long chains. Tables for the various games were arranged around the walls of the room, each with a cluster of anxious players around it, while other guests wandered about conversing or flirting with one another.

'A bit dreary for a gaming room, isn't it?' Richard said as they paused in the arched doorway.

'I think it's beautiful,' declared Jane beside him.

'The masks make everyone look so mysterious, and the chandeliers are like fairy lights.'

He grunted, sceptical. 'Fairy lights to hide how much you lose.'

'Perhaps,' she admitted. 'But it's one more pretty sight I wish to remember against some unhappy day in the schoolroom when none of my charges is behaving.'

'Here now, no more talk of wretched school-rooms.' He didn't like hearing her speak of her future without him in it, and he squeezed her hand fondly now, hoping to reassure her. 'We're supposed to be enjoying ourselves, mind?'

'That is true,' she said, and smiled up at him. 'I doubt Columbina's ever seen the inside of a school-room.'

'Hah, I'd lay a guinea that she hasn't.' Without thinking Richard began to shrug out of his cloak, and an anxious footman hurried forwards to stop him.

'He says you must keep the cloak on, Richard,' Jane said, interpreting for the servant. 'He says it's the custom, as part of the disguise.'

'I knew that,' he admitted ruefully, and sighed. 'It was just my custom as an Englishman to take it off. Ah, well, Columbina, let's find a place, and pray that I'll have better luck at the tables than at pretending to be Arlecchino.'

She looked up at him swiftly. 'You're going to play?' she asked, clearly surprised. 'You'll wager?'

He chuckled, remembering that she'd been raised in a country vicarage. 'Of course I'll play. Why else come to a gaming house? Ah, here's a faro table.'

'You know how to play faro?' she asked anxiously. 'You've done it before? I've heard it's a most perilous game.'

'Not if you don't let winning and losing go to your head.' He grinned. He'd never been a confirmed gambler, not like other gentlemen he knew, but he was too competitive by nature not to relish the sport of it. Success at faro was more random chance than sharpster's skill, and for that reason he'd always liked it. 'Don't worry, sweet. I'm not about to wager the deed to Aston Hall.'

'But faro, Richard,' she protested, scandalised. 'What would your daughters say if they knew?'

'They'd likely ask me to teach them how to play,' he said easily, teasing. 'For me it's the sport, my dear, not the winnings. I vow that if I claim so much as a farthing, I'll give it to the nearest Venetian orphanage. Will that settle your doubts?'

'That would be generous of you,' she admitted

reluctantly, 'and I suppose such charity would help ameliorate the sin of gambling.'

'Quite,' he said. 'Pray stand behind my chair, Columbina, and bring me *bella fortuna,* eh?'

'*Bella fortuna,* indeed,' she said primly as he took an empty seat at the nearest table. 'You are a constant surprise to me, your Grace, a constant surprise.'

He laughed, but none the less was pleased when she rested her hands on the high, carved back of his chair. Most likely she'd done it more so to be ready to whisk him from harm rather than for the good luck he'd asked for, but her concern pleased him. It had been a long time since he'd had a woman care for him like that, and he hadn't realised how much he'd missed it, almost as much as he'd missed having someone dear to him that he could spoil and fuss over in return. No wonder he was so happy in Jane's company.

Happy, and now lucky. As soon as his cards had been dealt, he tossed several coins into the well in the centre of the table. To his right, at the far end of the oval table, sat the banker with a fresh deck of cards, while the croupe sat at the other end of the table, already shuffling the next deck. These gentlemen, as well as every other at the table, were as shrouded and masked as Richard was himself, making it impossible to discover any of the little ticks, frowns or other give-aways in the other players' expressions. This truly *would* be a game of chance, and with that fatalistic thought, Richard folded down the corner of his first card to signify a double, or whatever it was called here in Venice.

The banker turned over his cards, one each on his left and right. He nodded to Richard to signify he'd won, and at once the croupe doubled the little pile of coins in the well before him. Richard nodded back, the only acknowledgement it seemed anyone was permitted to make. He left the now-doubled coins as his stake, folded his next card the same way, and won again.

And again. The pile of coins in his well had grown to a glittering heap, in marked contrast to the others at the table.

'Richard,' Jane whispered with awe behind him. 'You're winning.'

Richard nodded, concentrating on his next play. Though the mask would hide his face from the others, his heart was thumping with excitement. Another double, he decided, and when the banker dealt and showed his cards, he'd won again.

Gasps and low whistles accompanied the croupe as he pushed another pile of coins across the green cloth. Richard might not know every language being spoken around the faro table, but he could recognise the fervour of an oath in any tongue. Clearly his luck was both admired and envied, and he was wise enough to realise what a mixed blessing that could be. He knew perfectly well that the cards were just as likely to fall against him with the next hand and that he'd lose all he'd won, but damnation, who would have guessed he'd have such a run?

He rubbed his hand across his jaw, all the response he'd let himself display. It wouldn't be wise to show more. But excitement was making his mouth as dry as a desert, and impatiently he glanced about for one of the servants who'd brought wine to several of the other players.

'Where the devil have those fellows with the wine gone?' he muttered, more to himself than anyone else.

But of course Jane heard him. 'I'll fetch one,' she said, and before he could stop her, she'd vanished from behind his chair into the crowded room.

'Jane!' he called after her, half-rising from his chair to try to look beyond the crowd that had clustered around the table to watch. She didn't have to jump to obey him like this; she was here *with* him, not as his servant.

'*Signor,*' murmured the man seated beside him, recalling him to the game and the banker waiting for his play. Reluctantly Richard turned back to the table. Most likely Jane would be back soon enough, and, given her usual efficiency, with an entire vineyard in tow, too.

Jane herself would have been content to have found a single waiter. The room had grown far more crowded since they'd first arrived, and the costumed and masked figures that she'd found so enchanting then now felt oddly menacing as they pressed too closely around her, jostling her in the crush. She knew she was being foolish, scolding herself for imagining too much. Behind every white or black mask was an ordinary person, laughing and chatting and flirting and finding amusement just as she and Richard were.

Determined to find a servant, she tried to push her way through the bobbing sea of black cocked hats and cloaks. She gasped as someone brazenly fondled her bottom, yet when she jerked around to confront him, all she saw were more masks, more blank faces. She backed away, her heart racing, and as she did, someone clasped her arm and held her fast. She gasped again and struggled to pull free.

'Hush, hush, *cara mia,* I intend you no harm.' The man released her arm, and tipped his long-nosed mask up to show her his face. 'I cannot express how happy I am to see you.'

'Signor di Rossi!' she exclaimed, flushing with dismay. 'If you please, I cannot linger. I must find a waiter for wine for his Grace.'

She saw the disappointment flicker across his face at the mention of Richard. 'You are here with the duke?'

'Of course,' she said swiftly. 'I'd never come to such a place without him.'

He nodded. 'Then you've no choice but to please him, yes? The banqueting room with the wine isn't far. I'll show you.'

She hesitated, wondering if she could trust him.

'So that is how it is between us now, *cara?*' he asked wearily. 'And to think that once we were such grand friends!'

That was enough to prick her conscience. It had always been her nature to smooth over misunderstandings and make things peaceable, and though the rift between her and the *signor* certainly wasn't her fault, she couldn't bear for him to believe she'd been the one who'd broken their friendship. He had been exceptionally kind to her when she'd first arrived in Venice.

'Is it far to the banqueting room?' she asked. Truly,

what could happen among so many others? 'I can't seem to find anything for myself in this crush.'

'Then pray let me once again be your guide,' he said, and dropped his mask back in place. 'This way, if you please.'

'Thank you, *signor*,' she said, and before she'd finished speaking he'd taken her arm again and begun leading her through the crowd. Jostled left and right by other revellers, she had to hurry to keep pace with di Rossi, her breath short from haste and from the unfamiliar stays of her costume. They left the gaming room, and turned down a hall that was also full, then turned again into a small, elegantly furnished parlour lit by a single candelabrum. But there was no banqueting table, no wine, and worse, no others in the room, and at once Jane realised she'd been misled.

Her heart racing, she jerked her arm free and turned swiftly towards the door, but the *signor* had no intention of letting her escape. He caught her about the waist and blocked her path.

'*Signor*, please,' she said, her voice sharp with fear. 'Let me go. Let me go *now!*'

'That's not what you want, *cara*, not at all,' he whispered. 'In your heart, you know the truth. You want me, my little dove, not him. You want me.'

He pushed her against the wall and pinned her

with his body, trapping her there as she struggled. He was so much larger than she was, so much stronger. Her fists flailing to defend herself, she managed only to knock off his hat and his long-nosed mask. Beneath it, his face was mottled and fixed, and her fear grew. She tried to strike him again, and he grasped her wrists together with one hand and held them over her head against the wall. He shoved aside her veil and seized her jaw, keeping her face steady, and kissed her hard. She gasped with shock as he plunged his tongue into her mouth, and she writhed against him as her revulsion grew with his demands. His kiss reminded her of a slobbering dog, or worse, of a dog worrying a bone, and at last she managed to free one of her hands. Blindly she reached between them to find one of the long straight pins that held her bodice in place. She pulled it free, and, before he'd notice, stabbed it into the underside of his arm.

He swore from the pain and jerked away from her to grasp at his wounded arm. Without pause, Jane fled, bolting from the room and into the hall as fast as she could. Though he called after her, ordering her to stop, she didn't. She owed him nothing, not now.

She caught one high heel in the hem of her skirts and felt it tear, but still she plunged onwards through the sea of black cloaks. She didn't care who she pushed aside or bumped or jostled, only that she got away from di Rossi and back to Richard's side. Her breath now came in great sobbing gulps that racked her chest as she ran, and in a way she was grateful that the mask hid her face and tears that she couldn't keep back. Richard would save her, her own great bear of a love; no one would dare harm her when she was at his side.

Yet as distraught as she was, she still realised the folly of such thoughts. Earlier she'd ignored the fact that he'd worn his sword beneath his cloak; as unhappy as it made her to see him armed, she knew it equally pleased him to do so, and for that reason she'd said nothing. But everything had changed now. Richard's temper was formidable. If he learned of how di Rossi had treated her, he'd immediately be off to challenge the Venetian, and that—that terrified her. Somehow she must convince Richard to leave without telling him why, and she must do it at once, before the *signor* found her.

At last she reached the faro table, pushing her way through the ring of spectators. The pile of coins before Richard had grown larger since she'd been away, and clearly his luck had held. He smiled as soon as he saw her, so warmly that fresh tears started in her eyes.

'You're back, Janie,' he said fondly, his smile fading as he realised something was wrong. 'What's amiss, sweet? What has happened?'

'Forgive me, Richard,' she said, 'but I wish to leave. I—I'm not well.'

'Of course.' Instantly Richard rose, his concern for her overshadowing everything else, and glanced at the startled banker. 'I'm out, sir. Pray send my winnings tomorrow to my lodgings at the Ca' Battista.'

'But you cannot leave so soon, most illustrious sir,' protested one of the other players. 'You must grant us the chance to regain our losses.'

'I'm sorry, gentlemen,' he said, bowing slightly as he took Jane's arm. 'But the lady requests, and I obey.'

The crowds parted for them as they left the room, for by now, mask or not, most knew he was the English duke with the extraordinary luck. Richard wouldn't deny that he'd enjoyed it, but now all he cared for was Jane. Though he couldn't see her face, she somehow seemed bedraggled, her whole small figure drooping.

'What has happened, Jane?' he asked again. He slipped his arm protectively around her shoulders, and felt how she shivered. 'Should I summon a physician, or—?'

'No, no, please don't make a fuss, I beg you,' she begged. 'I'll be well enough when we're outside in the open air.'

He said nothing more as he guided her down the long staircase, out the door, and across the Campo San Moise to the canal. A long line of gondolas lay alongside the walk, waiting for those inside the Ridotto, but since Richard and Jane had left much earlier than they'd intended, their own gondola was nowhere to be seen within the bobbing lanterns' light—as bad, thought Richard, as the carriages before Buckingham Palace. A gondolier's boy came trotting up to them, touching his straw hat and offering in pidgin English to find their gondola. Richard nodded and tossed him a coin, and turned back to Jane.

'Let's hope the little scoundrel returns,' he said, unfastening his mask. 'Do you need to sit, sweet?'

She shook her head. She'd already taken off her mask and turned her veil up over her hat, breathing deeply of the cool night air. Damp tendrils of her hair were pressed flat against her temples, and her carefully applied paint was streaked down her face.

'I'm well enough now,' she said. 'It was the heat and the crowd, that was all.'

But Richard was sure there was more to it than

that. She was clinging to his arm too tightly for it to be otherwise, and her eyes had a rare fearfulness in them that made him want to protect her all the more.

'We'll take you home and put you straight to bed,' he said. 'That's what any proper governess would say, wouldn't she?'

'A proper one would, yes.' Her smile crumpled. 'Oh, Richard, why did I trust Signor di Rossi again? Why was I so foolish as to believe he'd wish to assist me?'

Richard stopped. 'What has happened, Jane? So help me, if he—'

'Nothing happened,' she said quickly, raising her chin with a little show of pride. 'I surprised him, and defended myself and that—that was that. I was the ninny for letting it go as far as it did.'

'It's hardly your fault, Jane,' Richard said, his anger rising on her behalf. 'I should go back and find that bastard, and teach him how—'

'You will not,' she said firmly, placing her hand on his arm to hold him back. 'That's why I didn't tell you before. It is done, and I will never speak or see the gentleman again.'

'He's hardly a gentleman,' Richard grumbled, placing his hand protectively over hers. He hated to think of her having to defend herself at all—that was what he was for, wasn't it? 'Ahh, here's that boy at last to lead us on our way.'

'Will you truly give away all the money you won?' she asked as they followed the boy along the walk and away from the lights of the campo. 'To orphans?'

'I promised you I would, didn't I?' he said with a heartiness he meant to cheer her. 'Orphans need it. I do not.'

She laughed softly, a most reassuring sound to him, and then patted his arm. 'You are a most excellent man, your Grace.'

But as much as Richard enjoyed her compliments, he was paying almost no attention to this one, and a great deal more to their surroundings. The boy had led them away from the first canal and down this darker *rio,* little more than a watery alley with the only light coming from the moon overhead. The place did not feel quite right to Richard, and instinctively he shoved back the edge of his cloak to find the hilt of his sword. Trouble, he knew, often came to those who were least prepared to face it.

And sometimes it came anyway.

The two masked men jumped from the shadows into their path, the moonlight glinting off the blades of their drawn swords. Jane gasped, and swiftly

Richard pushed her behind him, trusting she'd the sense to stay there.

'Your winnings, Englishman,' the first man demanded. 'Your gold, or your life.'

'I won, yes,' Richard said slowly, biding his time. There were two of them and one of him, but they were small, scrabbling bandits, and he'd have the advantage in size and strength to even the numbers. They spoke a manner of English, too—most likely sailors, then, and he'd never met a sailor who was good with a sword.

'Then give over your gold,' the man repeated. 'Give it now.'

Richard snorted derisively. 'Do you believe I'm fool enough to take my winnings with me?'

'I'm no fool, neither,' the thief said. 'Deliver, Englishman, or die.'

'Give him what you have, Richard,' Jane begged behind him, her voice shrill with fear. 'Don't play the hero, I beg you. Please, Richard, please!'

'Stand back, Janie,' he said without taking his gaze from the two men. He wasn't playing the hero; he was simply doing what any gentleman would. 'I'll tend to these.'

'Listen to your whore, *signor.*' The second man sniggered. 'Maybe we should take her, too.'

'That's enough,' said Richard curtly, and he drew

his sword with a scraping sweep of steel. 'No one takes what's mine.'

The two charged towards him together, and deftly Richard caught their blades against his. They flailed at him, and he met them swiftly, lunging forwards to attack rather than simply defend. They didn't expect that, and fell back, slashing wildly. With practised assurance, Richard attacked again, and again. This wasn't the elegant parry and thrust of the master swordsman he visited for practice in London, but the same moves applied even in a rough fight like this. Look for weakness, protect yourself, be quick, be relentless, be ruthless—he might be nearly forty, but by God, he'd put his experience against any man half his age.

But having Jane there made it different. Was she still fearing for him, he wondered, still frightened?

And in that half-second that he let his concentration wander, he felt the blade slice across the back of his wrist and his own blood spill out, not deep enough to sever any muscles, but more than enough to snap his attention back to where it belonged.

Falsely confident, the first man raised his sword high to strike again. Before he could, Richard struck first, catching the man beneath his upraised arm. Richard felt the blade cut through the rough cloth of the man's coat and shirt and then sink into his flesh, stopping only when it hit and glanced off a rib.

The thief cried out with pain and surprise and slid off Richard's sword to fall to the paving stones. Clutching at his side, he babbled to his comrade in anguished Italian, and to Richard, too.

'Misericordia, misericordia!' he cried weakly, begging for mercy. *'O, Jesu!'*

To Richard's surprise, the man dropped his sword and rushed to his wounded friend. He pulled the man to his unsteady feet and half-dragged him away as swiftly as he could, back into the shadows of a nearby alley.

'Richard!' Jane flung herself at him, wrapping her arms tightly around his waist. 'Oh, Richard, Richard, if anything had happened to you!'

'Nothing did, sweet, nothing at all.' Awkwardly he sheathed his own sword and wrapped his arms around her. 'It's over now, Janie, over and done.'

She turned her face to gaze up at him, her cheeks wet with tears. 'You can—cannot know how I feared for you, Richard,' she sobbed. 'I know we've vowed to live each—each day as it came here in Venice, but if—if I'd lost you—'

'But you didn't,' he said softly. 'Come, let me take you home.'

Once again he glanced past her to where the

thieves had vanished, with all that remained was a ragged dark trail of blood. So much blood, thought Richard wearily, still breathing hard himself. Now that the excitement of the fight had passed, his hand hurt like the devil. He felt exhausted, and worse, he felt every bit his age. He hadn't intended to kill the man, but his blade must have slipped deeper than he'd intended. Hell. It had been undeniable self-defence, of course, but he'd no wish to squander his final days with Jane here in Venice becoming embroiled in some sort of public inquiry.

He led her away, back towards the safety and the light of the busier piazzas, and it was then she saw the gash on his hand.

'Oh, dear God!' she cried softly. 'They did hurt you! Hurry, hurry, we must fetch a surgeon!'

'It's nothing, Jane,' he said in the way of all wounded men. Self-consciously he wrapped his dark cloak around his hand, as much to hide the blood and his crimson-stained cuff from her as to bind up the cut, and offered her his other arm. 'Besides, it's my own fault. I let my thoughts wander, and this is the result.'

Her face still wet with tears, she ignored his offered arm. Instead she'd drawn out her own handkerchief and reached for his wounded hand, briskly undeterred by the blood.

'That's foolishness,' she said, tending to him with her usual efficiency. 'I saw how *determined* you were. What could possibly scatter your thoughts in such a situation?'

'You,' he said. 'I thought of you.'

Chapter Twenty

Jane was always at her best when she was busy, and the more things she had to manage, or arrange, or settle, the better. So it was that night near the Ridotto once she'd realised that Richard had been wounded. Once she'd seen that Richard needed her, that she'd things to *do,* she'd been able to put aside Signor di Rossi and the ambush and everything else that had so frightened her this evening. Instead she could simply be capable Miss Wood.

Richard could protest all he wanted that the blood streaming from his hand was nothing; she knew better, just as she knew he'd be far too stubborn and gallant to admit it. With her usual calm efficiency—and her best Italian—she'd made sure their gondolier showed the greatest haste in returning them to the Ca' Battista. She'd sent for a surgeon, she'd roused the cook to produce a late, fortifying supper for Richard, and she'd ordered a footman to build the fires in Richard's rooms and to bring warm water for washing.

Though Richard's manservant Wilson had rushed to take possession of his master, Jane had insisted on accompanying him upstairs herself, and had only left Richard and Wilson alone when the manservant began to strip away Richard's blood-stained Arlecchino costume. She hurried to her own rooms just long enough to replace her own frivolous costume with her woollen dressing gown, and was back in Richard's bedchamber before the surgeon arrived. Now in a fresh shirt and a quilted silk banyan, he was sitting beside the long table where he'd conduct his business affairs, his injured hand resting gingerly on the edge and a glass of brandy in the other.

'That's not for you to do, Jane,' Richard said as she insisted on gently unwrapping the sodden handkerchief from his hand. 'Leave it for the doctor.'

'It's not good to let this sit any longer,' she insisted, her concern growing. For all his bluster, she thought he looked pale and drawn. 'Who knows when the fellow will decide to show his face?'

He grimaced. 'Janie, please.'

'I'm sorry,' she said softly, pouring warm water over the wound to clean it. He'd been caught on the heel of his hand, dangerously close to the underside of his wrist. The flesh gaped open, bleeding afresh now that it was unbound, and the rest of his hand was mottled and swollen. Now that she could see the gravity of the cut, she realised how difficult it must be for him to remain so stoic before her. She wasn't squeamish or afraid of nursing when required, but this was no ordinary scrape or bruise, and once again her emotions welled when she thought of how he'd risked his life to defend her.

'There now, Jane, you'll need a sterner face if you're to play surgeon,' he said, striving to lighten the mood. 'You're so doleful, I'd swear you're preparing me for an amputation.'

'Hush, Richard, don't even jest like that,' she scolded, but all the same she was vastly relieved to see Signora della Battista usher the black-clad surgeon into the room. The man bowed, and immediately set to work with a quiet confidence that reassured Jane. As he did, the *signora* pulled Jane aside.

'The authorities have arrived to question his Grace,' she whispered. 'About the fighting.'

Jane gasped with dismay. 'Oh, I was afraid of that! I'll go speak to them myself, and—'

'No, no, Miss Wood, please, it is not necessary,' the older woman said quickly. 'I have sent them away for now. But when they return in the morning, you must make sure that his Grace is mild and gracious. Venice is a republic, and peerages mean nothing here. We do not care for murderous foreigners.'

'He was defending us from thieves who would as soon have murdered us as not!'

'Then that is what they must be made to understand, Miss Wood,' the *signora* insisted. 'They will listen, if the explanation is civil. His Grace must be made to put aside his English temper. Be agreeable, and our authorities in return will be obliging and forgiving. But if he blusters—ah, who can say?'

'Thank you, *signora,* and I promise to speak with his Grace.' Jane glanced over her shoulder to Richard. He was sitting with his eyes squeezed shut and his head bent, fighting the pain as the surgeon finished stitching the gaping cut closed. The brandy glass was empty. 'Though I do not believe his temper will have much fire to it tomorrow.'

Swiftly she returned to Richard's side, resting her hand lightly on his shoulder. At once he reached up to take it, clasping her fingers so tightly she caught her breath. He opened his eyes at the sound, and looked up at her, and purposefully not at his hand.

'Is it so very bad, Janie?' he asked, little drops

of sweat glistening on his forehead. 'You'd tell me, wouldn't you?'

'There is nothing to tell, your Grace,' the surgeon said as he tied the final knot on the new bandage. 'The cut was deep, but clean. I have dressed it simply with a mixture of egg yolk, oil of roses and turpentine against putrefication, and while it is still early to predict entirely, I do not believe there will be much lasting damage. A scar, of course, but what gentleman does not relish such a hard-won scar?'

Sceptical, Richard at last frowned down at his bandaged hand.

'Another glass of brandy, your Grace, and you shall sleep like a babe,' the surgeon promised. 'I shall return tomorrow to dress it again, and—'

'Go,' Richard said sharply. 'All of you. Leave me with Miss Wood.'

As the others obeyed, Jane began to busy herself with clearing away the water basin and the surgeon's soiled cloths. She couldn't help herself; it was so much easier to fall into her old familiar patterns of usefulness than to confront everything else that had happened this dreadful evening.

'Here now, enough of that,' Richard said impatiently, reaching out to stop her. 'That's not why I asked you to stay with me.'

'You didn't have to ask,' she said. 'It needs doing regardless.'

'It can wait,' he insisted. 'It's your company I want, Jane, not you pretending to be a maidservant.'

She gave her head a little shake, and left off cleaning as he'd bid, instead filling his glass with more brandy. 'The surgeon said you were to drink this.'

'Blast the surgeon!' he exclaimed, knocking the glass from the table and scattering brandy across the floor. 'If I want to drink more brandy, I'll damn well drink it myself, and not wait for the by-your-leave of some prattling foreigner!'

At once Jane knelt to wipe up the spilled wine, and as she did Richard rose from his chair and awkwardly pulled her back to her feet.

'If I want a servant, Jane,' he thundered, 'then damnation, I'll call for one.'

Indignantly she jerked her arm free of his grasp. He didn't look pale now, and he certainly didn't seem weak, not when he was overflowing with bluster and spark like this. 'I can understand perfectly if you're cross, Richard, but I—'

'Can you understand?' he asked. 'Because if you can, than that's one more way you're better than I'll ever be.'

She shook her head again. Perhaps he'd drunk

more of the brandy than she'd realised, because no matter what he was saying, she didn't understand any of it. 'Richard, please, be calm. Don't do yourself harm.'

'Harm!' he exclaimed. 'Damnation, how can you speak of harm after the wreck this night has become? Do you believe this is what I planned, what I wanted, for us?'

Suddenly it all made sense to her. 'Oh, I am so sorry,' she said unhappily, bowing her head and clasping her hands in a tight knot. 'I spoiled everything, didn't I? You'd arranged such a lovely evening for us, and then I spoiled everything by asking to leave the Ridotto so early.'

'You, Jane?' he said, incredulous. 'How could you spoil anything when you are as close to perfect as any woman I've ever known?'

Swiftly she looked up at him. She wasn't the perfect one, not by half. But Richard was: her golden-haired duke with the broad shoulders and laughing eyes, kindness itself, a gentleman beyond measure, beyond gallantry. *That* was perfection, a perfection she couldn't dream of matching.

'I'm not perfect,' she said with regret. 'Not at all.'

'Yes, you are,' Richard said, and he'd never meant anything more in his life. 'Perfect for me.'

'But I'm not,' she protested again, shaking her head, her voice breaking with a troubled little sob. 'When I think of the terrible risk you put yourself through this night—'

'For you,' he said softly, reaching for her. He slipped his hands inside her dressing gown to find her waist and pull her close. He'd held her earlier when she'd been bound by silk and whalebone, and he much preferred her this way, with only the thinnest layer of well-worn linen over her soft, warm body. He'd wanted to do this ever since she'd come to his door in her nightgown on that first night, and despite all the times he'd imagined it, his imagination fell far short of this reality.

'I'd do it again a hundred times over, too,' he said, his voice suddenly hoarse. 'I'd slay any dragons you wanted slaying.'

'It's not the dragons that frighten me.' Her fingers splayed lightly across his chest where he was sure she must feel the racing of his heart. She looked up at him, her eyes enormous, and at last he kissed her.

He meant to kiss her only once, and lightly at that, as a kind of reassurance for her after she'd been so frightened. She was trembling still; he could feel it as he held her. He would keep it quick and chaste, and not let himself be lost in the heady, hot temptation he'd discovered when he'd kissed her before. A single kiss, that was all. She was too fragile tonight for anything more.

But while he'd planned to be so honourably restrained, he'd forgotten about Jane herself. As soon as his lips touched hers, her arms were around the back of his neck, drawing him down to her level. Her lips pressed and slipped over his, soft and eager, and then tipped to one side to part for him. There was nothing cool about her mouth, as warm and rich and sweet as he'd remembered, and he couldn't quite help himself from kissing her in return. It was quickly begun, yes, but not chaste, and not finished in an instant, either, the way he'd planned.

The sash on her dressing gown came unknotted, and the gown fell backwards over her shoulders. Impatiently she lifted her hands from around his shoulders only long enough to shake the dressing gown away, letting it fall into a woollen puddle behind her. Now when she kissed him again, her breasts with their thin linen covering crushed gently against his chest. He forgot the pain from his wounded hand, forgot everything but her. Instinctively, and against his own wiser and infinitely better judgement, his hands slid from her waist and over her rounded hips. It was nothing at all to pull that linen nightgown higher, to bunch it upwards so he discovered skin, bare, velvety, lovely-to-touch flesh, all the while drinking in the heady intoxication of her kiss.

He *would* stop. She didn't understand what they were doing, though God knows he did. Jane was clever in countless bookish ways, but not about this. He must stop, now, while he was still able to heed such cautionary warnings in his head.

But he wasn't thinking, at least not with the brains that were in his head. He was tasting, and touching, and discovering, and savouring every marvellous bit of her, even as he cursed his bandaged hand for making him clumsy. It had been a long time since he'd been with a woman, and longer still since he'd been with one he'd cared for the way he cared for Jane Wood.

She was the one who finally drew back, her breathing ragged and shallow and her eyes heavy-lidded, her arms still curled about his shoulders as if she'd never wish to let go.

'My darling, darling Richard,' she whispered, her voice breaking. 'What if I had lost you?'

'You'll never lose me, sweet,' he said, his voice hoarse, his hands sliding low enough to grasp her bottom. She gasped and tensed with surprise, but she did not pull away as his fingers spread to caress her, his senses reeling.

'That is—that is very nice,' she stammered, her hands sliding to his waist for support. 'That is... *nice*.'

It was considerably better than 'nice,' thought Richard with a desperation that was growing in direct proportion to his desire. His mouth was dry with longing, his blood hammering in his ears as if he'd just climbed to the top of that bell tower Jane loved so much. It didn't help that she'd slipped her hands inside his dressing gown, too, and was now sliding her hands up his back, exploring him the same way as he did her.

'Your hand,' she murmured. 'I don't wish to hurt you further.'

'You're not,' he said, and in that moment he'd quite forgotten all about it. 'Especially not now.'

He'd bet his life she was a virgin, and that she'd no notion of what she was doing to him. If he'd any morsel of honour, that alone should have sobered him enough to stop. Instead it had the opposite effect: she could be truly his, and he'd become the only man in the world who could ever say that.

He kissed her again, featherweight kisses of genuine sweetness, while his hand eased gently beneath her gown to her belly, to the tangle of dark curls, and lower, to steal into the honey-sweet place between her thighs. She shuddered as he touched her, stroking with infinite, tantalising care, and then she gasped again, breaking away from his kiss to squeeze her eyes shut and press her cheek into his shoulder. Her fingers clutched convulsively at his nightshirt, the last barrier between them and open disaster.

'Richard, Richard,' she whispered hoarsely as she moved awkwardly against him, her rhythm, like her pleasure, too new and unpractised to have any grace. 'I—*oh!* Oh, my, oh!'

She was so tight around his finger, small enough to make his guess about her inexperience a certainty. Small and tight and trusting and hot, all enough to make him want to howl with frustration. And there, too, in that sweet, narrow cleft, he found the proof that she wanted him as much as he wanted her.

'My God, Jane,' he muttered, the beginning and likely the end of his vocabulary under the circumstances. 'My God.'

'I—I don't know what to say,' she whispered as she swayed into him. 'I can't seem to—I shouldn't—oh, Richard, please, *ohh!*'

He was in perilous danger of losing more than merely his honour, and before the two of them toppled over on to the unforgiving floor, he guided Jane the last two steps to his bed. She gasped as she fell backwards on to the feather bed, and gasped again as she saw the mirror in the canopy overhead.

'Oh, Richard, that is wicked,' she said with wonder. 'It's so—so Venetian.'

'Pay it no heed,' he said, shrugging himself free of his dressing gown to join her. 'I don't.'

'But I want to,' she said. 'Pay it heed, that is. I will be brave, and I will be bold. That's what I've learned here from you, you see. I must seize what I want for myself, because I might not ever be granted another chance. Especially after tonight.'

Her face crumpled as she fought back tears.

'Here now, Janie, don't cry,' he said gruffly, reaching for her. Damnation, the last thing either of them needed now was tears. 'Don't cry.'

To his surprise, she rolled away from him to the head of the bed, beneath the gilded cupids. Before he could join her, she grabbed the hem of her nightgown and yanked it over her head. She balled the gown in her hands and threw it to the floor, then sat back on her heels. She met his gaze evenly, almost challenging him to look at her, her now-bare breasts rising and falling rapidly with her breathing and her cheeks flushed as she tossed her hair back over her bare shoulders.

'There,' she said quickly, as if afraid of losing her

nerve. 'I'm done being shy, Richard. If it pleases you, that is.'

'Jesus, Jane.' She was already brave and bold, and had always been so, and he loved her for it. How could she not realise that about herself? He'd tried to imagine her so many times without her clothes, but the vivid reality before him made those dreams seem poor and faded. Her skin glowed ivory pale by the candlelight, her hair tangled chestnut around her face and a darker, burnished colour in the tri-angle of curls below her belly. Her breasts sat high and round on her chest, with dark crests that begged for his caress, and her lips, too, were dark and swol-len from the kisses they'd already shared.

'You don't agree?' she asked, her words rushed. She shook her hair again, her breasts bobbing like small ripe fruit. No wonder the cupids behind her grinned. 'That—that I am being brave?'

'Yes,' he managed to croak. If she happened to glance downward to the front of his nightshirt, she'd know she might need every bit of that damned courage, and soon, too.

She smiled, her mouth ruddy and inviting, the way he'd made it. 'Then let me see you, too. If you are brave enough, that is.'

Still he hesitated, even as his whole body throbbed with need. She *was* daring him, and this time it wasn't merely another visit to another picture gallery that she was proposing. How much did she truly know of men, anyway? She hadn't done particularly well guiding his daughters in that area. Did she know the consequences she risked of losing her maidenhead to him, of taking his seed into her body? What, for that matter, would he do if he got her with child? He wasn't like a score of other carelessly single-minded gentlemen he could name who'd sired bastard after bastard on their female staff. He *thought* about these things, double damn him for a fool, especially with Jane, because Jane was—Jane was Jane.

His Jane.

But Jane herself knew none of this. Too late he realised that all she could see was the doubt that must be painted like a signboard across his face, and in those few moments he watched her brave invitation begin to falter and fade. She pulled one of the pillow-biers from the bed and clutched it in her arms over her breasts.

'You've come to your senses, haven't you?' she said, her voice flat with a shame she'd no right to feel. 'You've remembered that you're the Duke of Aston and I'm a governess, and a powerfully foolish governess at that. You're going to do what you meant to do long ago. You're going to turn and leave, and that will be that.'

She gave her shoulders a sad little shrug for emphasis, as if to prove she didn't care, even as she bowed her head and dug her fingers into the pillow to keep from crying. She was, after all, the bravest woman he'd ever known.

And it was that, then, that decided him. To leave her now would crush her, and he wouldn't do that. He *couldn't*. He knew he loved her, didn't he? Wasn't that enough?

And his conscience and propriety and whatever else was gnawing at him could just damned well go to blazes where it belonged, and where he could retrieve it later. *If* he chose to.

'No, Jane, I'm not leaving,' he said hoarsely as he began to pull his nightshirt over his head. 'And I swear to you I'll never leave you again.'

She didn't answer, but looked and watched as he undressed, her violet-blue eyes intent on him as she hugged the pillow in her arms. He wasn't ashamed of what she saw. He was a well-made man, especially for his age, and proud of it. Yet as he drew the shirt over his head, he didn't miss her stifled gasp—of fear? surprise? approval?—and when he looked up, her cheeks were flaming.

'I am not frightened,' she said fiercely. 'I am not, so do not even think that of me.'

'Then you won't need that to strike me,' he said as he took the pillow from her hands and lay beside her on the bed. 'Though I'll grant you goose feathers are a good deal more agreeable than most weapons.'

'You know I'd never wish to harm you, Richard.' She laughed, a little trill of nervousness as he traced the long sweep of her hip and waist with his unbandaged hand. 'But if you can kiss me again and—and touch me the way you did before, then I won't even have to consider it.'

'Striking me or more being afraid?' He kissed her gently, wooing her to put to rest the fears she swore she didn't have, and pulled her closer against him, letting her grow accustomed to the feel of his body beside hers. He didn't want to hurt her, though he couldn't forget how small and tight she was.

'Either one,' she breathed, nearly forgetting to answer as he began to touch her again the way she wanted, and the way he wanted, too. 'I told you I am determined to be very brave.'

'I've never doubted it,' he said. 'My own dear, darling Jane.'

'And you are mine, Richard,' Jane whispered,

overwhelmed by how impossibly sweet such simple words had become. 'You're mine.'

He smiled as he nudged her knees apart, and she could feel him, all of him, hard and insistent against the inside of her thigh. She knew what would happen next; she was innocent, not ignorant, though she wasn't entirely sure how the act was accomplished. She would trust that to Richard, just as she'd come to trust him in so many other ways. With any other man, this would mean she'd be ruined, but not with Richard. He wasn't claiming her maidenhead for boasting afterwards, or making a male trophy of her inexperience. She was giving it freely, a gift to him of the one single valuable thing she had to offer.

But as he touched her again, she forgot everything else but her desire for more, more of the strange, agonising, wonderful tension that he was building within her body. She ached for him in a way she'd never thought possible, and wouldn't be, if she hadn't loved him as much as she did. She pushed her hips forwards, seeking more, her breath coming in short gulps as she clung to his shoulders.

'Be brave now,' he said, his voice taut, and distantly she wondered why she needed to be brave at all.

Then he moved over her, and that part of him that had seemed so alarmingly large began probing where his fingers had teased her. Instinctively she fluttered against him, realising too late that this would *hurt*. Too late, and he was driving deep within her, forcing her open, and she couldn't any more stifle her cry than she could get away.

'There now, sweet, it's done,' he whispered, though from his grimace he didn't seem to be enjoying this any more than she was. 'It will be better now, I promise.'

She swallowed hard and nodded. She must trust Richard in this, too, as she had in so much else, for what other choice did she have?

But to her amazement, the searing pain she'd first felt began to fade as he moved within her, and in its place came the same sort of enjoyable tension she'd felt before, gathering and growing low in her belly. Tentatively she began to move with Richard, and he groaned in response, the kind of gruff animal sound he'd made when she'd hugged him close. She liked being able to do that to him, giving him the same sort of pleasure that he was giving her. The strange part was that the more she tried to give to him, the more she, too, seemed to garner for herself.

She arched her back to meet his thrusts, bracing herself against his shoulders. This felt good, very good, and as she closed her eyes she realised the animal sounds were now of her own making. Yet still the pleasure built, rising higher and sweeping her with it like the wind would carry a ship, carrying her higher and further until she feared she couldn't bear it any longer, and then, with wonderful, staggering abruptness, she was falling into the most beautifully blissful, calm sea, floating weightless in a safe harbour of purest joy.

She opened her eyes, and saw their reflection in the looking glass above them: his broad, muscled back, his tousled golden hair, her dark hair fanned around her face against the pale linen, her legs still wrapped wantonly around Richard's waist and her arms around his shoulders, a sight enough to make her blush, not with shame, but love. Love had made her as one with Richard, the love they'd discovered when neither was searching for it. Or maybe, without realising it, they had, and her smile twisted with emotion that was far too much for her heart alone to contain.

'I love you,' she whispered, her lips close to his ear and her fingers tangling in his curling hair. 'I love you, oh, so much!'

He sighed, a rumbling sigh of contentment that she felt as much as heard. 'Then marry me.'

She froze, not believing what she'd heard.

He pushed himself up on his forearms to look at her. 'Marry me, Jane,' he said. 'Please.'

'Oh, Richard.' Tears welled in her eyes. 'Do not believe that because of—of this, that you must wed me.'

'Why the devil not?' he asked, mystified. 'I love you, and you love me. Isn't that reason enough for two grown folk such as us?'

She shook her head. 'I cannot think that—'

'Then for this once, let me think for both of us,' he said. 'I love you, and you love me. You suit me better than any woman I've ever known, Jane, suit me in ways that it outright bewilders me, they're so perfect. I cannot imagine my life now without you in it.'

'But if this night—if we—oh, Richard.' She looked away, her face hot. She was not usually at such a loss, but then, she'd never had to speak of such a subject. Although at nearly thirty years she was no longer young, she still maintained her monthly courses, and thus it was possible that she might yet conceive a child, perhaps even likely, given Richard's unquestionable virility. She swallowed, and tried to begin again. 'That is, if we were now to—to—'

'Become parents?' He chuckled softly, making it clear that the possibility was a pleasing one to him.

'I would welcome another chance, if we were to be so blessed. And if you bore me a son—'

'Your son,' she said, awed by everything those words represented. 'Our son.'

'My heir as well,' he said happily. 'Oh, I know my brother will grumble behind my back to lose his chance at the dukedom, but to have a son—our son—would be worth it. Consider that, Janie. You could be mother of a duke.'

'That is not why you have offered, is it?'

'What, because I am the rare gentleman who does not believe in scattering bastards across the countryside?' he asked wryly. 'No, Janie, though I don't, if that's a comfort to you. But what I truly wish for is to have you with me always. My wife.'

'Then you are serious?' she asked uncertainly. 'You know your grand friends in the county and in London will judge you mad.'

'And I don't care a whit about their judgements. I'm the one marrying you, not they.'

'But I'll become your duchess as well as your wife,' she said, 'and I've never been more than a governess.'

'What you are is the woman I love,' he said firmly, 'and the woman I wish for my wife. I'd be the greatest fool in Christendom to let you go. I'm not sure I could.'

She searched his face with wonder. 'You *are* serious.'

'I am.' His smile twisted with something close to doubt of his own. 'I know I'm not a young man, Jane, not so young as you deserve, but I vow I'm still in my prime, and you won't find another who'll love you more, or—'

'Yes.' She was crying, her tears sliding down her cheeks and on to the pillow, yet she didn't try to stop them. 'Yes, I will. Oh, Richard, I love you so much!'

'My love,' he said, and his eyes, too, were bright with tears. 'My life. My Jane.'

The Signor di Rossi was in a black humour. His little English virgin had escaped him not once, but twice, and with the most humiliating ease, too. When he'd first learned that her great English oaf was bringing her to the Ridotto this night, he'd made what should have been perfect plans. He'd already observed her independence and had guessed that she'd leave the duke's side on her own, and she'd done exactly that. He'd only had to wait in the crowd a short time before he'd plucked her up and made her his prize. How delectable she'd looked, too, a perfect Columbina in her pink-and-white satin, a plump and delicious dove ripe to be claimed!

And yet he had failed, and let her escape. When he should have been rough, he'd been too gentle when he'd had her alone. Fear could make a virgin flutter with distress, and the only proper way to subdue and ravish her was with absolute force. Her humble defence and attack had been like the sting of a little bee, more of a pinprick to his pride than any real wound, but it had been enough, and the memory of it now was enough to make him wince with shame.

He'd worked swiftly after that, sending two rascals of his acquaintance to attack the duke as if to rob him, to kill him and toss his wretched English corpse into the canal that swallowed all such secrets. Unprotected, the girl would then have been gathered up and brought here, to the Ca' di Rossi. The men knew their trade, and it should have been the work of a few moments against a man as old as the duke.

But the thieves, too, bumbled and failed, with the one even daring to come whining here to di Rossi, begging to be paid still for the trouble of having his fellow killed. With disgust di Rossi himself had had him likewise dispatched soon after by one of his most trusted servants, an accident near the canal. It could not have been helped, really. There was nothing less trustworthy than a whining rogue, and the last thing di Rossi wished was to have had this one go tattling to the authorities.

He sighed irritably, and poured himself another glass of wine. The girl was in his blood like a madness, and the only cure would be possession. He knew now what must be done. He'd send his own servants this time, people who he knew could be trusted, and he'd have them carry the girl to another house, a secret place he used for assignations. There he could take her as it pleased him, and punish her, too, for the trouble she'd caused him.

He smiled, anticipating her cries of anguish, of pain, of surrender. What pleasure he'd find in such a conquest!

And if the English duke still wanted her after he was done, then he was perfectly welcome to what was left.

Chapter Twenty-One

Jane lay curled beside Richard, blissfully warm and drowsy. The morning sun streamed into the room, for they'd not bothered to draw the bed's curtains last night, and dappled reflections off the canal danced across the ceiling. With his large arm resting across her waist and her back curled against his chest, she felt safe and protected, but most of all, *loved*. That made her smile again, sleepy as she was.

Richard loved her, and she loved him, and now they were to wed. She'd long ago given up dreaming of ever finding such happiness, or being worthy of inspiring such a degree of love in any man that he'd offer to marry her, yet now she'd inspired exactly that in the Duke of Aston. He wished to marry her soon, too, here in Venice, as quickly as it could be decently arranged. Her Richard, her *husband* Richard—ah, was there anything more wondrous than those few words?

She chuckled softly, nestling more closely against him. He'd certainly proved his devotion to her last night, first defending her against the thieves, and then again, in this bed, several times over. She'd never dreamed the act of love could be so—so thrilling. It was undignified, yes, but it was also so full of pleasure and delight that she'd quickly forgotten the undignified part and had instead shamelessly, even eagerly, agreed to everything that Richard had suggested. She knew she was beyond fortunate to have a duke ask for her hand, but she suspected she was far more fortunate still to have such a skilled and pleasing lover, too.

She was truly blessed, beyond all measure and expectation. It was only a handful of weeks since she'd arrived in Venice, burdened with an unfortunate past and an uncertain future, and now, thanks to Richard, she'd wakened from her own nightmare to find herself in a world full of love, kindness and security.

'Janie,' he murmured gruffly, more asleep than not. He curled his arm more closely around her waist, pulling her to him. 'Don't leave, mind?'

She smiled, settling her hand over his. 'I'm not, Richard,' she whispered. 'Not ever.'

'As it should be,' he said, and with a grumbling sigh of contentment, slipped back into sleep.

Still smiling, Jane closed her eyes and began to drift back to sleep herself, lulled by the peaceful, steady rhythm of Richard's breathing. In the distance, she could also hear the sounds of Ca' Battista coming to life with the day, the bustling footsteps of servants, someone complaining, someone laughing, and doors opening and closing, the same sounds of any great house in the morning.

Yet in an instant, it wasn't.

A young woman's voice, light and lilting, and her hurrying step on the marble staircase as she called to another in English.

'Come along, Mary, don't dawdle,' she said merrily. 'I can't wait to see Father's face when we surprise him!'

At any other time, Jane would have been delighted by what she heard: Lady Diana's voice, with Lady Mary answering. Richard's daughters, her own former charges, as dear to her as any true daughters, here in Venice five days before they were expected. Here, now, at the Ca' Battista, here on the stairs, here outside Richard's bedchamber and ready to surprise him.

'Richard, wake, please!' Jane whispered urgently, shaking his arm. 'Richard, please, the young ladies are here, your daughters—'

But the door to the room was already swinging open

and the two young women were crowding through it together, dark-haired Lady Mary Fitzgerald and her blonde and pregnant sister Lady Diana Randolph, their horrified faces reflecting what they saw as clearly as any looking-glass: their father and their governess, naked and in bed together.

As an English duke, a peer of the realm and a gentleman long beyond the age of rash youth, Richard expected most matters in his life to be ordered without surprises. Falling in love with his daughters' governess in Venice, however, had been well outside his expectations, and was most likely the largest and most pleasant surprise in all his life. But he'd welcomed it happily, and now that he and Jane were to marry, he expected everyone else to be happy for them as well.

Yet from the looks on the faces of his two daughters, sitting solemn and stiff-backed before him with their new husbands standing behind them, these expectations, too, were going to be challenged. He and Jane had dressed quickly, joining the others in this drawing room. He'd been imagining his first meeting with his wayward daughters and their new husbands with them begging his forgiveness, but somehow instead everything had turned topsy-turvy, and now he was the one being judged.

'You must admit it was a shock to us, Father,' Mary began carefully. She was the more sensible of the two, and the one, too, who'd always been closest to Jane. 'To discover you and Miss Wood in—in—'

'*In flagrante delicto,* as it were,' said her husband cheerfully, an Irish lord who seemed determined only to see the entertaining side of this whole wretched situation.

'There was nothing *flagrante* about it,' Richard answered irritably, keeping his hand firmly on Jane's shoulder. 'Janie and I had already planned to wed, as soon as the thing could be arranged with a respectable English minister. Not that I need answer to you, Fitzgerald.'

'Be easy, Richard, please,' Jane said. She placed her little hand over his, both to calm him and as an unspoken caution against losing his temper, and smiled warmly, once again the oil that had always soothed the conflict in his family. 'Of course it must be a shock to you. It's been rather a shock to us as well. Love seems to do that. Who would have guessed all of us would find the Continent such a romantic place?'

Richard smiled at that, unable to help himself as he gazed down at Jane with more love than he could ever hope to express. How could his daughters not see how happy she made him?

But Mary did not smile in return. 'I suppose it is romantic, yes,' she said. 'But even you must admit, Miss Wood, that the circumstances surrounding my marriage and my sister's are very different from this, ah, this alliance.'

'I would rather you call me Jane, than Miss Wood,' Jane said gently. 'A simple thing, I know, but it might help ease us all through this.'

But Mary's expression did not change. 'I do not believe that is possible,' she said slowly. 'You shall always be Miss Wood to me, and I cannot imagine you otherwise.'

Richard felt Jane's shoulder tighten beneath his hand, and at once he came to her defence.

'Then perhaps you'd rather call her your Grace,' he said sharply. 'Once I marry her, she'll outrank you, whether you like it or not.'

Mary flushed. 'That's not what I meant, Father. Miss Wood has been so important a part of our lives for as long as I can recall, and now to learn she's to wed you is a very great change.'

She rose from her chair and came to stand before Jane.

'If you truly are in love with Father, Miss Wood, and he with you, then I shall be happy for you both,' she said, and at last she smiled—a shy, uncertain smile, but a smile none the less.

'Thank you, Mary,' Jane said, and held out her arms. To Richard's relief, Mary at once embraced her with the same affection he'd seen between them a thousand times before.

'I only wish you to be happy, Miss Wood, exactly as you wished for me,' Mary said, still hugging Jane close. 'I don't give a fig that you were my governess. You were always our friend first.'

'Well, I do give a fig about it,' Diana said fiercely, her hand spread over her belly as if to protect her unborn child from such indignity. 'I won't fault Miss Wood, but you, Father! What possessed you? Have you lost your wits entirely? Don't you realise the scandal this will cause?'

Richard snorted with disgust. 'That's a fine question for you to ask, Diana, considering all the mischief you contrived at home. Or have you conveniently forgotten that only this good lady's intervention saved you from thoroughly destroying whatever reputation you had left?'

'That was her place,' Diana insisted tartly. 'She was our governess. You paid her to look after us, though now it would appear that she was tending to you as well.'

'Enough, Diana,' Richard said curtly. It had always been like this between him and Diana, the two of them scrapping ever since she'd been a tiny girl. He'd spoiled her shamelessly, of course; he'd spoiled both his girls, his perfect right as a father. But it was more than that with Diana. She'd not only inherited his golden hair and his fearlessness, but his temper and stubbornness as well, and while he had come to recognise how much alike they were, it still didn't make their quarrels any easier to bear. 'I won't have you speak of Jane with so little regard.'

'She doesn't mean it, Richard,' Jane said swiftly. Though she still held Mary's hand, she was ready to defend Diana, too, as she always had. 'Please don't make it worse.'

'What will be worse, Miss Wood, is if Father insists on continuing this intrigue with you,' Diana said, her voice turning plaintive as she turned once again towards Richard. 'Can't you conceive of what will be said, Father, or how people with laugh behind your back when it becomes known? A governess for your duchess! Everyone has always respected you in the county, but if you return to Aston Hall wed to one of your servants—'

'Hush, *cara*, please,' interrupted Diana's husband gently, his English laced with the accent of his native Rome. 'This is between the two of them, not you. Your home is with me in Rome. Why do you care what gossips may say out of your hearing?'

He brushed his lips against her cheek, then kissed

her hand for good measure. These had been the first words he'd spoken after the introductions, and, to Richard's mind, most sensible words they were, too. Lord Anthony Randolph was a handsome, dark gentleman, exactly the kind of half-Italian rogue that would have swept Diana off her feet, but now he also appeared to have the rare patience necessary to cope with her as well.

'Calm yourself, *carissima,* please, please,' he continued, bending over her with tender solicitation. 'It's not good for you to be so vexed, nor good for our child, either.'

'Very true, Randolph, very true.' Richard's new son-in-law was rising in his estimation by the minute. 'You're going to be a mother, Diana, and you must learn to put the welfare of your child first above all things.'

A single fat tear slid down her cheek. 'Then why aren't you doing that for me, Father? Why are you being so mean to me? I'm still your child, aren't I?'

Richard sighed with exasperation. 'Of course you are, Diana. But there's nothing to be gained from the sort of hateful, slandering gibberish that you're flinging at poor Jane. Be reasonable at once, Diana, and consider someone other than yourself.'

'But I *am,* Father!' she cried, rising clumsily to

her feet. 'Don't you see that? I've been trying to put the welfare of my innocent babe first, yet here you've gone and spoiled *everything!*'

Before anyone could stop her, Diana rushed from the room, her hand clasped dramatically over her mouth.

'Oh, hell and thunder,' Richard said. 'Mary, go fetch your sister back here.'

'I'll go after her,' Jane said softly, slipping free of his hand to stand.

'You don't have to go,' Richard said, not wanting to be apart from her even for a few minutes. 'You're not her governess any longer.'

'No,' Jane said, 'but I am to be her stepmother, and I don't wish to begin like this.'

'I'll come with you,' Mary said. 'She'll listen to me.'

Jane shook her head. 'Thank you, Mary, but no,' she said. 'It will be better if we resolve this between us alone.'

Though Jane smiled over her shoulder at Richard as she hurried after Diana, she wasn't feeling nearly as confident as she pretended to be. Diana was always unpredictable, and her pregnancy had clearly made her even more so. Now Jane didn't have far to follow her. With two uncertain servants hovering nearby, Diana stood in the hallway with her head bowed and shoulders quaking, sobbing as if her heart had been broken.

'Oh, sweet, no,' Jane said, hurrying to her side. 'Don't cry, not over this.'

'But I've—I've missed you so, Miss Wood!' Diana wailed, and threw her arms around Jane. 'I can't tell you how much!'

'You don't have to, my dear,' Jane said, tears of her own smarting her eyes as she hugged the younger woman. 'I've missed you as well. But now we're together, so there's no need to weep, is there?'

'But there is!' Diana cried miserably. 'Seeing you now makes me realise all over again how much I love you, and need you, and—and, oh, Miss Wood, how will I ever manage without you?'

Jane smiled, deeply moved, and hugged her close. 'You will manage perfectly, perfectly well, Diana. I've only to look at you to know that you're happy and prospering.'

'But that's *now*,' Diana said through her tears. 'What will happen after the baby comes? When I must be a mother? What will I do?'

'You will do exactly as every other new mother does,' Jane said, patting her back. 'You will love your new babe, and the rest will follow. You're far stronger than you realise. You're a Farren, you know.

And pray don't forget your husband. His lordship will be there with you as well.'

'I do love Anthony, with all my heart, but I—'

'Then all will be well,' Jane said firmly, using her own handkerchief to dry Diana's eyes. 'Now come, there's a lovely courtyard behind this house, and a path beside the canal. Let's go for a small walk together, Diana, just as we used to do at Aston Hall. You remember that. There's nothing for clearing one's head like a walk, is there?'

She called to the servants to bring their cloaks, and in a few minutes' time she and Diana were walking arm in arm, their heads close together in conversation. It was, in fact, much like the old days—just as Richard was often restless without sufficient exercise, so it was with Diana, too, and Jane had long ago learned that the best way to calm Diana was a brief, brisk walk. The morning was clear and cool and the breeze ruffled their skirts around their ankles. They'd the walkway along this narrow canal to themselves, with only their own reflections on the water for company.

'It was Anthony's idea, you see,' Diana was saying. 'He thought that we could bring you back to Rome with us, and then make you a permanent part of our household. You'd be my companion for now, and later our child's governess. It would have been perfect.'

Jane smiled. There'd been a time when Lord Anthony's suggestion would have seemed like the sweetest deliverance from all her worries. Now, however, she'd the chance of a love and a life of her own, perhaps even motherhood. How could she think of anything else, when they were so near to the arching footbridge where she and Richard had first kissed?

'It would have been perfect, yes,' she said, 'and I thank both you and his lordship for considering me. But now that your father has—'

'Oh, Father!' cried Diana petulantly. 'Father has simply ruined everything!'

'By falling in love with me?' Jane asked. 'You believe our love is ruination? That is why you so objected?'

Diana sighed heavily. 'Not exactly a ruination, no. That's not what I meant. But for him to claim you—'

'Will make him happy, and me as well.' Jane's smile was wistful, for to her it did not seem a ruination at all. 'You and His Lordship have found your love together. How can you wish us any less than you have for yourself?'

Diana stopped as another fresh round of tears overtook her. 'Oh, Miss Wood, I am sorry!'

'I do not want you to be sorry, Diana,' Jane said softly, 'only that you understand. I love your father with all my heart, as he does me. It's quite a miracle, one I never expected, but then love is like that, isn't it?'

'Miss Wood,' Diana whispered, and squeezed Jane's hand. 'Dear, dear Miss Wood!'

'Not Miss Wood,' Jane said tenderly. 'Call me Jane, if you can. I'd never dare to claim your mother's place in your heart, but I'll always love you as a mother should, if only you'll let me.'

Without waiting for a reply, she hugged Diana close, her heart so full of love that she doubted she could speak another word. No matter if she and Richard were blessed with children of their own: she now had two daughters that she already adored, and one with a grandchild on the way, too. She closed her eyes, both to squeeze back her tears and to savour the moment all the more. How could she ever be any happier than this?

With her heart so full, she did not hear the lapping of the canal as the hired gondola glided close to the pavement. With her eyes shut, she didn't see the two men, their faces hidden by long-nosed Carnevale masks, jump from the gondola to the paving stones. She wasn't aware that they'd clambered up on to the walk to rush towards them. She didn't realise their size or strength until one of the men had grabbed her from behind to jerk her away from Diana, nor see the heavy black tarpaulin, reeking of fish, until it was thrown over her head and bundled around her. Her cry of surprise and fear was smothered inside it, and as she twisted and struggled to escape, the man grabbed her around the knees and slung her over his shoulder.

She could see nothing, hear nothing, and the heavy, disorienting blackness terrified her even more. She felt herself lifted through the air and then dropped hard enough to knock the wind from her lungs. Yet even as she gasped for breath, her first thought wasn't or herself, but for Diana and her unborn child.

'Diana!' she cried frantically as she flailed against the heavy cloth. She must be in the bottom of a gondola. She could feel the now-familiar motion of gliding across the water, and hear the squeak of the single sweeping oar in the oar-lock at the stern. 'Diana, sweet, are you with me? Can you hear me?'

'*Silenzio!*' The man jabbed at her roughly through the tarpaulin to give extra emphasis to his order, and another man laughed. '*Avverbio, abberbio, eh?*'

Fighting her panic, Jane forced herself to be silent as he'd bidden. She'd achieve nothing against them if she couldn't be calm, and think, *think*.

There were at least two men, maybe more. The sound of the water beneath them had changed, enough that she knew they'd left the narrow canals and were headed for the open sea of the Bacino di San Marco. There, too, were the distinctive bells of the Basilica, tolling the hour. That much she could discern.

Yet none of this made sense. Everyone had assured her that the particular neighbourhood of the Ca' Battista was among the safest in the entire city, a most unlikely place for a woman to be kidnapped at random in the bright morning light.

Unless, of course, it wasn't random. Immediately she thought of Signor di Rossi, and again she struggled to control her fear. He had to be the one behind this. There was no one else in Venice who it could be, nor another who would dare be so desperate. Whatever had she done to make him so fascinated with her? What unwitting encouragement had she offered to him that he'd so wrongly misread, and contrived such an unwanted attachment to her? And why now had he ordered her stolen away like this?

The only good she could find in it was that he'd wanted her, not Diana. Left behind, Diana would be distraught, but safe, and she could also tell Richard what had happened. She'd no doubt that Richard would find her. Richard, and Lord Anthony, and Lord John, too, would join together as a family should to rescue her. It was a comfort, but a small one. Until they found her, she'd be entirely, entirely on her own, and if—

'Are you there, Miss Wood?' Diana's voice was a bewildered, muffled wail of terror. *'Miss Wood!'*

'Diana!' Again Jane struggled to free herself, kicking and clawing at the heavy tarp that surrounded her. 'Diana, sweet, I'm here, I'm here, be brave, and—'

'Silenzio!' This time the man struck Jane harder, knocking her so sharply on her shoulder that she yelped from the pain of it.

'Diana, sweet, I'm here!' she cried, ignoring the man's order. 'Everything will be fine, I promise you, everything will be—'

But the man's hand pressed roughly over her mouth through the tarp to stop her words. Jane closed her eyes, at last letting her tears flow. Not even the best governess in the world could keep cheerful now, and it didn't matter what she'd just told Diana. Diana might be frightened by the situation they were in, but grim as that was, Jane was more terrified of what might lie ahead for them, especially if the *signor* was involved.

And no matter how hard she tried, she could not think of how any of it would ever be half as fine as she'd promised.

Chapter Twenty-Two

Once again Richard drew out his watch, flipped it open with his thumb, and glanced at the face.

'They haven't been gone long, Father,' Mary said gently. 'Only a half of an hour at the most. Likely it's taken all this time just for poor Miss Wood—that is, for Jane—to speak a single word of her own. You know how Diana can be.'

'Hah, don't we all.' Resigned, Richard tucked the watch away. Diana had always been astonishingly absorbed with herself. If she followed her usual habit, it could take her an hour to air her unhappiness, and more beyond that for Jane to soothe her. He glanced across to Diana's husband. 'I expect you've discovered that about my daughter by now, too, Randolph, haven't you?'

The younger man smiled benignly. 'Love has given me patience beyond measure, your Grace.

Diana is so dear to me that I'm only vexed when we're apart.'

Richard nodded, surprised that the rogue would be so romantically sentimental. Yet what Randolph said *was* true. He didn't want to be apart from his Jane at all, even for such a good purpose as mending family fences with Diana. Likely he was being overprotective, but damnation, if it were up to him, she'd never feel a scrap of danger or fear again. He flexed his wounded hand, wincing a bit as he remembered the night before. He and Jane should both still be in bed, and they'd be there, too, if his daughters hadn't insisted on surprising them like this, and now—

The door to the room swung open and he looked up expectantly. But instead of Jane and Diana as he'd hoped, it was Signora della Battista who'd entered, so agitated that she'd not bothered to wait for leave to enter.

'My lord Duke, my lord Duke!' she cried, her face pale and streaked with tears. 'Sainted Mother in Heaven, that such a thing should happen before my own house!'

Another woman had uncertainly followed the *signora* into the room, a frightened, round-faced woman whose apron and hands were still dusted with flour from baking. She made a quick curtsy, then began speaking so hurriedly in Italian that Richard couldn't begin to follow it. Yet still, with a sick certainty, he understood.

Something had happened to Jane.

At once Lord Anthony stepped forwards. 'What is wrong, *signora*?' he demanded in curt Italian that even Richard could make out. 'What has happened? Are the two ladies—?'

'*Sequestrare!*' cried the anguished *signora,* wringing her hands before she and the other woman rushed into an unfathomable outpouring of Italian.

'What is it, Randolph?' Richard demanded, his dread rising by the second. 'What the devil are they saying?'

Anthony's expression had become fixed. 'They say that Diana and Miss Wood were walking beside the canal, when two ruffians jumped from a gondola. They seized Miss Wood first, and when Diana protested, they took her, too, and carried them both away in the gondola.'

'Who would do such an unspeakable act?' exclaimed the *signora* in English. 'Oh, my dear, gentle sirs! We must send for the soldiers, we must summon the Council! Who would dare kidnap two such fine English ladies like this?'

But Richard knew, just as he knew what he must

do to save both his daughter, his unborn grandchild and the woman he loved above all others.

And when he was done, he would be sure that the Signor Giovanni Rinaldini di Rossi would heartily wish he'd never crossed the Duke of Aston.

As his gondola glided swiftly through the narrow canals, di Rossi could scarcely contain his anticipation. He'd been disappointed so often by the incompetence of others that he'd never expected the servants he'd sent this morning to act so quickly, or with such success. When word had come to di Rossi that his little governess was waiting for him, he'd gasped aloud with joy. This time, she'd not escape. This time, at last, she'd be his.

He smoothed the black velvet along his fingers, one gloved hand over the other. He'd had Jane Wood taken to the Ca' Colomba—the House of the Dove—a small house he kept on one of Venice's many islands. The area had lost much of it past lustre, and di Rossi wore a sword against the chance he'd be attacked by petty thieves. But danger or no, it amused him no end that the house had begun its long life as a nunnery for an order that had been disgraced by scandal and dissolved two hundred years earlier on account of the lewd behaviour of its wanton sisters. Now he'd returned it to its illicit beginnings, using it to host licentious gatherings for his friends, assignations with courtesans who could cater to his tastes, and other debauchery he'd rather not have connected to his own palazzo. Venice was a city famously tolerant of its pleasures, but di Rossi's family was an old and revered one, and he understood the value of discretion.

Which was why he was particularly pleased with this day's success. To steal away the plaything of an English peer from beneath his very nose—ahh, could there be a more delicious trick? No matter how much Aston railed before the local authorities, they'd only shrug and wink and do nothing. A young female servant who wearied of the master's attentions and left for another household was a tale as old as servants themselves, and hardly against any law. And when it was the word of a foreigner against a di Rossi, there'd be no doubt in whose favour the magistrates would rule.

Di Rossi smiled behind his mask. He'd considered ordering the governess to be dressed as a penitent novice, in rough white linen with her little feet bare and her hair loose. He was fond of taking virgins dressed that way—the humble garb made their cries even more delectable—but he was already so inflamed by the little Englishwoman that the penitent's costume would be unnecessary, at least at first. There'd be time enough for such amusing re-finements once he'd enjoyed her maidenhead.

At last the Ca' Columba loomed before him, seem-ing to float on the island's mists, and it took all of di Rossi's will-power to remain on his bench while the gondola drew close and his servant landed first to have the door opened for him. Di Rossi climbed the landing and entered the door, where he was greeted by the housekeeper and the two servants in charge of capturing Jane Wood. Impatiently he motioned for them to rise.

'You've welcomed my guest, then?' he asked, glancing up the stairs. 'She waits in the first bed-chamber?'

'She awaits you, yes, *signor*,' the housekeeper said, hesitating just enough that di Rossi noticed and looked at her sharply.

'She awaits me, yes?' he repeated curtly. 'Or not?'

'She does, master, she does,' one of the men said. 'But because we were not sure which of the two English ladies was the one you sought, we took them both.'

'*Both?*' Di Rossi struck the man across his face as hard as he could, sending him staggering back-wards. Without pause he stormed up the stairway, determined to discover how badly these imbeciles had erred this time. He waved aside the footman who'd been posted as a guard outside the bedchamber, and unlocked the door himself.

As he'd ordered, only a single candlestick lit the room, but by its light he could clearly see that there were not one, but two, young women, sitting on the edge of their bed with their arms clasped around one another's shoulders for comfort.

'You have gone too far this time, *signor*.' Jane Wood rose at once, her round face glowing with foolish defiance. 'You have no right to keep us here against our will.'

'I have every right in the world,' he said, smiling. She was delightful like this, her outrage as impotent as a child's. 'You are in my house now, my dear, and I am your master.'

'You're nothing of the sort,' the other woman proclaimed, standing beside Jane. She was younger, tall and fair with golden hair, the sort of pink-and-white Amazon that the English favoured. Though she didn't match di Rossi's own tastes, he wasn't about to scorn the unexpected bounty of two young playthings for his amusement.

'You must release us at once,' she demanded. 'You cannot hold us against our wills. We are English.'

'And you believe that will impress me?' he asked, bemused. 'Arrogant creature.'

He beckoned to the servants behind him. They knew immediately what he expected and hurried to seize the two women, deftly pinning their arms behind their backs as they yelped and fought with indignation and fear. Di Rossi enjoyed that, too, for there were few things more pleasing to him than the forced conquest of a proud, pretty woman, to be followed by her inevitable submission.

'Villain!' cried the blonde woman, breathing hard. 'Don't you know who we are?'

Di Rossi bowed, enjoying her humiliation. 'I know Miss Wood, of course, and in time I shall have the delight of your acquaintance, too.'

'There will be no acquaintance between us, sir,' she said sharply, drawing herself up as straight as she could with her arms pinioned behind her. 'I am Lady Anthony Randolph, and my father is the Duke of Aston, and both of them will be eager to make you answer for this outrage!'

She tried again to shake free of her captor, and as she did her cloak fell open. For the first time di Rossi saw the rounded swell of her pregnant belly, and revulsion swept over him. He would have forgiven her a lack of virginity—besides, he'd his dear little governess for that—but breeding women disgusted him with their clumsy, misshapen bodies, swollen with another man's seed.

'Only if they would ever connect me to you,' he said with chill uninterest. 'They will not, of course. I have as little interest in you as you have in me, and you will simply be made to disappear. They say the Turkish slavers are always eager for gold-haired women like you, eager enough that they'd take your brat, too. You could become quite the prize of some sultan's harem, *cara.*'

It was gratifying to see how the woman paled and shrank away from him, her bravado gone in an instant. Harems and slavery always had that effect on ladies.

'But you, *dolce,*' he said, smiling as he turned towards Jane Wood. 'I won't part with you, not for all the gold the Turks might offer.'

'With all my heart I wish you would,' she said, as defiant as a governess could be. 'I want nothing to do with you, *signor.* Nothing!'

His smile curled upwards with anticipation. 'You say that now, *cara,* but I've planned many ways of changing your mind.'

Teasing himself as much as her, he unfastened the clasp of her cloak and pushed it from her shoulders. She held his gaze, not looking away, yet still unable to control her trembling. Pretty little creature, he thought fondly, and trailed his fingers along the slender column of her throat to feel her fear.

He liked that, too, and unable to resist any longer, leaned forwards to kiss her.

But as he came closer, she twisted her head to one side, and instead of the sweetness of her innocent mouth, all she offered was the side of her face and a tangle of her hair. Though she'd rebuffed him before, he hadn't expected her to refuse him now, when he was so clearly in control. To make sure she understood that he was to be her master, he circled his hand over the front of her throat and tightened his fingers.

Jane gasped reflexively, shocked that di Rossi would be so aggressively cruel. Shock soon turned to panic as his hand closed over her windpipe, squeezing her breath from her lungs. The harder she tried to free herself, the more tightly his fingers contracted. Everything seemed to narrow to his dark eyes before her, glittering as hard as jet, the pressure of his thumbs and the growing weakness in her limbs. Her heart was thumping so loudly in her ears that she could hear Diana crying her name only in the fading distance, as if a wide field stood between them instead of only a few feet.

She could not breathe, she could not breathe, and just when she was sure she could bear no more and di Rossi's face began to fade before her eyes, he released her. Her gulp for air was rough and strangled, and she sagged in the servant's grasp as she struggled to regain the air that had been throttled away from her.

Di Rossi smiled, a devil incarnate. Truly he *was* mad. She'd feared before that he'd meant to rape her; now she was terrified for her life as well.

'You must learn to be less insolent, *cara,*' he said mildly. 'I do not simply expect your obedience. I demand it.'

'You have no right to demand anything from Jane!' cried Diana. 'She owes you nothing!'

'But she does,' di Rossi said firmly. 'She is mine, you see, my pearl, my jewel. And when I finally ravish her maidenhead—'

'No—no,' Jane gasped, her throat raw. If this was all he'd wanted from her, then surely he'd let her and Diana go once he learned the truth. 'I'm not—not a virgin.'

Incredulous, di Rossi stared at her. 'You must be,' he insisted. 'You are.'

Jane shook her head. It had only been last night that she'd made love with Richard, only a handful of hours, yet now it seemed as distant as another lifetime.

'*Aston,*' di Rossi said furiously, practically spitting the word. 'He dared—what the devil?'

Through the open chamber door rose a growing

din from the front hall. Men were pounding on the front door, demanding to be admitted, while the maidservants wailed and shrieked with distress. Yet there was one word Jane could make out, over and over again: *soldato,* or soldier, and for the first time since she'd been brought to this house her hopes began to rise.

Perhaps Richard had somehow found them, perhaps he'd come to rescue them, to save her...

'I will not be disturbed,' di Rossi declared, his face twisted with rage. He swung his arm imperiously at one of the footman. 'Go below, and tell those wretched fools to be quiet, else they'll answer to me.'

The servant bowed and fled, clearly relieved to be permitted to leave. Jane saw how the man holding Diana shifted uneasily, glancing at her captor as if he, too, wished to be gone. In return she felt sure the man's grasp began to ease on her arms. Had soldiers been to this house before? Every Venetian feared answering to the city's dreaded authorities, and feared Venice's infamous prison even more. Households ruled by threats and violence were seldom loyal ones, and Jane's slender hopes rose a fraction higher. Perhaps they would be able to escape, and she'd return to Richard, and—

'Now you smile, *signorina?*' di Rossi said furiously, misreading her expression, and raised his hand to strike her. 'You who have cheated me of what I most desired?'

But his threat was lost in the crash of the heavy door below being broken open. Now the screams of the servants were drowned by the rough voices of the men who'd forced their way inside and the thump of heavy footsteps racing up the stairs. Drawing his sword, di Rossi swung around towards the door to face the intruders. The man holding Jane swore and shoved her away, as did Diana's captor, and the two of them fled through the narrow door to the chamber's serving stairs.

'Stop, you cowards!' screamed di Rossi after them, his voice quivering with fury. '*Madre dio*, stop and defend me!'

Jane could hear the soldiers running down the hall from the staircase, and if she and Diana could reach them, then they'd be safe. It wasn't far, only a few paces, but di Rossi and his sword still stood between them. If they were quick, they could escape while he was distracted by his traitorous servants.

'This way, Diana, hurry, hurry!' Jane cried, seizing Diana's hand to lead her. A crowd of soldiers in black hats and blue coats with swords and muskets were already filling the doorway, salvation if ever she'd seen it. But then over their heads she saw another face towering over the black hats, and she forgot everything else.

'Janie!' Richard roared, pushing past the soldiers to reach for her. 'Diana, here!'

'Richard!' she cried, and with a final effort she darted around di Rossi and flung herself into Richard's waiting arms.

But as she did, Diana's hand abruptly jerked away from hers. Jane twisted around, searching desperately for Diana, and to her horror, found her.

She hadn't been able to escape past di Rossi. Instead he'd caught her and dragged her backwards, pinning her against his chest with the blade of his sword pressed close below her throat. Now she was trapped there against him, her eyes squeezed shut and her hands clasped over her unborn child. One of the soldiers raised his musket to his shoulder, intent on shooting di Rossi, but before he could, Richard shoved the musket's barrel aside.

'No,' he said, the single word full of anguish for his daughter. 'The risk's far too great.'

Di Rossi smiled, his eyes bright with a madman's gleam. 'You are wiser than I believed, Aston. Sufficiently wise that perhaps we can reach an agreement between us. An arrangement between gentlemen.'

'I'll agree to nothing until you release my daughter,' Richard said. 'Free her, and we'll talk.'

'Now why should I do such a foolish thing as that?' di Rossi said. 'The instant I release her, one of these wretched soldiers will murder me. They're itching for my death, and so are you, Aston. You can hardly deny it.'

'I won't,' Richard said, his voice so sharp with anger that Jane lay her hand gently on his arm. 'To see you dead and delivered straight to hell would indeed give me the greatest of pleasures.'

'What I propose is simple enough,' di Rossi said. 'A trade that's more than fair by any standards. Your daughter for the governess, one for the other.'

Jane gasped, stunned. How could Richard ever make such a decision? As much as she loved Richard, she loved Diana, too, and there was also the unborn child to consider. Heartsick, Jane knew such a choice would be impossible for her, and likely for Richard as well, and as if to prove he shared her fear, his arms tightened protectively around her.

'I told you, di Rossi,' Richard said, 'I will not bargain with you.'

'I say you will,' the Venetian answered evenly. He'd regained his customary demeanour, as if they were discussing no more than a dish of chocolate, but Jane knew this was only one more mask to hide behind. Tension locked his smile in place, and the drops of nervous sweat that clustered across his forehead and soaked his dark hair betrayed the truth. 'Consider your stakes for bargaining. A humbly born governess, a servant in your house, a woman past her first youth, of no fortune, family, or remarkable beauty, a woman you've already bedded—'

'Enough, di Rossi,' Richard said sharply. 'Let my daughter go free.'

'Your daughter, your daughter,' di Rossi mused. 'She's my stake, yes? She is an English lady, your daughter, a noble lady wed to a nobleman. That alone should make her of more value than that chit of a governess. Your daughter also carries your grandchild in her belly, the grandchild of an English duke! How can you hesitate, Aston? How do you dare?'

Before Richard answered, di Rossi swept his sword away from Diana's throat, flipped aside her cloak, and pressed the blade instead across the swell of her unborn child. Diana whimpered, her fingers spreading as she vainly tried to protect the babe within her. She wept quietly, the tears trickling down her face, and it was only then that Jane realised she was crying with her.

She could end this herself, and spare Richard the agony of deciding. She had that power. To think of two lives hanging on the whim of a madman's blade, one that had scarcely begun before it was so brutally ended...

Behind her Richard swore, a vehement mixture of anger, frustration and despair.

'Surely that cannot be your answer, Aston,' di Rossi said, smiling with triumph. 'Consider well. One choice for eternity, for ever on your conscience. The other only until I weary of the lady. A month, a half-year. I doubt she'll hold my interest beyond that, and then you're welcome to what's—'

'May God curse you for ever for this,' Richard said vehemently, 'and may the devil himself claim you for—'

'Take me,' Jane said softly as she slipped free of Richard's embrace. 'Let the lady go free, and take me instead.'

'For God's sake, Jane, no!' Richard exclaimed, but she'd already begun walking away. Jane was counting on him not following from fear of startling di Rossi, and he didn't, nor did she look back, no matter how desperately she longed to. If she did, she knew she'd never be able to do this, no matter that it was the most honourable sacrifice she could ever make for love. For *love:* for Diana, her child, but most of all for Richard.

'If you please, *signor,*' she said, her hands clasped

resolutely at her waist and the calm in her voice surprising even herself. 'Pray release the lady, so that I might join you.'

Di Rossi's careful mask dropped away, and he gazed at Jane now with a raw hunger that terrified her.

'*Cara mia colomba,*' he crooned, his dark eyes glittering with lust as he held one hand out to her. 'My own little dove. At last you recognise your true master!'

Intent on Jane, he let his sword slide away from Diana's body, and with a desperate little cry, Diana scrambled away from him.

The pistol's shot exploded in the room, echoing so loudly that Jane gasped from the shock of it. The noise, and the acrid cloud of burnt powder, and the men's voices all speaking at once, and blood, so much blood, as di Rossi's now-lifeless body toppled to the floor. She saw the spent pistol drop from Anthony's hand as he reached Diana and held her, burying his face in her hair so none would see that he, too, wept.

'Janie,' Richard said as he gathered her up into his arms as if he'd never let her go again. 'My own brave, dear Janie! It's done now, love, it's done.'

She smiled up at his impossibly dear face, or tried to. She was so weak with relief, with happiness, with the complete contentment of love, that if he'd not held her, she was certain she'd collapse on the floor before him.

'I love you,' she whispered. 'Oh, Richard, how I love you!'

And fainted away in his arms.

Chapter Twenty-Three

Aston Hall, Kent—December 1785

'There you are, your Grace, everything fit to please his Grace.' Jane's lady's maid Polly gave Jane's elegantly dressed hair one final pat. 'You'll outshine the rest o' the ladies tonight, that's for certain.'

'Oh, I doubt that.' Jane smiled at her reflection in the glass, more as a compliment to the maid than from delight in her own appearance. She and Richard had married in Venice, in the front room of the English consulate with only a handful of guests. Mary and Diana had served as both witnesses and bride's maids, and their combined blessings had added an extra measure of joy to the wedding.

The only dark part of their days in Venice had come from the investigation of Signor di Rossi's death. With so many having seen his last moments, however, there'd been no question of any charges of murder against Anthony. Though the *signor* and the wickedness he represented were gone for ever, Jane could not recall that day without trembling, and thinking of how a gentleman she'd first thought a friend had proved himself so thoroughly the opposite. And yet, ever the governess, she still could find a lesson in it—if she'd not come so perilously close to losing everything, would she have been able to treasure quite so dearly her life and the love she shared with Richard?

From Venice they'd travelled back to Rome with Diana and Anthony, lingering there long enough to see the birth of their child, a beautiful, golden girl named Marianna, honouring both her mother and her doting aunt. By the time that Jane and Richard had finally sailed for England, Jane herself was with child as well. This was a miracle that had made Richard crow like a proud rooster one moment, and then fuss like a broody hen the next, treating Jane with such infinite tenderness that she could only love him all the more for it.

She had been wary of her welcome at Aston Hall, dreading how the staff would respond to her being raised so unexpectedly high. A few had given notice, unable to bring themselves to take orders from a former governess, but the majority had rejoiced for her good fortune and the happiness that she'd brought to their master. Richard had gladly turned the household affairs over to her, and considering how much she'd already been in the habit of doing with Mary, her transformation into the Hall's mistress had proved remarkably easy.

Becoming a duchess, however, was far more of a challenge. She'd never considered herself a beauty, and a lifetime of quiet, serviceable dresses had been a difficult habit to shake. She'd been overwhelmed by the dressmakers and milliners who'd eagerly sought her patronage, each of them infinitely more fashionable than she ever would be herself. The lavish collection of family jewels that Richard had presented to her had felt more like a burden than an honour, and the more he'd tried to spoil her with finery, the more she'd panicked, and feared she'd never be the great lady Richard deserved. Finally, after one particularly teary afternoon that had had as much to do with her pregnancy as with a certain emerald necklace, they'd reached an understanding that satisfied them both: he agreed to show his affection for her by way of flowers, pictures and books, while she agreed to let him order her gowns when an occasion demanded it for the Duchess of Aston.

Yet these had been minor quibbles, easily resolved with love to ease the way. And when on the first snowy day in late November Jane had presented Richard with the much-desired son and heir, their joy and happiness as new parents had been boundless.

'A single plume in your hair, your Grace?' coaxed Polly. 'Here, to curl winningly over your temple?'

'I'd prefer a rose,' Jane said, plucking one of the velvety red blooms from the silver vase beside her. Each month, on the anniversary date of their wedding, Richard would bring her an enormous bouquet of roses from the Hall's greenhouses, roses that he'd had specially forced to bloom on that day for her. To Jane it was both impossibly romantic and impossibly perfect, and if the duke and duchess always remained alone together in the duchess's bedchamber for the remainder of those 'rose days', as the staff called them, then that was quite perfect as well.

'Tuck the rose into the curls, Polly, if you please,' Jane said. 'You know best how—'

'Where's my Janie?' boomed Richard, throwing open the door to her dressing room. Against his broad shoulder was the tiny Marquis of Brecon, wide-eyed and open-mouthed at sharing his father's towering height, while his nursery maid hovered anxiously behind.

'Your men are here to see you, Janie,' Richard

continued, 'and to learn what has kept you dawdling here so long. It's our first supper since your lying-in, you know, and I thought you'd be eager for company.'

'I'm dressing, not dawdling,' Jane protested, rising from the bench as both Polly and the nursery maid curtsied. 'Have a care with Brecon, Richard. He's not even a month old.'

'Twenty days on this earth, and already master of it,' Richard said happily, cradling his son's small, bonneted head with his palm. 'Isn't that so, little rogue?'

Jane sighed, though in truth there was no finer sight to her eyes than her husband with their son. Unlike most men, Richard was completely at ease with a baby in his arms, nor could he keep the unbridled joy that the child brought him from his face.

'It's not so much that I fear for Brecon,' she said, 'as I do for your coat. You're already dressed for our guests, and if he spits upon your shoulder—'

'Then I shall shift my coat for another,' he declared, turning so that the baby could peer over his shoulder at Jane. 'Isn't that so, my Lord Brecon? Now come with us, Janie. While you've been about up here, your Christmas present has arrived.'

'Mine?' Jane asked, frowning. She'd been working a needlepoint wallet for Richard, flame stitch in wools with his monogram stitched in the centre, but because she'd wanted to surprise him, her progress had been slow. 'But it's not Christmas yet, Richard, and besides, my gift for you isn't quite ready.'

'But mine is,' he said grandly, offering her the crook of his arm. 'Ready and waiting for you in the dining hall. Come now, I'd like you to see it before our guests appear.'

'In the dining hall,' she mused as the three of them made their way down the stairs. 'Does that mean you're giving me a glazed ham, or perhaps a dressed goose for Christmas?'

'Or a great festive pudding, full of fruit and brandy,' he suggested, teasing her in return. 'You like those, too. But I fear it's something to admire, not to eat.'

A footman held the door open for them to enter the dining room, and then closed it gently behind them. From habit Jane made a quick, critical survey of the long table, the snowy linen cloth already laid and the sterling set out for the guests who would be joining them tonight. The fires in the twin hearths were dancing merrily as well, warming the large room for later, and though the chandeliers and the candelabras on the table were still dark, Richard had ordered the sconces at the far end of the room lit. There stood an easel with something long and framed resting upon it, draped and covered by a cloth.

'What is it, Richard?' Jane asked curiously, standing before the easel with her hands at her waist. 'What are you hiding?'

'I thought you said you wanted to wait,' he teased. 'I thought you—'

'Hush,' she said sternly. 'Show me.'

'Very well, your Grace.' He handed Brecon to her, and the babe made a contented cooing as he settled against her. Just like Richard, she'd risk every silk gown in her wardrobe for that happy little sound.

With a conjurer's flourish, Richard tweaked the corner of the cloth to build her suspense. Then, at last, he swept the cloth aside, and stood back to watch her reaction.

And Jane reacted. How could she help it? Her eyes filled with tears, and she bit her lower lip to keep them from spilling over. He'd known exactly what would delight her, the one thing she'd never realised herself that she wanted the most.

The painting was a beautifully detailed scene of Venice, similar to the ones that a great many English gentleman brought home as souvenirs of their Grand Tour. But this one was different. This one showed the corner of Venice where she and Richard had fallen in love, and captured that magical place exactly as she wished to remember it.

There was the Ca' Battista, with its balconies as lacy as spun sugar. There were the windows with the pointed arches that had belonged to Richard's bedchamber, and the filmy red curtains that had filtered the sunlight as they'd lain together in his bed. There was the narrow arched bridge where Richard had first kissed her in the moonlight, and there in the distance was San Marco's square tower, whose tolling bells had called the hours of their day. Even the sky was the same, the bright enamel blue that had marked the Venetian winter when they'd been there, with the gondoliers and others on the water and at the windows all bundled in bright hats and coats exactly as Jane remembered.

'Love, love,' she said softly in wonder, unable to look away from the painting. 'How did you know?'

'I knew, Janie, because it was what I wanted, too.' He came to stand beside her, looping his arms fondly around both her and Brecon, who'd fallen peacefully asleep against Jane's shoulder. 'But here, sweet. You've missed the best part. Look down in this corner, directly in front of the Ca' Battista.'

Jane leaned forwards to study the part of the painting he was pointing to. A black gondola with two passengers sitting closely together, a small, dark-haired woman tucked beneath a fur coverlet, holding hands with a broad-shouldered blond gentleman, his hat pulled low over his brow against the cold.

'Oh, Richard, it's us,' Jane whispered. 'The way we were. It's *us,* there in Venice, for ever and ever.'

'The way we'll always be, Janie,' he said, bending over their now-sleeping son to kiss her. 'In love, for ever and ever.'

* * * * *

HISTORICAL

Large Print

LORD PORTMAN'S TROUBLESOME WIFE
Mary Nichols

Forced to marry Harry, Lord Portman, Rosamund must produce an heir in return for a comfortable life! But self-controlled Harry is unsettled by his attraction to Rosamund, his convenient wife, and keeps her at arm's length. But Rosamund falls into danger and he has to find the courage to let go of the past and fight for the woman he loves…

THE DUKE'S GOVERNESS BRIDE
Miranda Jarrett

Dreading the end of her Grand Tour, former governess Jane Wood awaits the arrival of her employer, Richard Farren, Duke of Aston, with trepidation… Richard finds mousy Miss Wood unrecognisable as the passionate, carefree Jane. Will Richard overcome the shadowy demons of his past…and convince Jane to be his wife?

CONQUERED AND SEDUCED
Lyn Randal

Two years ago former gladiatrix Severina had no choice but to flee from Livius Lucan. Their fiery relationship threatened his safety – a risk she couldn't take. But now she needs his help. In his turn, Lucan is determined to conquer this runaway woman – and claim the wedding night he never had!

MILLS & BOON

HISTORICAL

Large Print

REAWAKENING MISS CALVERLEY
Sylvia Andrew

Lord Aldhurst rescues a cold, dazed lady one stormy night – and now the nameless beauty is residing in his home! Horrified at her growing feelings for her handsome protector, she flees to London, where she regains her status as the *ton*'s most sought-after debutante. Until she sees James's shocked and stormy face across a ballroom…

THE UNMASKING OF A LADY
Emily May

While she dances prettily by day, the *ton* doesn't know that by night Lady Arabella Knightley helps the poor – stealing jewels from those who court her for her money. Upon discovering it's Arabella, Adam St Just should be appalled. Instead, captivated by her beauty, he proposes to unbutton Lady Arabella…or unmask her!

CAPTURED BY THE WARRIOR
Meriel Fuller

With the country on the brink of anarchy, Bastien de la Roche will do what it takes to restore calm. So when he captures the spirited Alice Matravers, a servant to the royal court, he charms her into gaining an audience with the King. Could Alice's courage and kindness begin to mend Bastien's shattered heart…?

 MILLS & BOON

HISTORICAL

Large Print

INNOCENT COURTESAN TO ADVENTURER'S BRIDE
Louise Allen

Wrongly accused of theft, innocent Celina Shelley is cast out of the brothel she calls home and flees to Quinn Ashley, Lord Dreycott. Lina dresses like a nun, looks like an angel, but flirts like a professional – the last thing Quinn expects is to discover she's a virgin! With this revelation, will he wed her before he beds her?

DISGRACE AND DESIRE
Sarah Mallory

With all of London falling at her feet, wagers abound over who will capture the flirtatious Lady Eloise and her fortune. Dashing Major Jack Clifton has vowed to watch over his late comrade's wife, but her beauty and behaviour intrigue him. The lady is not what she seems, and Jack must discover her secret if he is to protect her…

THE VIKING'S CAPTIVE PRINCESS
Michelle Styles

Dangerous warrior Ivar Gunnarson is a man of deeds, not words. With little time for the ideals of love, Ivar seizes what he wants – and Princess Thyre is no exception! But to become king of Thyre's heart, mysterious and enchanting as she is, will entail a battle Ivar has never engaged in before…

 MILLS & BOON®

HISTORICAL

Large Print
COURTING MISS VALLOIS
Gail Whitiker

Miss Sophie Vallois has enthralled London Society, yet the French beauty is a mere farmer's daughter! Only Robert Silverton knows her secret, and he has other reasons to stay away. However, Sophie is so enticing that Robert soon finds that, instead of keeping her at arm's length, he wants the delectable Miss Vallois well and truly *in* his arms!

REPROBATE LORD, RUNAWAY LADY
Isabelle Goddard

Amelie Silverdale is fleeing her betrothal to a vicious, degenerate man, while Gareth Denville knows that the scandal that drove him from London is about to erupt again. In Amelie, Gareth recognises a kindred spirit also in need of escape. On the run together the attraction builds, but what will happen when their old lives catch up with them?

THE BRIDE WORE SCANDAL
Helen Dickson

From the moment Christina Atherton saw notorious Lord Rockley she couldn't control her blushes. In return, dark and seductive Lord Rockley found Christina oh, so beguiling… When Christina discovered that she was expecting, Lord Rockley knew he must make Christina his bride…before scandal ruined them both!